I0746354

Stories of Crime & Detection

Volume Eight

Hard-Boiled

James Ronald

Edited by Chris Verner

Moonstone Press

This edition published in 2024 by Moonstone Press
www.moonstonepress.co.uk

Hard-Boiled originally published in 1937 by *The Thriller Library*.
Hanging's Too Good originally published in 1937 by *The Thriller Library*.
The War Makers originally published in 1939 by *The Thriller Library*.
Partners in Crime originally published in 1932 by *20-Story Magazine*.
Stories of Crime and Detection, Vol VIII: Hard-Boiled © 2024 the Estate of
James Ronald.
The right of James Ronald to be identified as author of this work has been
asserted in accordance with the Copyright, Designs and Patents Act 1988

ISBN 978-1-899000-86-9
eISBN 978-1-899000-87-6

A CIP catalogue record for this book is available from the British Library
Text designed and typeset by Moonstone Press
Cover illustration by Jason Anscomb

Royalties from the sale of this book will be donated to MND Scotland,
who fund ground-breaking MND (motor neurone disease) research and
world-class clinical trials to combat an uncommon condition that affects
the brain and nerves, and causes weakness that gets worse over time,
eventually resulting in death.

Contents

INTRODUCTION

This volume contains the final three Mendoza tales in order of publication. They all first appeared in The Thriller Library, published by Amalgamated press—a weekly newspaper in circulation from February 1929 to May 1940, that during its eleven-year run published stories by the top thriller writers of the day and built the reputation of others who contributed to its pages.

This eighth volume of *James Ronald, Stories of Crime and Detection* is the third of three consecutive volumes to feature James Ronald's six stories about fictional crime reporter Julian Mendoza of the *London Morning World*. Mendoza is neither young nor good-looking, nor blue-blooded, nor in love with anybody at any point. In actual fact, he smokes a filthy pipe, has a marvellous landlady from Scotland, walks with a limp, is kind to down-and-outs but unkind to policemen, is rude to Society ladies; and is quite prepared to do anything to ensure his reputation as the greatest crime reporter in Fleet Street.

The first story is the fourth Mendoza yarn, *Hard-Boiled*. It is a brutal and compelling story of the race gangs in London during the interwar years when Soho had the reputation as being Britain's criminal capital. Mendoza battles the violence of organised crime. This hard-hitting story, though fictional, reflects the true menace of British-Italian mob bosses like the notorious Charles 'Darby' Sabini, considered protector of Little Italy in Clerkenwell. Such mobsters are represented in this story by Mike Flannery.

"When Mike Flannery entered, everything came to a dead stop. The place looked like a waxwork museum: one man was frozen into immobility in the act of dealing cards; another, bent over the billiards-table, sighting a shot, remained like that with his eyes on the intruder; a darts-player stood like a statue, his hand, holding a dart, poised in mid-air. No one spoke. They all looked at Mike with the emotionless eyes of dead fish."

Hard-Boiled was first published on 8 May 1937, in *The Thriller Library* No 431. In July 1938 Rich & Cowan published three Mendoza novelettes in one book, with the overall title *Hanging's Too Good*. The stories were *Hanging's Too Good, Angel Face* and *Hard-Boiled*. This version is from the book with the original Chapter titles from *The Thriller Library* restored.

The fifth Mendoza novelette *Hanging's Too Good* began life as *The Sucker*, first published on 18 December 1937 in *The Thriller Library* No 463. *The Sucker* was subsequently revised and republished as the title story in a three-story, aforementioned book, *Hanging's Too Good*—Rich & Cowan, July 1938.

"When he stood up, there was a fierce light in his eyes and his mouth was grim. One thing at least he could do for Old Dan; he could track down the slayers and see that they got their deserts. This was one crime for which hanging was too good."

The sixth and final Mendoza story is *The War Makers*, a novelette written before Britain declared war on Germany on 3 September 1939, but published after on October 7 1939, in *The Thriller Library* No 557.

The main crux of the story is the formula for a 'Weapon of Mass Destruction' and the demonstration and political ramifications of such a weapon. Considering when it was written, the story was prophetic and remains still topical today, considering that humanity has lived with—and been manipulated by—the threat of WMD's as a daily occurrence since the end of WW2.

> "This gas is infinitely more deadly than any used in warfare before. It could wipe out a trenchful of men without warning. Ordinary poison gas can be seen coming or smelt soon enough to enable a gas mask to be put on, but this gas is colourless and odourless. You breathe it in unsuspectingly and in breathing you die. Think what a weapon like that would mean in the hands of a power hungry for conquest."

Detective Inspector Howells of the C.I.D. again meets up with Julian Mendoza who uncovers the truth about 'The Secret of World Power!'

The short story *Partners in Crime*, evolves into gentle blackmail within a dysfunctional aristocratic family. It is also a delicious social satire on the inability of the privileged classes to exist without inheritance when forced to survive by earning a living through honest work.

The story was published in *20-Story Magazine* No 116, February 1932. Now defunct, *20-Story Magazine* (sometime called Twenty Story Magazine) was a monthly pulp fiction magazine with an emphasis on adventure and mystery stories. Authors included; W.E. Johns, Agatha Christie, Edgar Wallace, and James Ronald. The magazine was published 1922-1940 by British publishing firm Odhams Press.

ABOUT THE AUTHOR

James Jack Ronald, to give his full name, was born 11 May 1905, in North Kelvinside, Glasgow, Scotland. He was the son of James Jack Ronald, a Chartered Public Accountant, and Katherine Hamilton Ronald. He was educated at Hillhead High School, Glasgow, established in 1885.

Until he was five, James Ronald says he was chubby, happy, and irresponsible; but in 1911, his sixth year, he was run over by an automobile causing a very real morbidity to creep in. For ten years following the accident he suffered recurrent dreams about a wheel that became larger and larger as it turned faster and faster. He was invalided over a long period during which, with his mother Catherine's encouragement, he enjoyed a prodigious amount of reading. He later claimed he owed his literary gift and resultant career to this near-fatal automobile accident, which caused him to change from a sunny little extrovert to a cloudy introvert.

When he was fourteen he wrote an account of the accident, setting down all the details in a somewhat light vein, not forgetting to note that the candy he had purchased with such delight on that foggy morning was found sticking to the wheels of the car as he was being carried off. The piece won him first prize for composition and congratulations from the masters at the school and even the headmaster wished him well, but that did not prevent corporal punishment for his appalling handwriting. He was called into the headmaster's office, but kept waiting so that everybody knew that he, James Ronald, was going to receive a beating from the headmaster. This injustice obviously affected him very deeply, because it remained with him all his life, and crops up in interview after interview:

> After all, I taught myself to read before going to school and could see no reason for accepting a beating because they failed to teach me how to write, so I bolted.

In a spirit of rebellion against repeated punishments for bad handwriting for compositions for which he invariably got an 'A', Ronald came home from school one day announcing he would never return. It was time to leave. His mother Catherine was understandably distressed, concerned her elder son leaving school at such a young age would diminish his career prospects. Aware of the scarcity of jobs just then in Glasgow, she told him he could only stay away from school if he remained active in some useful employment, making it clear she would not condone an idler in the family.

Within three days James Ronald was an errand boy for the *Glasgow Evening News*, a paper into which he had smuggled a poem some months earlier. But there was 'no writing, nothing editorial' in his set up and he thoroughly disliked it and lost the job. He found another post immediately with the *Glasgow Sunday Mail* and kept this one until he printed his own rival paper on the office mimeograph. He broke the machine and, failing to cover his tracks by leaving a sheet in the copier, he was fired. Then came a dozen jobs, including one with an art dealer for whom he gilded statues and washed windows. His mother told him, 'It is no disgrace to wash windows, James, but it is a disgrace to wash them like that.'

By the age of seventeen, James Ronald had run through all prospective employers in Glasgow, including every newspaper.

He felt the need of open space—'a lot of it'—and after various and sundry abortive departures, finally won grudging permission to seek his fortune in the New World.

For some reason, Chicago stuck in the mind of the young Ronald as a magic word. He became determined to travel to the United States of America. The main method of crossing the Atlantic Ocean in the 1920s was by steamship and ocean liner. The passengers aboard the *SS Saturnia* included seventeen-year-old James Ronald, who arrived at his destination on 6 December 1922, at the Port of Québec, an inland port located in Québec, Canada. From there he continued his journey across the Great Lakes to Chicago, Illinois, United States. He managed to survive in Chicago; the fastest-growing city in world history, with a flourishing economy approaching three million people, attracting huge numbers of new immigrants from Eastern and Central Europe. Ronald stayed in Chicago for five years, wanting to write, but unable to afford the time because he was forced to earn money to live. He was taken on and fired from a variety of jobs with monotonous regularity. Like his experiences in Glasgow, he exhausted all potential employers, dabbling in some forty jobs ranging from short-order cook and dishwasher to muslin salesman; from dance promoter and theatre manager to washing dishes again in a Greek restaurant. He edited ten trade journals at one time for a Chicago publisher; and gave new life to a women's religious magazine. A chain-smoker, he confessed slyly to have worked for the Anti-Cigarette League, his excuse being 'a man must eat don't you know'—at that time eating being the only philosophy he could afford to practise. It was in the Windy City that he learned about life.

Working in the U.S. as 'a visitor' to avoid immigration may have caught up with Ronald because, in 1927, he returned to Britain on a more permanent basis, and secured a well-paid job with an English newspaper chain, and a promise of future advancement. However, during his first holiday in the job, a car accident disrupted this promising career trajectory. Whilst driving a small open two-seater Rover 8, Ronald was struck by a two-ton truck and thrown out against the radiator of another vehicle. Left with a broken hip and temporarily crippled (and without the newly acquired job), he settled down to write.

Ronald's writing developed in three stages. First, he hammered out serializations and short stories which were syndicated in newspapers, both at home and abroad; and a number were also published in obscure pulp magazines. Some stories then became lost and forgotten and this has unfortunately contributed to a lack of recognition for an impressive body of work. These early narratives were very difficult to track down, but searching has provided me with an enjoyable and rewarding task—a treasure hunt for lost tales. This was not made any easier because many of these stories were published under pseudonyms; Peter Gale, Mark Ellison, Kenneth Streeter, Alan Napier, and even women; Cynthia Priestley and Norah Banning—in addition to known pseudonyms Michael Crombie and Kirk Wales. Those I have discovered have all been gathered together for republication in this series.

A second writing stage followed; the full-length mystery stories which have made him so popular with Golden Age of Detection aficionados. They are out-of-print, elusive to find, and first editions are very expensive.

Finally, late in life, James Ronald embarked on his Dickensian-style life drama novels. He received enthusiastic praise for his ingenuity, freshness, and sharp sense of humour by many critics and writers of the time, such as August Derleth. Orville Prescott, the main book reviewer for *The New York Times* for 24 years, called James Ronald 'a born novelist', and that he 'has in full measure the two basic of fiction—the urge to create characters and to tell stories about them. Mr. Ronald does both naturally, directly and well.' His work received praise and has been compared to William de Morgan, H. G. Wells, Rudyard Kipling, J. M. Barrie, and Somerset Maugham.

James Ronald is a writer who has not gained the long-term recognition he deserves. His work has received high praise for his ingenuity, freshness, and sharp sense of humour by many critics and writers of the time and current enthusiasts, highlighting him as one of the leading storytellers of the day, yet barely anything has been republished since his death in 1972. I hope the reader will enjoy these imaginative and entertainingly written stories as much as I have collecting them.

Chris Verner
Berkhamsted, Buckinghamshire, UK
April 2023

HARD-BOILED

Mistaken Loyalty

With his God-forsaken hat at a rakish angle, Julian Mendoza perched himself on the edge of a littered desk in the newsroom of the *London Morning World*. He filled an ancient briar with tarry black tobacco and struck a match. Through a haze of pungent blue smoke, he said:

"You wanted to see me?"

The news-editor, hard at work in his shirt-sleeves, looked up with a scowl. His lean, sour face was topped with a shock of white hair which contrasted oddly with the jaundiced yellow of his cheeks. He looked as though he had eaten something that disagreed with him; it was his habitual expression. "When I send for a man it's usually because I want to see him. What's this?"

He held out a grubby piece of paper on which some words and figures were scribbled in pencil in Julian's sprawling handwriting. Julian squinted at it.

"The cashier asked for a detailed account of how I spent the twenty quid I drew from him last week."

"A nice expense account this is. The cashier went into hysterics when he read it. Take the first item alone: 'To getting Little Pete drunk…£3 8s. 3d.'"

"Getting Little Pete drunk is no light task," said Julian solemnly. "You have to fill him with whisky till his tonsils float."

"How do you explain these items: 'Skit-Skat…£5 1 1s. 4d.; Blue Bottle…£2 18s. od.; Wind Blew Inn…£2 4s. 6d.'?"

"Those are night clubs. Little Pete's crazy about night clubs."

"It's nice to know he's had a good time. And just who the hell is this Little Pete?"

"Little Pete Papadoupolis, the gangster. His father was Greek, his mother is Italian, but Pete himself is naturalised English.

You ought to meet him. You'd like him. When he's drunk, he sings 'Tiger Rag' in seven different languages."

"One would be enough for me. And I'd have to love him before I'd spend twenty pounds of the paper's good money on him. What was the idea of giving Mr. Papadoupolis the time of his life at our expense?"

"I was trying to get him to talk."

"Well, what did he say?"

"Nothing," said Julian sadly. "Not a word. By the time he was drunk enough to loosen up he was too drunk to talk."

The news-editor made his chair rear back on its hind legs like a horse. "One day I'll be carried off by a stroke, and it'll be your damned fault. You're supposed to be my best man—a fat lot of good you've been to me for the past couple of months! Greyhound racing gangs—that's all you think about nowadays. Oh, I know you've turned in some good stories about them. But the subject's going stale. For quite a while nothing's happened—"

"Nothing but the extortion of money from bookmakers and the beating-up of those who won't pay."

"That's an old story. The fact that it's true doesn't make the public any less tired of hearing it. This race-gang stuff is no longer big enough to warrant the time you're spending on it—not to mention the money!"

"In a few days," said Julian, "this race-gang stuff is going to be bigger news than ever before."

"Oh. Why?"

"Mike Flannery came out this morning."

"How did that happen? It's only nine weeks since he was sentenced to eighteen months' hard for half-killing his wife."

"A convict went crazy and attacked a warder. Mike rushed to the rescue. Some of the smart boys say that it was a put-up job, but that's neither here nor there. The point is that Mike's bravery so touched the authorities that they remitted the rest of the big thug's sentence."

"Well, who cares? Mike Flannery is only another gang-leader—and the public is fed to the teeth with gang-leaders."

Julian sighed. "Where's your famed nose for news? Mike is the toughest crook in London. In his absence Nick Rossi has taken over his gang. Mike won't stand for that —and Nick isn't likely to abdicate without a fight. It means murder. But if you want the exclusive story, I've got to be on the spot when hell starts popping."

For a few moments the news-editor stared in silence at his star crime reporter.

"You may be right, at that," he said grudgingly.

"I'm always right," responded Julian complacently. He tossed a slip of paper on the desk.

"What's this?" growled the news-editor.

The question was unnecessary. He knew what it was.

"It's an order on the cashier for another twenty pounds expense-money," replied Julian cheerfully. I'm going to need it."

The news-editor ground his teeth. They made an audible gritting noise. But he signed the order.

"Alright. You've promised me a murder. Now go out and bring it in!"

*

Through the velvet dusk snowflakes as large as postage stamps fell steadily from a heavy purple sky. In the yellow glare of a street lamp Julian Mendoza looked like a down-and-out as he turned the corner from Shaftesbury Avenue into Dean Street. An icy wind hunched his shoulders and made him thrust his hands deep into the pockets of his shabby greatcoat. His collar was turned up to his chin, his battered hat drawn down over his eyes. Snow encrusted his shoulders with white epaulettes.

He plodded along Dean Street, his head bowed before the wind, until he came to a sooty old house as cold and shabby as himself. He went through a narrow doorway and stood in a gloomy passage, shaking his coat to dislodge the snow, while his eyes roved over the visiting-cards which were tacked up above a row of bell-buttons. He found the name he was seeking, but he did not ring the bell below it. His stick tapping on uncarpeted boards, his crippled right leg dragging, he limped up four flights of stairs to a dark landing at the top of the house.

There was only one door on the landing. Julian knocked loudly on it. He heard the soft padding of feet on carpet, and a woman opened the door. There was a welcoming smile on her lips, but the sight of Julian wiped it off.

"Oh," she said dully; "it's you."

"You remember me, then?"

"You're Mendoza, the newspaper reporter." Her tone was far from pleasant.

"You don't sound pleased to see me."

"Why should I be pleased?"

"Aren't you going to ask me in?"

She stared wearily at him. For a moment he thought she was going to slam the door in his face. Then she shrugged her shoulders and stood aside. "Come in if you wish."

She led him into a small sitting room which had a scoured, polished appearance. A cheerful fire was burning in a freshly blackened grate. The chairs were covered with bright-flowered chintz, the windows curtained with the same material. The walls were distempered pale yellow. No two pieces of furniture quite matched—it had probably been picked up cheaply, piece by piece, after long ferreting in street markets and hole-in-the-corner sales-rooms—but the effect was pleasant and liveable. Through an open door Julian glimpsed another room, furnished as a bedroom.

The reporter's glance seemed casual, but his shrewd grey eyes took in everything there was to see. They travelled to the woman, and their expression softened. Mary Flannery was not yet thirty, but she looked ten years older. Already her thick dark hair was turning grey, and worry and sorrow had etched deep lines at the corners of her mouth and beneath her fine, large eyes. Looking at her, it was difficult to believe that only a few years before she had been one of the loveliest and most brilliant actresses on the London stage. Her features were still beautiful but, even so, she was no more than a tragic shadow of her former glowing self. If she followed the path she was treading, in a few years she would be haggard, unlovely; old.

"They let Mike out of jail this morning," he said, watching her face.

"You didn't come all the way up here to tell me that?"

"Now that he's out he'll be searching for you—and you won't be hard to find."

"He won't need to search. When I moved here after the trial I wrote and told him my new address."

"You must be mad!" declared Julian angrily.

"Maybe I am. It's hardly your affair."

"He almost killed you—he would have killed you but for your screams being heard and the police being summoned—and yet you're willing to have him back!"

"He's my husband," she said simply. "Besides, he didn't know what he was doing. He was drunk."

"He'll get drunk again. Next time he may finish the job."

Mary Flannery said nothing. She was looking out of the window at the white flakes swirling down through the darkness. Julian felt like shaking her.

"I can't understand you. You've got looks, brains, ability—everything an actress needs. You could go back to your profession tomorrow and earn enough to surround yourself with luxury. And yet you're willing to live in a dump like this, to stick to a swaggering bully who knocks you about every time he has a drop too much."

"He's my husband."

"He's a filthy brute. Perhaps when you married him you thought you could reform him, but surely by this time you know better? Nothing will ever change him until the hangman stretches his neck or a rival thug sticks a knife in his back. In the two years since your marriage, he hasn't altered in the least—but take a look in the mirror and see what he's done to you!"

Mary Flannery reddened with shame and annoyance. She stared at Julian; her eyes hot with resentment. "You said all this before—at the time of Mike's trial. I told you then to mind your own business. How many times must I repeat it?"

"I can't stand back and see a woman as fine as you dragged down. Can't you see what's in store for you if you stick to Mike? You'll get the heavy end of it always. When he's got money he'll throw it away on other women, and when he's broke he'll come back to you. When he's drunk, he'll ill-treat you, and when he's sober he'll forget you. When your looks are gone he'll kick you out."

"Maybe you think I don't know all that."

"If you do—and you still want to stick to Mike—you're crazy. He's a criminal, and in the long run he'll make a criminal out of you. He'll make you do things you'll shudder to think of. You'll despise yourself, hate yourself; and one fine day you'll find yourself behind prison bars, all because you stuck to Mike. What's wrong with you? Why are you throwing yourself away on a worthless crook?"

"It never occurred to that great brain of yours that I might be in love with him?"

"I see. You're funny that way. All right, be a fool if you must. There's only one end for Mike, and it'll be your end as well as his. One day he'll kill someone—it may be you. Or perhaps you'll be an accomplice instead of the corpse and in that case, you'll hang with him."

"I'm sticking to Mike," retorted Mary firmly, although her eyes were haggard. "Whatever comes of it, he's my man and I'm sticking to him. I'll even risk my neck for Mike."

Julian swore under his breath. "Alright," he said savagely; "it's your neck."

Mary Flannery opened the door. "I don't want to hurry you," she said.

On the landing Julian paused and fumbled in a pocket for one of his cards. "Take this," he said, handing it to her. "It's got my 'phone number on it. If you change your mind, you'll need help. Give me a ring and you'll get it."

Looking straight into his eyes, Mary Flannery tore the card to shreds and let the bits flutter over the banisters.

"I'm sorry," she said. "I know you mean well." And then she went into the flat and shut the door.

Julian swore again. Limping down the stairs, he found himself wishing there was a woman in the world for him as steadfast as the one Mike Flannery had had the luck to find.

Little Pete's Alibi

The falling snow had spread a layer of white over a saloon car parked without lights in one of Soho's drab alleys, making it look more like a snow model than the real thing. Inside, hidden from view by the white coating on windows and windscreen, two men were sitting in dour silence, smoking.

One was short, slim, dapper, with a little black moustache like a misplaced eyebrow, thin, predatory lips and cruel dark eyes. His coat fitted almost as tightly as his skin—Little Pete Papadoupolis fancied himself as a dandy—and all the colours of the rainbow mingled in his tie. A diamond as large as a pea gleamed on his right hand—but his fingernails were in mourning.

The other man, Mike Flannery, had the chest of a gorilla, the bulging muscles of an all-in wrestler. His face was broad, heavy, pugnacious; but his eyes were surprisingly shrewd. He was smoking a cigar—his first for nine long weeks—and obviously enjoying it.

Now and then Little Pete shot a sulky glance at the big man. His lips moved and a faint mutter issued from them, as though he were arguing with himself. Suddenly he said aloud:

"I wouldn't do it if I was you."

"You said that already," retorted Flannery.

"I'm sayin' it again. Walk into the Blue Spot alone and you'll come out on a stretcher. Listen to reason, will ya? Lemme put Nick Rossi out of the way before you start anything. There's an empty room above a fruit shop across the street from where Nick lives. The man who runs the shop is a pal of mine—at least, you can call him that. I know enough about him to hang him. He'll lend me the room for a few hours and forget afterwards that he ever saw me. When Nick comes home tonight, I can put a bullet through his head as easy as spitting in a pail. With

Nick in the morgue there won't be nobody to argue when you walk in and take over the gang."

"Nothing doing. If I couldn't take on ten rats like Nick Rossi at once I'd jump in the river."

"It ain't only Nick. I keep tellin' ya, he's got the whole gang on his side. I know you're hard-boiled. I've seen you wipe up four blokes at once. But this ain't no four blokes—it's a dozen. If they start on you with coshes and brass-knuckles and broken tumblers, they'll chop you up as fine as though you'd been through a mincin'-machine. I'm tellin' ya—"

"Then pack up telling me. You're giving me a headache." Mike looked at the illuminated clock on the dashboard. "It's gone eight. Most of the gang will be at the Blue Spot by now. Start the car and let's be on our way."

Scowling, Little Pete touched a switch and the twin arms of the windscreen-wiper swished across the glass, clearing two semi-circular patches. He stabbed the self-starter with his toe and a powerful engine sprang to life.

"You're crackers," he snapped, as the big car moved off.

"If you're so keen to rub out Rossi," said Flannery, "I might give you the job later."

"It'll be a pleasure," said Little Pete.

Purring like a sleek cat, the car weaved through the slums of Little Italy and drew up in front of a dingy café in Little Denmark Street. Above the entrance an electric sign winked on and off. It read simply: THE BLUE SPOT.

"I'll come in with you," said Little Pete.

"Nothing doing. I'm going in alone."

"Then take this." Little Pete slid a hand under his armpit and brought it out holding an automatic pistol.

"I'm going in with nothing but my two fists," said Flannery, swinging open the door at his side. "I'll show 'em I'm a better man than the whole gang put together!"

He crossed the pavement and parted the swing doors of the café with a thrust of his shoulder. Inside was a long counter and some tables spread with blue-spotted cloths. A door in the rear wall led to an inner room, the headquarters of the gang of which Mike Flannery had been leader until he was sent to prison.

But for a fat, middle-aged Italian standing behind the counter, with a soiled apron round his middle, the outer room was deserted. At the sight of Flannery the Italian's eyes widened and he made a dive for a button set in the wall which would ring a warning bell in the inner room.

Before he could reach it, Flannery crossed the space between them in two rapid strides, grabbed him by the tie and yanked him bodily across the counter with a jerk that almost dislocated his neck. Half-strangled, his face purple, the Italian kicked like a dying rabbit. Drawing back his fist, Mike chopped it down on the point of the man's jaw. The Italian's eyes rolled upward and he sagged limply in his captor's grasp. Mike dragged him behind the counter and left him on the floor out of sight.

Kicking open the door in the rear wall, he walked through. A hum of conversation died abruptly at his entrance, replaced by a silence that was almost audible.

The room was large, but the windows were tightly shut and curtained and the atmosphere was blue with smoke and stale with human breath. To the left a game of cork-pool was in progress on a full-sized billiards-table. To the right some of the gang were playing darts. At a table in the middle of the floor another group was engrossed in poker.

When Mike Flannery entered, everything came to a dead stop. The place looked like a waxwork museum: one man was frozen into immobility in the act of dealing cards; another, bent over the billiards-table, sighting a shot, remained like that with his eyes on the intruder; a darts-player stood like a statue, his hand, holding a dart, poised in mid-air. No one spoke. They all looked at Mike with the emotionless eyes of dead fish.

At a desk in a corner sat a lean, hook-nosed man in the middle thirties, with black, glittering eyes, a mouth like a knife-gash and hair smooth and glossy as patent leather. He stared bleakly at Mike Flannery and his lips twisted into a mirthless grin, cold and repellent, like that of a snake on the point of striking.

Behind the door a smart fawn overcoat and a grey velour hat were hanging on a peg. Mike lifted them down, glanced at them contemptuously, and tossed them into a corner. With elaborate care he took off his own hat and coat and hung them on the peg. No one moved or spoke. The gang was watching him silently, hungrily—a wolf pack ready to rend and tear at the first sign of weakness.

With steady fingers Flannery struck a match and applied it to his cigar. Sauntering to the desk, he glanced down at the man who was sitting there and said: "You're in my chair, Rossi."

"There's been some changes, Mike," said Rossi coolly. "It ain't your chair any more. While you was in jail the boys decided they didn't want you running the show. Nothing personal—but you're too fond of the rough stuff, and we've come to the conclusion that it don't pay. You think with your fists. Maybe that was all right in the early days when we was getting our noses in at the Kenley Greyhound Stadium—a sock in the jaw was the best argument then—but now we've built up the racket into a big-money proposition, the less trouble we stir up the better. We still use a cosh when necessary, but every time we do, it gets in the papers, and publicity is bad for our business. Peaceful persuasion's the game today—and you never learned to play it. That's why you're out, Mike."

"You're in my chair, Rossi."

"I'm staying in it, Mike."

"The hell you are," said Flannery.

He heaved the desk over on its side. Nick Rossi kicked his chair away and jumped back. One hand flew to his pocket and came out holding something tightly. There was a click, and the long, sharp blade of a knife slid out between his fingers.

Nick sprang forward like a panther, jabbing the gleaming blade at Flannery's stomach. With the heel of one hand Mike struck the knife down, with the other he gripped Rossi's wrist and twisted it relentlessly. There was a sharp crack. Rossi screamed with pain and dropped the knife. Mike let the arm drop and it dangled grotesquely, broken between wrist and elbow.

Hooking two fingers into the V of Rossi's waistcoat, Mike pulled him closer and delivered a smashing punch to his hooked nose. A sickening crunch of splintered bone accompanied the thud of the fist. Rossi dropped to his knees, his eyes shut, his head lolling on one side, blood streaming down his ashen face. When Mike released him, he sprawled on his face in a crumpled heap on the floor.

As calmly as though he were alone in the room, Mike picked up the desk. Hooking the chair nearer with his foot, he dropped into it. His eyes travelled round the room. No one had moved. "A nice bunch of rats," he said. "I walk in and beat up your elected leader and none of you moves a finger."

"Nick was supposed to be quick with the knife," mumbled one of them.

"So, you thought you'd wait and see what happened. If he'd got me with his first jab you'd have pitched in and finished me off, but because he bungled it you left him to it. You make me sick. I thought some of you had guts."

"Maybe some of us wasn't so keen on Nick bein' chief as Nick thought," said another gangster.

"Well, you've just witnessed another election and Mike

Flannery's running things again. If any of you don't like it, now's the time to say so."

Silence. Mike smiled grimly. "Carried unanimously," he said. "Well—ain't any of you mugs going to say you're glad to see me?"

The man who had been dealing at poker when Mike came in rose from the table and threw down the cards. Ex-prizefighter was written all over him—on his flattened nose, his cauliflowered-ears. At one time he had been a fair performer in the ring, but as he grew older he had become a punching-bag for younger fighters who were trying to make names for themselves. During the latter period he had earned the nickname of One-Round Reilly by his promptness in hitting the canvas and staying there, and the name stuck to him, although he had long ago hung up his gloves. He walked over to the desk and grinned sheepishly at Flannery.

"We're all glad to see you, Mike." He looked to the others for support. "Ain't that right, boys?"

There was a murmur of assent.

"You were quick enough to throw me over when I went to jail."

"Well, Mike, someone had to boss the show."

"I left Little Pete in charge."

"Little Pete ain't you, boss. Nick kept sayin' Little Pete was no good. He said you was no good either, or you'd have kept yourself out of jail. That's what a gang-leader is for—to keep the boys out of jail—and if he can't keep hisself out, what good is he? I'm only tellin' you what Nick said," he added hastily. "Nick's smart, and he talked us over. But we've been wonderin' lately if he was any good hisself, for a couple of the boys are in Brixton this minute, waiting for trial—and they look like bein' in jail for a long time."

"What were they pinched for?"

"Beatin' up a bookie at the Stadium."

Mike Flannery smiled. "I thought the rough stuff was out?"

"As a rule, boss. But every now and then you gotta give one of them a good goin'-over, as a warning to the others. Shorty Egan and Skats Manusco was sent out on this job, and they bungled it. They nearly killed the bloke, and they was seen by three witnesses. The lawyer says they'll get ten years apiece."

The gang leader looked thoughtful. His eyes travelled to the prone figure of his beaten rival. "Nick couldn't think of a way to save 'em, eh? Well, maybe I can. Maybe I've got more brains than Nick gave me credit for." He called forward another member of the gang and said: "Spike, you and One-Round take Nick home and call a doctor. Keep your mouths shut about how he got hurt. You can use my car, it's parked outside. Little Pete's waiting in it. Tell him to come in."

The two gangsters obeyed. Mike Flannery tilted his chair, put his feet on the desk, and stared at the ceiling, deep in thought. In a few moments Little Pete came in and hurried over to the desk. "Mike, are you crazy? You can't let Nick go. When he comes to, he'll be after your blood. If you let him live, he'll bump you off sure as eggs is eggs."

"Who said I was going to let him live?"

Little Pete smiled. His hand slid to the gun that was holstered beneath his armpit. "You're going to let me bump him off?"

"Not with a gun. Sit down. I want to talk to you. You know someone who would swear to a false alibi?"

"Sure," said Little Pete. "My woman."

"Big Annie? God knows what you see in that baby elephant."

"Annie's fat," said little Pete huffily, "but I like 'em fat. It gives you more to get a grip of."

"Every man to his own taste. This is what you've got to do: first see Big Annie and make her understand that you're supposed to be spending the rest of the evening with her; then go out and steal a car—a big car…"

Nick's Accident

For a time, Mike Flannery and his lieutenant had their heads together, talking in whispers. One of the card-players rose and slouched out for cigarettes. He came back in a hurry. Leaning over the desk, speaking out of the corner of his mouth, he said: "Mendoza's out there."

"The reporter? What's he doing?"

"He's behind the counter, helpin' himself to coffee. I told him he ain't welcome, but he only laughed. Shall I take a couple of the boys and throw him out?"

"I'm surprised at you, Joe," said Flannery. "Don't you know better than be rude to a newspaperman? Show the bastard in."

Joe looked astonished, but hastened to obey. Several minutes passed, however, before he returned with the reporter, who carried a cup of coffee and some doughnuts.

"Sorry to keep you waitin', boss," said Joe apologetically.

"I fancied a doughnut," said Julian. "Joe didn't know where they were, so I had to forage about a bit. Careless of you, Mike, leaving the front shop untended. Poor Tony isn't feeling up to his work. It seems that someone gave him a sock in the jaw. I saw Nick Rossi being helped into a car. So, you won the first round, eh?"

"The first and last, Mendoza," said the gang leader. "Nick knows when he's licked. He won't make any more trouble."

Julian perched himself on the desk and munched a doughnut. "He won't make any more trouble. What do you mean by that? Thought up a way to get rid of him for good?"

"Keep on shovin' that nose of yours in where it don't belong," said Little Pete, with a scowl, "and one day you're gonna lose it."

"That's unkind, Pete," said Julian reproachfully, "after the nice time I gave you the other night. I thought we were pals."

"Sure," retorted Little Pete. "This kind of pals." He went through the motions of cutting a throat. Turning to his chief, he added: "I'll be goin'. Got a date with my woman."

"Love's young dream," sighed Julian. "Still going with Big Annie Verucci? How do you take her out? In a truck?"

"Aw, phooey to you!" snapped Little Pete. Yanking his hat down over his eyes, he stamped out, slamming the door behind him.

"You're a great little kidder, Mendoza," said Mike Flannery. "I hear you were like a mother to my wife while I was in jail."

"I gave her some good advice, if that's what you mean. I warned her to avoid you like the plague."

"Yes," said Flannery. His voice was steady, but his eyes smouldered. "Yes, that was pretty good advice. But she wouldn't take it?"

Julian was silent, and Flannery added: "Y'know, Mendoza, many a man would resent you running him down to his wife. Ain't you afraid of getting your block knocked off?"

"By you? Oh, no. You're tough with women, Mike, and little blokes like Rossi, but you steer clear of men your own size."

Flannery reddened and clenched his fists. For a moment Julian thought the gang leader was going to spring at him. The reporter measured with his eye the exact spot on which he was going to punch Flannery when the trouble started; but Flannery forced a smile and let his fingers relax.

"If you wasn't a cripple," he said scathingly, "I'd make you eat them words."

"Don't let the game leg worry you, Mike. I'll take you on any time."

The gang leader's smile wavered, but it did not flicker out entirely. That puzzled Julian. An insult usually made Flannery fighting mad. The door opened, and Spike and One-Round Reilly came in. At sight of Julian, seated on the desk, they blinked with surprise.

"You boys are back quick," said Flannery.

"We left Nick's mother and the doc lookin' after him," said One-Round. "We thought we better bring your car back in case you wanted it."

"Good! I was thinking about going home. Haven't seen the wife since I came out this morning. You two boys come with me, and we'll have some beer and a hand of poker after I've said 'Hello' to Mary. Care to come along, Mendoza?"

Julian hesitated. There was something behind the invitation, of that he was certain. But what? "Alright," he said quietly.

Flannery said 'Goodnight' to the other members of the gang and went out, followed by Spike, One-Round, and Julian. Passing through the café, the gang leader paused at the counter and smiled at the middle-aged Italian in the soiled apron, who backed away with a frightened look on his plump, pallid face.

Flannery held out his hand, with a five-pound note in it. "No hard feelings, Tony," he said.

The Italian grinned feebly and took the note. "No hard feelings, boss," he agreed.

A few minutes later the four men trooped up the stairs of the drab house in Dean Street in which Mary Flannery had her small flat. In answer to Flannery's knock his wife opened the door with a welcoming smile. Her face fell when she saw Julian and the two gangsters standing behind Flannery.

The gang leader swept her into his arms and gave her a long, passionate kiss. She clung to him tightly, her eyes ecstatically shut, and when he released her, she looked as though she were coming out of a dream. With an arm round her waist, Flannery walked into the sitting-room.

"You were expecting me?"

"Yes," she said, in a low tone, "I've been waiting for you all day. I—hoped you'd come alone."

"I wanted a little fun after being shut up for nine weeks, so I brought a few friends up for a drink and a game of cards."

"Friends!" Mary Flannery repeated. "Mendoza's no friend of yours! He'd like nothing better than to see you back in jail."

"Sure, he's a friend. He don't know what a good friend he's going to be. Come on, now, take that sour look off your pretty dial and fetch us some beer and four glasses."

With a puzzled, resentful look at Julian, Mary Flannery left the room. Mike took a pack of cards from a drawer and threw them on a table, which he drew closer to the fire. Removing his overcoat and jacket, he hung them on the back of a chair and pulled the chair up to the table. He pushed his hat to the back of his head and began to shuffle the cards with the technique of an expert.

Mary Flannery returned from the kitchen with the glasses and some quart bottles on a tray. She set the tray on the table and walked away without a word. Her husband poured himself a glass of beer and drank it at one gulp, smacking his lips.

"Help yourselves," he said.

He spread the cards flat with a stroke of his hand.

"Cut for deal."

Taking from his pocket the expense-money he had drawn that evening, Julian placed it on the table at his elbow. From the opening hand he won steadily. Although Flannery was the major loser, the gang leader did not seem to mind. It was Flannery who had suggested the game, but now that they were playing, his mind was not on it.

"I feel good tonight," said Flannery, a moment after Julian, with a pair of sixes, had bluffed him into throwing in a straight. "The only thing is, I'm sorry I had to beat up Nick. He ain't a bad bloke; all that's wrong with him is a swelled head. He's got brains. We need him in the racket. I think I'll call him up and see if we can't make friends."

Julian looked up swiftly. Flannery met his suspicious gaze with a bland smile. The gang leader reached for the telephone and dialled a Temple Bar number.

"That Mrs. Rossi?" he said, a few moments later. "This is a friend of Nick's. I want to speak to him. In bed? Ask him to shove on something and come to the 'phone. No, I can't give you no message. Tell Nick it's important."

He waited, with the receiver to his ear.

"That you, Nick? This is Flannery. Aw, that's no way to talk. I'm surprised at you, using a word like that. I've been thinking; there's room in the racket for both of us. A bloke with your brains is always useful. Why can't we be friends? Yes, I said 'friends'—what did you think I said? Aw, don't talk like that. You got the wrong idea. This is on the level. You're a good man, and I don't want to lose you. I'm at my wife's new flat in Dean Street. You know the number. Why don't you come over for a chat? Maybe we can come to terms. Yes, I know you don't feel well, but I wanna talk to you. No, no, this ain't no double-cross. Mendoza's here. Sure, Mendoza the reporter. I wouldn't try any funny stuff with him looking on. Sure, if you want to."

The gang leader offered the telephone to Julian. "Nick wants to talk to you," he said.

Julian took it. "Mendoza speaking."

"Is this on the level?" demanded Rossi, at the other end of the wire. "I know your voice. You're really at the flat?"

"I'm at the flat," replied Julian, "but I don't guarantee anything. If you take my tip, you'll stop stay away."

A pause.

"I'm coming," said Rossi finally. "I'll have a gun with me— tell Mike that. Tell him, at the first sign of trouble, I'll use it."

"Don't be a fool, Rossi!" said Julian sharply. There was no answer. Nick Rossi had hung up. Julian replaced the receiver.

"He's coming," he said. "He'll have a gun, and he'll use it if you start anything. What's the game, Mike?"

"The game's poker," laughed Flannery. "Come on, give me a chance to get my money back before Nick comes. He ought to be here in about twenty minutes. It'll take him that long, coming on foot."

"On foot?" echoed Spike. "In the state he's in?"

"Nick's got a suspicious mind," smiled Flannery. "He won't risk taking a taxi. How would he know it wasn't a plant? No, he'll come on foot."

Half an hour passed, but Nick Rossi did not come. Suddenly, Mary Flannery, standing at the window, uttered a sharp exclamation. She turned a frightened white face to her husband.

"Mike! A police car! It's pulling up to the kerb!"

Spike and One-Round Reilly dashed to the window, but Flannery did not move. He said coolly: "Maybe some of the Yard boys have come to welcome me home."

Tramping of feet on the stairs, a thunderous knocking at the door. Mike rose calmly and opened it. Two plainclothesmen walked in. One of them was tall, spare, angular, with a clipped iron-grey moustache and the matter-of-fact air of an accountant—Detective Inspector Howells of the C.I.D., who for months had been devoting most of his time to the growing menace of the greyhound-racing gangs.

"Where have you been for the past half-hour, Flannery?" he demanded curtly.

"Right here, playing cards with some friends. You know Mendoza? He'll tell you I haven't left the room for an hour or more."

Looking at the reporter, the inspector's eyes narrowed. He was surprised to find Julian, apparently quite at home, in the enemy's camp.

"That the truth, Mendoza?"

"Yes, it's true. Why? What's happened?"

"Ten minutes ago, Nick Rossi was knocked down and killed while crossing the street. The car that hit him was travelling fast and didn't stop. An onlooker took the number: it is that of a car which was stolen an hour ago."

"Poor Nick!" murmured Flannery. "Who'd have thought a smart guy like him would end in a street accident?"

"If it was an accident," retorted Howells. "About twenty minutes ago Rossi's mother rings up the Yard in great agitation and says Nick has started out to come here and she's sure he's walking into a trap. On the way here Nick's killed by a stolen car. It looks funny to me."

"Well, what can I know about it? I was indoors when it happened."

"Little Pete," said Julian suddenly.

Inspector Howells looked at him questioningly.

"Fifty to one it was Little Pete who drove the car," said the reporter.

"Pete's spending the evening with Big Annie Verucci," said Flannery.

"Yes," said Julian sardonically, "Pete will have an alibi all right. Smart work, Mike."

"What d'ya mean? Me, smart? You're crazy. Why, only this evening Nick was telling me I hadn't any brains."

"Perhaps," said Julian soberly, "in the split second before the car hit him, he realised how wrong he was."

On the way back to Fleet Street Julian stuffed into a hospital collecting-box the money he had won at poker—it was too much like blood-money for his liking.

They gave Nick Rossi a lovely funeral. All Little Italy turned out to bid him goodbye.

Over a hundred cars followed the hearse to the cemetery, and a dozen of them were heaped high with flowers. Near the head of the procession was Mike Flannery's big saloon car, the gang leader, in silk hat and cutaway coat, sitting bolt upright in the rear seat. Mike scanned the impressive array of flowers for his own offering, but failed to see it. He had sent a wreath of white roses with 'Good-bye, Old Pal!' picked out on it in red. It was five feet high and shaped like a greyhound. Nick's aged widowed mother—an impulsive Italian who had never learned to control her emotions—had kicked it to pieces and put the fragments in the dustbin.

The neat and expeditious dispatch of his rival made Mike Flannery's prestige with his followers greater than ever.

A couple of hours after the funeral the more important members of the gang met in the back room of the Blue Spot Café to discuss what could be done for Shorty Egan and Skats Manusco, who were languishing in Brixton Prison, awaiting trial for assault with deadly weapons on a bookmaker at the Kenley Greyhound Stadium. Mike Flannery took the chair, and the others present were Little Pete, Spike Pinoli, One-Round Reilly, Joe Colombo and Dapper Dan Magee.

"An alibi's the thing," said One-Round Reilly, his mashed features wrinkled with the strain of unwonted thought. "We oughta cook 'em up an alibi."

"What good's an alibi," demanded Little Pete caustically, "when they was seen by three witnesses?"

"Did the bookie see who hit him?" asked Flannery.

"He didn't even know he was hit until he woke up in hospital," replied Spike. "He was lookin' the other way, and they came up and clouted him with an iron bar. From the first clout he didn't take no interest in nothing."

"It was bad luck they was seen," said One-Round sadly.

"Bad luck be damned!" snapped Little Pete. "They was careless. They oughta made sure the coast was clear. They always was a pair of slipshod workers. No system."

"Who saw them?" asked Flannery.

The others looked at Dapper Dan. He had been in the magistrate's court when Manusco and Egan came up for a preliminary hearing. He took a slip of paper from his pocket.

"I've got the names of the witnesses written down here. Albert Henry Wiggin, plumber, of 183, Kenley Street; Abraham Bloomberg, an old man with an antique shop near the Stadium; and Major General Sir Arthur Cope Hammond, managing director of the Stadium."

When he heard the third name, Mike Flannery uttered a low whistle. The others looked glum.

"We might have done something about the others," said Little Pete gloomily, "but we can't fix the General. We can't buy him and we can't scare him. I hate the sight of the old swine, but I got to admit he's got all the guts in the world and a yard over."

"Maybe so," said Flannery, "but we've got to have a crack at it. No man of mine is going to jail for ten years if there's anything I can do to prevent it."

A murmur of approval came from the others.

"Forget the General for the present," said Flannery. "We can come back to him later. Let's see what can be done about the other witnesses."

"Me and Spike here—" said One-Round Reilly.

Flannery shook his head.

"No rough stuff, if we can help it. Remember what Nick said. Nick had brains. We'll see what a little palm oil will do. That's where you come in, Dan."

It was as a confidence man that Dapper Dan Magee had first embarked on crime. He had no stomach for violence, but was valuable to the gang at times when a glib tongue and a good appearance were required. It was Dapper Dan who always made the first approach to bookmakers from whom tribute was demanded, trying by smooth speech to convince them that to pay up and look pleasant would be wisest in the long run.

At dusk that evening a car drew up outside the plumbing establishment of Mr. Albert Henry Wiggin. Dapper Dan climbed out and sauntered across the pavement into the shop. Behind the counter stood a doleful little man in soiled overalls and a dusty bowler hat. He had a pessimistic mouth and the nose of a hard drinker, and between them sprouted a chunk of moustache like an untrimmed hedge.

"Mr. Wiggin?" said Dapper Dan.

"That's me."

"I dropped in to see you about a mistake you made."

"I never make no mistakes, mister. I'm the best dam' plumber in the districk."

"You didn't make this mistake with your hands; you made it with your eyes."

"Wot d'you mean?"

"One night a couple of weeks ago you thought you saw two men at a certain place and all the time they were miles away."

"Wot are you talkin' about? Wot two men?"

"Their names are Manusco and Egan. Get me?"

Mr. Wiggin looked frightened.

"'Oo are you?"

"I'm a friend of some friends of theirs. Those two boys have some hot-tempered pals, Mr. Wiggin, and they're feeling annoyed with you."

"I don't want no trouble," said Mr. Wiggin nervously.

"That's what I thought. But, believe me, you'll cop a packet if you give evidence at the Old Bailey."

"But, mister, I've got to. I've already pointed 'em out at an identification parade."

Dapper Dan took a wallet from his pocket and slowly counted out fifty one-pound notes. As he did so, he said softly:

"You made a mistake. At the identification parade you were flustered, and the cops kept badgering you to make up your mind. Now that you've had time to think, you realise that Manusco and Egan are not the men who attacked the bookie."

"But—but—that's perjury," stammered Mr. Wiggin, with one eye on the money.

"Sure," said Dapper Dan, "but your only choice is between perjury and suicide. Take a look out of that window. There's a car outside with two men in it. They're a couple of tough guys, Mr. Wiggin. I wouldn't want either of them to have a grudge against me."

Mr. Wiggin shivered.

"Perhaps I was mistaken. On thinking it over, I'm sure I was. My eyes ain't been too good lately. I—"

Pushing the notes across the counter, Dapper Dan said:

"Take these and buy yourself some spectacles. The cops will be pretty wild when you withdraw your identification, but stick to your guns, no matter what they say. You made a mistake. You identified the wrong men."

In a tone that was quite mild and yet chillingly sinister, he added:

"I wouldn't double-cross us, if I were you. It'll be too bad what'll happen to you if you do."

"D-don't w-worry, I-I w-won't," stuttered Mr. Wiggin, clutching the notes.

Dapper Dan went quickly out of the shop. Swinging open the car door, he climbed in and said:

"Mr. Wiggin listened to reason. Now I'll have a word with the old man. He ought to be easy."

The antique shop of Abraham Bloomberg was dim and dusty and quiet, a jumbled storehouse of forgotten treasures. When Dapper Dan pushed open the door, a piano wire stretched above it emitted a nasal twang. A grey-bearded man in a velvet jacket whose body was bent like a question mark, came from the shadows at the rear of the place. His face had the texture of parchment, his hands were like old ivory.

"What can I do for you, sir?"

"I've called about a case of mistaken identity."

"I don't understand."

"You will in a minute. Remember the identification parade you attended at the local police station a couple of weeks ago?"

"Yes, I remember."

"Well, you picked the wrong men."

"That is not so. The men I identified were the rogues who attacked and almost killed the bookmaker. I saw it all clearly. Who are you, please? Are you from the police?"

"I'm from some friends of the men you identified. They think you made a mistake. They're giving you a chance to put it right."

"There was no mistake," said Abraham Bloomberg firmly. "Is that all you wanted to know? I am busy."

"Don't be hasty. There's money in this for you. Those two men never did you any harm. Why should you want to get them sent to prison? Listen to reason and you can earn yourself fifty pounds. All you need do is go to the cops and tell them you made a mistake. The cops won't like it, but there's nothing they can do about it. Anyone can make a mistake. What do you say? You can find a use for fifty pounds, can't you?"

"Get out of my shop!" exclaimed Abraham Bloomberg, livid with anger.

"With your own eyes you saw what happened to the bookie. It could happen to you." "Out!"

"You're asking for it," said Dapper Dan.

He went out to the car and put his head in through the open window. "I did my best," he said, "now it's up to you boys."

Leaving the engine running in case they had to make a quick getaway, Spike Pinoli and One-round Reilly climbed out of the car.

"Keep your eyes peeled for the cops," said Spike, out of the corner of his mouth. Followed by the ex-prize-fighter, he crossed the pavement briskly and entered the antique shop. Dapper Dan stood beside the car, as nervous as a week-old kitten—the mere thought of physical violence always made him feel sick—and his sharp eyes jumped restlessly from one end of the street to the other.

Spike wasted no time in preliminaries. He took a grip of the old man's lapels with one hand and smacked his face with the other. He shook him until his teeth rattled. Bloomberg's eyeglasses fell off and Spike ground them under his heel.

"You made a mistake when you identified Manusco and Egan," he rasped. "You made a mistake, see? Are you going to admit it, or must I pound some sense into your silly fat head?"

Abraham Bloomberg was very pale—except for the red imprint of Spike's hand on one cheek—but his weak eyes did not falter.

"I made no mistake," he whispered. "You will be sorry for this. This is England, not—"

Spike punched him on the mouth. "You made a mistake," he said.

Speechless, his lips bruised and bleeding, Bloomberg shook his head.

"You old bastard," hissed Spike. "Have I got to kill ya?"

Another vicious punch sent Abraham Bloomberg sprawling among his treasures. Spike kicked over a table on which stood a blue Chinese vase. A cry of anguish burst from the pulped lips of the old dealer.

Half an hour later, Dapper Dan, Spike and One-Round swaggered through the Blue Spot Café to the back room. Flannery was there, sitting at his desk. He gave them a questioning look.

"We can forget those two witnesses, boss," reported Dapper Dan. "The plumber took fifty quid and agreed to change his story. We had some trouble with the old man, but he finally listened to reason."

"It was funny," said Spike: "at first he wouldn't budge, although I give it to him good and strong. Then One-Round and me started smashin' up the place. That was a different story. You'd have thought he was a mother and we was stranglin' his baby. He caved in and agreed to do anything we said if we'd only leave his stuff alone. He won't cross us; I warned him if he did, we'd come back and wreck the joint, and that put the wind up him good and proper."

"He was a game old basket," grunted One-Round Reilly moodily. "We coulda butchered him and he wouldn't have given in, but he couldn't bear to see his junk smashed. He loved that old rubbish of his better than his life."

"Every man has his weak spot," said Mike Flannery shrewdly. "If we could only find Hammond's—By God!" he said suddenly. "I have it!"

He snatched up a crumpled newspaper which was lying on the floor beside his desk, shuffled it swiftly until he came to the picture page which he flattened on the desk.

"What do you think of that?" he said.

The others stared at the photograph to which his finger was pointing—a picture of a chubby little boy of about four who was running along, bowling a hoop as big as himself.

"Little Jimmy Hammond, Sir Arthur's only son," said Flannery meaningfully. "It says here his nurse takes him for a walk in Kensington Gardens every morning at ten."

"For the lova God, Mike! You're not suggesting—"

"Mike, you're crazy!"

Flannery tapped the photograph.

"The General's weak spot," he said grimly. "Tomorrow at ten," he added, "a couple of you boys have a date in Kensington Gardens…"

Mendoza Takes Charge

The following afternoon, shortly after one, the news-editor of the *Morning World* telephoned to his star crime reporter. To Julian, whose working hours were from early evening to the small hours of the morning, one p.m. was the break of dawn. When he answered the telephone, his voice was irritable with sleepiness.

"A nursemaid in Kensington Gardens this morning," said the news-editor, "stopped to pass the time of day with a polite stranger. Her charge, a little boy, wandered on by himself. That was at ten. Since then, the gardens have been searched from end to end and the child can't be found."

"You want a bloodhound," yawned Julian, "not a reporter."

"An old lady claims she saw the child being lifted into a car by a dark-skinned stranger."

"I know these old ladies. Wherever they go they see sinister men lurking. The kid's probably playing hide-and-seek with himself in the bushes."

"His father is Major General Sir Arthur Cope Hammond, managing director of the greyhound stadium where your boy-friends play their pretty pranks."

"You think Flannery's gang may have kidnapped him? No, that's hardly in their line. And yet—" Julian frowned and bit his lip. "I'm going to look into this."

"Do! Give us a ring later—if you're not too busy buying drinks for Mr. Papadoupolis!"

In record time the reporter was dressed and in a taxi. Outside Sir Arthur Cope Hammond's house in Sloane Square he ran into Inspector Howells, who was leaving.

"You on the missing-child story, Mendoza?" asked the Scotland Yard man. "It's a false alarm. The General's sister rang up a few minutes ago. She met the boy wandering by himself in Kensington Gardens and took him home with her. If she'd had the sense to ring up earlier a lot of grief and trouble would have been spared. Going my way?"

"No," said Julian quickly, without asking which way that was.

He watched Howells out of sight, then went up the steps of the General's house and rang the bell. The door was opened by a butler of sober and forbidding aspect. When Julian offered his card, the man glanced at it loftily and shook his head.

"Sir Arthur is not at home," he said heavily, and started to close the door.

Julian pushed it open and walked in. The butler spluttered a protest, to which Julian did not listen. He tried all the doors in sight until he found the General's study. Going in, he shut the door in the face of the indignant butler.

Sir Arthur, tall, thin, grey-haired and soldierly, was sitting at a desk with his head in his hands. A widower, his whole life was centred round his small son. He looked up and stared at Julian, his haggard eyes filled with surprise and annoyance.

"Please forgive this intrusion. Your butler wouldn't even consider admitting me, so I had to take the matter into my own hands. I'm from the *Morning World*."

"I have nothing to say to the Press," replied the General stiffly. "Good day, sir."

"I've already heard about your son being found," said Julian, making no move to go. "I only wanted to ask which of your sisters found him."

Sir Arthur looked at Julian for a while before replying. "My sister Caroline," he said at last.

"That was clever of her, considering that she's in Vienna with her husband. Your other sister's in Scotland. I'm afraid your story doesn't hang together very well, Sir Arthur."

They gazed squarely into each other's eyes. Julian said quietly:

"You need help. I may be able to give it to you. I'm a newspaper-man, but I'm not so desperate for a story that I'd do anything to harm your boy. You can trust me."

The General was a judge of men. "

"I believe I can," he said, after a long pause. "God knows I've got to trust someone, or I'll go mad. I don't know what to do, where to turn. For the first time in my life, I'm afraid, terribly afraid. My son has been kidnapped. A man who wouldn't give his name spoke to me on the telephone. He said: 'Your son is in safe hands. Get rid of the police, or you'll never see him again. This evening I'll ring up about eight and tell you what to do to get the boy back.'"

"Sounds like Mike Flannery," said Julian, "but I'm hanged if I know what his idea is. Kidnapping has never been in his line."

"Flannery? I know a man of that name. Used to be a doorkeeper at the Stadium. Runs some sort of employees' union now."

"A union is what he calls it. Actually, it's a gang. His men have bogus jobs at the Stadium as a cloak for their activities."

"Why should Flannery kidnap my son? For money?"

"Hardly. He can get all the money he wants in easier ways. You haven't been making trouble for him?"

"No, I didn't realise what kind of man he is. I understood that this union of his—"

"Wait a moment," said Julian. "Weren't you a witness to the attack on Parker, the bookie?"

"Yes, that is so. A disgraceful affair."

"Then that's why your son's been stolen. Manusco and Egan are two of Flannery's men. To get him back you'll probably have to promise not to testify against them."

"But—good God, man—this is England! That sort of thing—the intimidation of witnesses, the organised thwarting of justice—belongs to America. How on earth has such a state of affairs come about in this country?"

"Speaking plainly," said Julian, "you are personally to blame for the rise of Mike Flannery. To keep a gang going it's necessary to have a racket from which plenty of easy money can be extracted. No easy money, no gang. You've allowed Flannery and his men the free run of Kenley Stadium. It's been a gold mine to them. They screw large sums of money for 'protection' out of the bookies, they take toll from the pickpockets who work the stands, they even control the results of half the races. With wads of easy money to play with, Flannery's built up an organisation that can fight back when the Law attacks it. And it's your fault. You could have wiped out Flannery's gang long ago by denying admittance to the Stadium to every thug connected with him."

"I had no idea of all this. Oh, I'd heard stories, but I was assured that they were grossly exaggerated. The secretary of the Stadium, who is closely in touch with the bookmakers and the police, told me definitely—"

"What's the secretary's salary?"

"Five hundred a year."

"Has he any private means?"

"None I know of. Why?"

"A few months ago," said Julian, "he bought his wife a mink wrap. About the same time, he paid seven hundred pounds for a new car. He's fond of night clubs, too."

"You mean—But this is terrible!"

"I'm kicking you when you're down," said Julian. "I'm sorry. The important thing is to get your boy back. I don't know quite where we start. We could arrange to trace the call that is coming through this evening, but I don't suppose that would help. It's sure to come from a public booth. I'm going to see if I can find Flannery."

"What can I do?"

"Nothing. Wait for that 'phone call. Don't worry. It wouldn't do Flannery any good to harm your boy."

*

On leaving Sir Arthur, Julian called on the late Nick Rossi's widowed mother at her delicatessen shop in Soho.

"You'd like to be revenged on Flannery for killing your son?" he suggested.

"That Flannery!" cried Mrs. Rossi. "If I were a man, I would tear his heart out with my two hands!"

"A little boy is missing," said Julian. "He may be hidden in Soho. If he could be found and it were proved Flannery's gang had him, Flannery would go to prison for a long, long time."

The dark eyes of the wrinkled old Italian woman stared up into his.

"I have many friends in Soho. Perhaps one of them has seen something, heard something. I will find out. Come back later."

The reporter's next visit was to the Blue Spot Café. He found the door locked, the shutters up. A friend of his ran a shady hotel two doors away. Without asking any questions, he agreed to let the reporter go up on his roof. Julian picked his way over the slates to a skylight window in the roof of the café. He kicked in the glass and dropped through, twisting his crippled leg in landing. He limped through the building from attic to cellar, but it was completely deserted.

Going on to Dean Street, he climbed the stairs to Mary Flannery's small flat and knocked, but got no answer. He picked the lock with a useful little instrument which he carried on his keyring and went in, but the flat was void of human occupants.

From Dean Street he went to the sprawling redbrick tenement in Drury Lane in which lived Big Annie Verucci. He was not sure which of the one roomed flats was hers, so he knocked on several doors to inquire. Although Big Annie had been born in the tenement and had lived there all the thirty years of her life, everyone he asked denied ever having heard of her.

The eleventh door he knocked on was opened by Big Annie herself. She tried to shut it again in a hurry, but Julian had his foot in the way.

"Where's Flannery?"

"How should I know?"

"Where's Little Pete, then?"

"I dunno."

"When did you see him last?"

"I don't remember."

Impatiently, Julian pushed the door open and walked in. The room was full of smells, that of garlic predominating. Big Annie swung an arm like a leg of beef and gave him a punch on the ear that sent him staggering across the room. Straightening up, he saw her coming for him with a carving-knife. He snatched up a broom and held her off with it. Shoving her back, he shot a swift glance under the bed, then opened the door of a cupboard.

Something hard was jabbed into his stomach.

"Drop that broom and put your hands up," said an icy voice. It was the voice of Little Pete, who had been hiding in the cupboard. Julian did as he was told—he could not argue with a gun. The gangster smiled thinly and prodded the reporter in the stomach with his automatic. "Stand back a bit."

Julian obeyed. Keeping the reporter covered with the gun in his right hand, Little Pete put his left hand under his right armpit and brought out another automatic. With this he struck Julian a vicious blow on the bridge of the nose.

"That's for buttin' in without an invitation. And that"—he hit him on the mouth— "that's just because I like sockin' ya."

Blood streaming from his nose, his lips pulped and bleeding, Julian dropped to his knees. Little Pete laughed harshly.

"So you can't take it!"

He aimed another savage swipe at the reporter's head. Julian sensed it coming and fell forward on his face and the blow went wide. The reporter's fingers fastened round the handle of the broom. He thrust it between the gangster's legs and jerked it sideways, throwing him off his balance. Before Little Pete could right himself, Julian butted him in the abdomen with his head. The gangster gave an agonised gasp and sat down hard and suddenly on the floor, the guns dropping from his limp fingers.

Stumbling to his feet, Julian kicked the automatics under the bed. Out of the corner of his eye he saw Big Annie rushing at him with the carving-knife. There was no time to be nice about it. Dodging a jab from the big blade, he put out a foot and tripped up the furious fat woman. The floor shook with the bump. Wrenching the knife from her hand, he threw it under the bed with the other weapons.

Bending over Little Pete, who was groaning and holding his stomach with both hands, Julian gripped the gangster by the lapels and dragged him to his feet. He shook him and said:

"Where's Hammond's kid?"

Little Pete stared at him, white-faced and speechless with pain. To be butted really hard in the lower regions is a particularly painful experience.

"Where's the kid?" Julian repeated.

"I—don't—know—"

Julian shook him again. "Tell me the truth, you little rat."

"I—tell—you—I—don't—know—"

Where's Flannery, then?"

"I—haven't seen him—since—last night."

Big Annie panted to her feet and made an attack on Julian, pummelling his back with both fists. "Leave him alone!" she screamed. "You're killing him."

Julian twisted round so that the gangster was between him and Big Annie. He slapped Little Pete across the face and said: "Spit it out. Where's Flannery?"

"Lemme alone—you cowson! You've ruined me, damn you."

The fat woman wrapped both arms about Little Pete's middle and pulled with all her might. Julian kept a firm grip of the gangster's lapels. A tug-of-war ensued which ended when Little Pete screamed and fainted.

Big Annie ran out to the corridor and bawled: "Pietro! Luigi! Antonio! Venite subito!"

Following her, Julian saw doors opening all along the corridor. The Italians who had denied all knowledge of Miss Verucci came rushing out with knives and sticks in their hands. Discretion being the better part of valour, Julian went down the stairs as fast as one sound leg and a crippled one would take him. A block of wood came flying after him, narrowly missing his ear.

He spent the rest of the afternoon in a further fruitless search of Soho for a trace of Mike Flannery or the missing boy. In the early evening he went back to see Mrs. Rossi. She greeted him with a sad shake of the head.

"If anyone in Soho knows anything about the leetle boy, the secret is well kept. I could discover nothing."

Returning to Sir Arthur, Julian confessed himself beaten. The General seemed to have aged years that day. In silence they sat waiting for the telephone-bell to ring. The wait seemed interminable. When it rang at last, the General snatched up the receiver and said 'Hello?' in a desperate voice.

He listened for a time, then said harshly:

"Give me a minute to think."

Covering the mouthpiece with his hand, he said to Julian:

"You were right. My son will be returned in exchange for my promise to withdraw my identification of Manusco and Egan. I must also agree to keep quiet about the kidnapping."

"Give them all the promises they ask. After you've got the boy back you can do as you see fit. A promise given under pressure to a rat like Flannery is not morally binding."

"If I give my word," said the General stiffly, "I must keep it."

His face was distorted with emotion as he struggled to make the most difficult decision of his life.

"It is the duty of every honest man to refuse to compromise with crime," he said, almost in a whisper.

"If it were my son," said Julian, "I'd do anything to get him back. After I'd got him back, I'd set to work and kick Mike Flannery's organization to pieces."

The General took his hand from the mouthpiece.

"Very well," he said, in a dry, cold voice. "I agree to your terms. Yes, I give you my word of honour.

An hour later little Jimmy Hammond came home alone in a taxi. It was long past his bed-time, and all he could say—between yawns—was that some nice ugly men had played games with him and given him fish-and-chips and ice-cream for dinner.

Their Own Medicine

Two days later the following advertisement appeared in the *Morning World*:

> WANTED. —50 men who can use their fists and are not afraid of getting hurt. Wages, £1 per day. Liberal cash bonuses for injuries. All hospital expenses paid. Apply Box G 296, '*Morning World*.'

None of Mike Flannery's gang saw the advertisement, which might have made them think. They were too busy preparing a rousing welcome for Shorty Egan and Skats Manusco, shortly expected home from their sojourn at Brixton. Inspector Howells saw it. He read it three times, then cut it out and went to call on Julian Mendoza at the *Morning World* office.

"Know anything about this?" he asked, displaying the clipping.

"That's a leading question," replied Julian. "I don't think I can answer it until I've consulted my solicitor."

"Mendoza, if you or any of your friends are planning action which may constitute a breach of the peace—"

"If we are," said Julian cheerfully, "I shouldn't dream of embarrassing you by telling you anything about it."

At the Old Bailey trial of Manusco and Egan the judge made some pointed remarks about the witnesses, who formerly had been quite certain that the accused were the men who attacked the bookmaker and who were now equally certain that they were not. In the circumstances, he had no choice but to discharge the prisoners, who left the court with broad grins on their faces.

A 'coming-out' party in their honour, given at the Blue Spot Café, was attended by every member of the gang. An elaborate dinner was served on trestle tables in the back room. Two barrels of beer stood on boxes at one end of the room and there was a bottle of whisky at each place and more bottles in reserve. The gang settled down to make a night of it.

When the party was in full swing, a taxi drew up outside the drab hotel adjacent to the café and two men alighted from it. One was tall and broad and walked with a limp; the other was tall and thin and carried himself fiercely erect. They went into the hotel.

With a short interval between them, three taxis in succession halted at the same place and from each four burly men descended. They crossed the pavement swiftly, entered the hotel, and went straight upstairs. The two men who had arrived first were waiting for them in an attic bedroom. When they were all present the bedroom was packed like a sardine-tin. One by one they climbed through the window on to the roof and with the limping man in the lead made their way in Indian file across the slates to a shattered skylight on the top floor of the café.

At about this time a removal van stopped at the kerb outside the Blue Spot Café. Climbing down, the driver raised the bonnet and began to tinker with the engine—which was in perfect order. Inside the van a dozen large men were sitting on the floor, waiting.

Before his followers were too fuddled to pay attention, Mike Flannery rose to make a speech. This was the signal for thunderous applause. Smiling indulgently, the gang leader waited for few moments, then raised his hand for silence.

"Boys," he said, turning to the guests of honour, "we're glad to see you back. It's been no picnic for you at Brixton, but you can thank your lucky stars we were able to save you from ten years at Dartmoor. I've never been on the Moor myself, but some of the boys—who speak from experience—tell me it's hell with knobs on. If you hadn't had the organisation behind you to the last man—to the last penny—you'd have found out all about it for yourselves. Far be it from me to cast a damper on this merry party, but I want to point out it was your own faults you landed in the dock. You was careless. I might even say criminally careless. You ought to know enough to make sure no one's looking before you do a job. I don't want to rub it in, but if you take a little more care next time, you'll save the organisation a lot of trouble and expense.

"That brings me to another point. Funds are low. To a certain extent we can blame the late Nick Rossi for that. When I was sent to jail we had four thousand quid in the kitty. When I took over again there was less than three hundred. God knows what Nick did with it. Maybe he salted it away in his own name. Well, it won't do the bastard no good where he's gone.

"It's no use cryin' over spilt milk. We're short of dough, but we know where to find it. Get by and make the bookies toe the line. At present they're turning over fifteen percent of their profits to the organisation. That ain't enough. We want twenty percent from now on. I have a suspicion of them are cooking their books. It's up to us to prove it and teach the dirty crooks a lesson. A lot of money changes hands in the Stadium on race nights, and we've got to have a bigger share of it. We don't want to be tough about it, but—by God—if we have to—"

Spike Pinoli cocked his head to one side and frowned. Funny! He could have sworn he had heard a muffled sound from overhead. It was unlikely, for the upper part of the building was untenanted, but— There it was again; as though someone were tiptoeing through the room above. Turning to his neighbour, Spike said: "You hear anything?"

"Sure," said One-Round. "Mike talkin'. Don't you?"

"I didn't mean that, you mug. A noise, overhead."

"What kind of a noise?"

"Never mind what kind of a noise. Let's go and see if anyone's messing about up there."

Reluctantly, the ex-prizefighter rose. He took a swig at his bottle before following Spike through a door at the rear of the room. The passage behind was in darkness. Spike struck a match and held it above his head so that the flame shed a wavering light on the stairs that led to the upper floors.

"Nothin' there," said One-Round. "It musta been a mouse."

"Mouse be blowed," snapped Spike. "I'm going to look."

He went up the stairs, striking matches to light the way and dropping the spent ones over the banisters. Grumbling, One-Round Reilly plodded up at his heels. Crossing the dark upper landing, Spike peered in at the open door of an unused room. He heard a dull thud behind him.

Turning quickly, with a flickering match in his hand, he saw One-Round, glassy-eyed and open-mouthed, buckling at the knees and crumpling to the floor. The ex-prizefighter's limp body did not reach the floor; out of the darkness came an arm, which wound about his waist and held him up. Spike reached for the revolver which was holstered beneath his left armpit, but before he could draw it something hit him on the back of the head and he dropped without a sound.

Most of the gang had noticed Spike and One-Round leaving the room. Hearing the door opening again, they took it for granted that the same two were returning and did not bother to look round. Mike Flannery was still talking on the subject of increasing the turnover. The voice of Julian Mendoza interrupted, paralysing him into silence.

"Shut up and sit down!"

Hardly believing his ears, the gang leader turned his head and stared. As though they were hypnotised, the eyes of his men followed Flannery's gaze.

Julian Mendoza and Major General Sir Arthur Cope Hammond were standing in the doorway behind them.

"You've been talking long enough, Mike," said the reporter calmly. "The General has something to say."

Out of the corner of his eye, Julian saw Little Pete sliding a hand under his left armpit. Taking a stride forward, the reporter snatched up a bottle and threw it at the gunman. It flew through the air and struck Little Pete squarely on the forehead. With his automatic in his hand, the gangster went over backwards, chair and all, and lay in a twisted heap on the floor. Chairs fell with a clatter as the rest of the gang scrambled to their feet.

"Wait!" said Flannery. "We'll hear what the General has to say."

Squeezing through between two tables, Sir Arthur walked to the centre of the room and faced the gang. Julian limped to his side.

"I am here in person," said Sir Arthur, in an icily distinct voice, to tell you that none of you will ever again be admitted to the Kenley Greyhound Stadium. Most of you are nominally employed there by bookmakers who were forced, by threats, to engage you. A meeting was held this afternoon at which these bookmakers unanimously resolved to have nothing to do with you in future."

"They're making a big mistake," said Flannery. "A lot of tough mugs hang about the Stadium. Without protection I wouldn't want to be in the shoes of one of them bookies."

"Once you and your men are excluded from the Stadium, protection for the bookmakers will hardly be necessary."

"What makes you think you can keep us out?"

"You will find that out if you try to get in."

"I wouldn't be too hasty, if I were you," sneered the gang leader. "Maybe you haven't thought what'll happen if you try to go through with this. Take a look round the room, General. Do we look like a lot of sissies you can slap and put in a corner? Do you think we're goin' to stand back tamely and let you take our living away?"

"My decision is final. Whether you like it or not, the Stadium is closed to all of you from now on."

"We know a lot of ways to make stubborn people change their minds," said Flannery. "After a taste of them your decision may not be so final."

"For your information," retorted the General, "my son is now hundreds of miles away. Nothing you can do to me personally will affect my decision. If you're wise, you'll accept the position. If you want trouble, you'll get it!"

"Trouble!" cried Flannery. "You're talkin' about trouble! Why, you old buzzard, I'll show you what's in store for you if you meddle with us!"

He sprang on to the table, sending glasses and bottles flying, and in another jump landed beside Sir Arthur. Julian grasped the General's shoulder, spun him into a corner, and planted his own body as a shield in front of him. Flannery hit the reporter on the point of the jaw, smashing him back against the wall. Before the gang leader could strike again, Julian put a whistle to his lips and blew a shrill blast.

Ducking under another punch aimed at his chin, he drove his fists in rapid succession into Flannery's middle. And then, as though a wave had engulfed him, Julian went down under the furious onslaught of the rest of the gang. They scrambled over each other in their efforts to get at him. It was twenty to one—and the twenty were using bottles and boots. Although he had spent twenty years looking for trouble—and finding it—all over the world, Julian was never nearer to death than at that moment. A brutal death, a messy death, one which would leave the kind of corpse that is hard to identify.

At the sound of the whistle, men poured down the stairs at the rear of the house; from the removal van in front more men rushed in. Out-of-work prize-fighters, navvies, seamen, stevedores, retired policemen, ex-soldiers. Square-jawed, bold-eyed, heavy-handed, they were all of the breed of Briton who loves nothing better than a fight. The fact that they were being paid for this one gave it an added zest, although many of them would have been delighted to join in for nothing but the fun of it. They did not mind being hurt; every injury they could display later was to be paid for in cash. They waded in with itching fists and hit out lustily.

Snarling, cursing, the gang retaliated savagely with bottles and razors. Some of them had revolvers, but, with friend and foe tangled together in wild confusion, it was impossible to use them.

The pace was hot—too hot to last. The gangsters were dirty fighters—out to maim and mutilate, they kicked, bit, gouged, slashed with razors, jabbed with the ragged edges of broken tumblers and bottles—but their opponents had been through the mill and they, too, knew some unpleasant tricks. In a few minutes only half a dozen men were left standing, and not one of them was a follower of Mike Flannery.

Julian squirmed out from under a heap of men who had landed on him like a rugger scrum. He had a loose tooth, a black eye, a cut on the forehead from which blood was trickling down his cheek, and every bone in his body was aching, but he was still in one piece, which was all that mattered. Staggering up, he reeled over to the General, who was sitting in a corner ruefully fingering his scalp.

"You all right?" asked the reporter.

"All but this," replied Sir Arthur, exhibiting a lump on his head the size of an egg; "for which injury I have you to thank. I hit my head on the wall when you bundled me out of the way at the start of the fight. Why couldn't you mind your own confounded business? I may not be as young as I was, but I like a good scrap as much as the next man."

"I couldn't let anything happen to you," grinned Julian. "We need you to boss this campaign. Besides, hasn't anyone ever told you that generals die in bed?"

Sir Arthur's irregular army had suffered many casualties, but none of them was serious. Every man left the place on his own feet, although some of them walked unsteadily. Three of them carried with them a half-full barrel of beer. Julian was the last to go. Before he went, he pinned the following notice to a wall:

TO THE FOLLOWERS OF MIKE FLANNERY:

IF YOU WANT WAR, YOU'LL GET IT! FIFTY HAND-PICKED TOUGH GUYS ARE SPOILING FOR A FIGHT. YOU'VE HAD A SAMPLE OF WHAT THEY CAN DO. IF IT ISN'T ENOUGH, THERE'S PLENTY MORE WAIT-ING FOR YOU AT THE STADIUM.

£100 REWARD!

THE ABOVE REWARD WILL BE PAID FOR ADVANCE INFORMATION OF ATTEMPTS TO MAKE TROUBLE AT THE STADIUM. THE IDENTITY OF THE INFORM-ANT WILL BE KEPT IN STRICT CONFIDENCE.

It was not in Mike Flannery's nature to accept defeat. The wrecking of his headquarters, the beating-up of his men, the declaration of war and its offer of a reward to informants; these things lashed him to insensate fury. Raging like a madman, he swore to create so much hell in the Stadium that the General would bitterly regret ever having interfered with him.

He was faced with immense obstacles: to make trouble in the Stadium it was necessary for the gang to get in; and that was not going to be easy. His scouts reported that a heavy guard had been placed on the employees' entrance, through which the gangsters had been accustomed to swagger. It was Little Pete who suggested trying the turnstiles.

"Thursday is a big night at the Stadium," he said, "and there's always long queues at each of the ten payboxes. When the crowds are pouring through, the attendants are kept too busy to notice who's buyin' tickets. Here's the idea: we join the queues and pass through the turnstiles one by one. Inside, we meet behind the stands. Before anyone knows we're in, we come down like a cyclone on the administration building and smash it to hell."

"It might work," said Flannery thoughtfully.

"Sure, it'll work," said Little Pete.

They tried it on the following Thursday evening. As unobtrusively as possible, the gangsters mingled individually with the long lines of greyhound-racing fans which radiated from the payboxes. Spike Pinoli found a place near the head of the queue at entrance D. His hat was drawn low on his forehead, his coat collar turned up to his ears. When he reached the paybox he put down the exact price of admission and was passed through without having to utter a word. It was easy, dead easy.

The attendant did not even spare him a glance. With a smirk on his lips, Spike hurried towards the spot where the gang was to gather. A hand gripped his shoulder.

"Not so fast," said a hard voice.

Spinning round, the gangster looked into the grim eyes of a burly man with a silver greyhound on his lapel. Drawing back his arm, Spike aimed a clenched fist at the man's jaw. It did not reach its objective. Another burly individual, standing behind the gangster, jabbed a knee into the small of his back, throwing him off his balance, and at the same time bashed his hat over his eyes, effectively blindfolding him. The two men hooked an arm through each of his elbows and rushed him backwards at breakneck speed to an exit, where he was swung round and booted into the street.

As the other gangsters passed the turnstiles the same treatment was meted out to each of them in turn. Mike Flannery fought like a demon, but was mastered by five hefty guards, who rough-housed him unmercifully as they hustled him to an exit.

Almost insane with anger, he returned to his headquarters to meet the bitter eyes of his humbled followers. They stared at him in silence while he stormed about the back room of the café. Someone was going to pay, he vowed—someone was going to pay!

"Alright," snarled Spike Pinoli. "Someone is going to pay. Who? When? How? Unless Little Pete has another of his bright ideas"—this with a vitriolic glare at his fellow-gangster "we're out of the Stadium for good. How do we make 'em pay if we can't get at 'em?"

"Maybe we can't get in," growled Flannery, "but the bookies have to come out. They've got homes to go to, haven't they? Well, tonight things are going to happen to some of 'em on their way home. Who are the four biggest bookies?"

It was Dapper Dan Magee who supplied the answer. "Edwards, Massi, Davis and Greenbaum," he said.

"Alright! We'll make an example of them. You boys will split up into four squads. Each squad will steal a car and attend to one of those bookies."

Shortly after twelve that night one of the designated book-makers, driving home in a smart little two-seater, was crowded into the kerb by a powerful saloon car from which sprang four men. Armed with lengths of gas-pipe, iron bars, knuckle-dusters and razors, they swarmed over the two-seater, wrenched open the offside door and hauled the driver out on to the road.

Before they could give him the murderous beating they had planned, another car roared up and swerved across the road beside them. Out of it jumped six burly men with truncheons in their hands. They laid about them, and in a few minutes the bewildered gangsters were battered into submission.

All night Mike Flannery sat in the back room of the Blue Spot Café waiting for his men to return. With him was his lieutenant, Little Pete. On the desk between them stood a bottle and two glasses. At intervals Little Pete fetched a fresh bottle from a supply in a cupboard. Frequently Mike Flannery rose and paced the floor like a caged animal. With the passing of time his stride grew jerkier, his frown became blacker.

"Why don't they come? What the hell's happened to 'em?" he cried, when the grey half-light of the dawn was creeping into the room.

In gloomy silence, Little Pete shrugged his shoulders and poured himself another drink from a bottle which was two-thirds empty. Flannery snatched up the bottle and put it to his lips. When he set it down again Little Pete took one look at it and went to the cupboard for another. At half-past seven Little Pete went out for a morning newspaper. When he came back his thin, swarthy face was peaked and grey. "Read that!" he snapped, tossing on the desk a copy of the *Morning World*.

The veins at Mike Flannery's temples swelled as his eyes took in the sprawling headlines:

STADIUM 'FLYING SQUAD' FOILS GANGSTER ATTACKS ON
BOOKMAKERS

SIXTEEN ARRESTS

When Flannery was sufficiently calm to read the story beneath the headlines, he skipped the opening paragraph, which told of the attacks which had been launched simultaneously on four homeward-bound bookmakers: he knew all about that. The second paragraph ran:

> "Information received had prepared the Stadium authorities for the attacks, and car-loads of employees followed the threatened bookmakers as they set out to go home. In the act of assaulting their victims the gangsters were surprised and overpowered by superior numbers. Detained until the arrival of the police, they were taken to various police stations and charged with felonious assault with intent to cause grievous bodily harm. It is expected that further charges will be made in connection with the theft of the cars in which the attacks were carried out. Among the sixteen men in custody are Luigi (Spike) Pinoli, Joseph Colombo, Edward (One-Round) Reilly, Bryan (Shorty) Egan and Enrico (Skats) Manusco, all of whom are said to be known to the police as dangerous characters."

The gang leader ripped the newspaper across and crushed it into a mangled ball.

"How did they know?" he raved furiously. "There are fifty

bookmakers at the Stadium. They couldn't employ carloads of guards to follow all of 'em. How did they know we was goin' to pick on these four?"

"'Information received,'" quoted Little Pete grimly. "One of the boys turned squealer."

"Who? Tell me that! Who?"

"Dapper Dan was here yesterday evening when you planned the attacks. He left the room while you was arranging the final details. He ain't been in since."

"By God! I'll tear his guts out, the dirty—"

"Sure," retorted Little Pete; "when you catch him. A bloke can go a long way on a hundred quid."

Mike Flannery spent the day at a secret hideout in the Euston Road, chain-smoking and pacing the floor. In the early evening there was a loud double knock on the door, followed by a quieter single knock. The gang leader opened the door and Little Pete slipped into the room.

"The cops ain't lookin' for you," he said. "They ain't been near the Blue Spot or your wife's place all day. That means the boys are takin' their medicine without squealing. I told you they'd keep their mouths shut. They ain't the squealing kind."

"What about Dapper Dan?" objected Flannery. "He squealed to the Stadium authorities. Suppose he tells his story to the Yard? He knows enough to get me ten years' hard."

"I got a straight tip that Dan left town last night, so he's the least of your worries. What are you going to do about the boys in jail?"

"What can I do? The cops have got 'em dead to rights. There isn't enough money in the kitty to do 'em any good—and we've got a fat chance to fix the witnesses. If it was only three or four of the boys, we might be able to do something—but it's damned near the whole gang."

"Yes," said Little Pete gloomily, "the gang's busted up properly. Those who ain't in jail have taken it on the lam." He grinned sourly and added: "Wherever Nick Rossi is, I'll bet he's laughin' himself sick. Got a drink?"

"If I had I wouldn't give it to you. You're going to need a clear head. We've got work to do."

"What kind of work?"

Flannery was looking out of an unwashed window. Over his shoulder he said in a stifled voice: "Think I'm going to crawl into a corner like a whipped dog and admit I'm licked?"

"If you take my tip you'll lie low. This ain't no time to start anything."

The gang leader swung round fiercely. "I'm going to hit back, and hit hard! All that's happened to us is the fault of one man. I'm going to get him if it's the last thing I do."

"You mean Mendoza?"

"Mendoza!" Flannery laughed. "A cheap newspaper hack."

"You—you don't mean the General?"

"Who else?"

Little Pete uttered a low whistle. "Then it probably will be the last thing you do!"

"If you're afraid, say so, and I'll go through with it alone."

For a few moments Little Pete eyed his leader bleakly. "You're the boss," he said at last.

"Alright. Bring Big Annie to my wife's place at ten tonight. Meanwhile, steer clear of the booze."

"Honest to God," said Little Pete, "I won't touch a drop.

When he left Flannery he went straight to a pub, where he downed four large whiskies in rapid succession. He had a feeling that the near future, following Flannery's lead, was going to be about as safe as playing with dynamite. It did not occur to him to desert his leader, as the shattered remnants of the gang had done. Little Pete had no conscience, but his loyalty was unlimited.

Accompanied by Big Annie Verucci, he arrived at Mary Flannery's flat on the stroke of ten. His walk was steady, his speech was normal, but there was a glitter in his dark eyes which betrayed the fact that he had been drinking solidly for hours. Mary was sitting beside the fire in her living room. Playing-cards and counters were set out on a table in the middle of the room, flanked by a full bottle of whisky and some glasses.

"A poker party, eh?" said Little Pete, mildly surprised. "I

thought we had work to do." "The poker party's an alibi," said Flannery curtly. "You and me, Big Annie and Mary, we're supposed to be playing cards."

"I see. And what will you and me really be doin'?"

"The General's a punctual old bird. You could set your clock by him. Every night at two minutes to twelve he steps out of a taxi and crosses the pavement to his house. Tonight, he ain't going to reach it. When he gets out of the taxi, we drive up behind in a stolen car, and as he walks towards the house, we let him have it. One of us drives the car, the other does the shooting."

"Which does which?"

"That's a detail," said Flannery. He produced a coin. "Heads or tails?"

"Heads," said Little Pete, when the coin was in mid-air.

"It's tails. You do the shooting, I drive. You're the best shot, anyway."

Little Pete stretched out his hand for the bottle. Flannery moved it beyond his reach "That's only part of the stage setting. You can have all you want after the job's done, but until then, leave it alone. You look as though you've had a skinful already."

For an hour or so the two gangsters played banker, and Big Annie looked on, sitting on the groaning arm of her lover's chair and stroking his hair with a large, chubby hand. Mary Flannery sat by the fire, staring into the glowing coals.

"It's about time we knocked off the car," said Flannery at last, glancing at his watch. "If you're doing the driving," replied Little Pete calmly, "knockin' off the car is part of your job."

Flannery rose. "Alright," he grunted, "I'll be back inside half an hour."

He picked up the bottle, locked it in a cupboard and put the key in his pocket. "Just to be on the safe side," he said.

Twenty-five minutes later, having stolen a fast car and parked it nearby, Flannery re-ascended the stairs to his wife's flat. Between two landings he paused and listened with a black look on his heavy features. Overhead a fuddled voice was singing "Where's that tiger? Where's that tiger?"

It was the voice of Little Pete: and when the Greek-Italian-English gangster sang 'Tiger Rag' it was a sure sign that he was hopelessly drunk.

Taking the remaining stairs two at a time, Flannery burst into the flat in a towering rage. The door of the cupboard in which he had locked the whisky stood open, the lock wrenched off. The bottle was on the card table, empty. Its contents had not satisfied Little Pete; he had found another bottle in the cupboard and emptied that, too. He was sprawling on the couch with his eyes half-shut and a foolish smile on his face, and Big Annie Verucci—far from sober herself—was nursing his sleek, black head on her ample bosom.

Gripping his lieutenant by the tie, Flannery hauled him to his feet. Little Pete's legs gave at the knees, as though they were stuffed with sawdust. With an oath, the gang leader smacked his face and let him drop back on the couch. Clenching his fist, he swung it back, preparatory to driving it into Little Pete's vacant, grinning face.

Big Annie put her hand under Little Pete's jacket and drew out an automatic. Her eyes grim, she pointed it at Flannery. "Touch him again!" she hissed. "I blow your god-damned head off."

Looking into the barrel of the gun, pointing unwaveringly at his head, Flannery let his fingers relax. "To hell with the pair of you," he snarled, turning away.

To his wife, he said: "You can drive a car. Get your hat and coat."

Mary Flannery stared in horror at her husband. "No, Mike, please!"

"Get your hat and coat."

"Mike, I'll do anything you ask, anything but that. Think what you're doing! You're asking me to be an accomplice to a murder!"

"When you've killed as often as I have, murder is only another word. I've got to have someone to drive the car. That's all I'm asking you to do. I'll attend to the rest myself."

"Let him live, Mike. It can do you no good to kill him. You needn't worry about being broke. I'll go back to the stage and earn all the money you need."

He struck her across the face. "Get your hat and coat," he said.

Wearily, she turned and went into her bedroom. In a few moments she returned, dressed for the street.

*

"If you think I'm going to run away," said Sir Arthur angrily.

Kenley Greyhound Stadium was closed for the night, and Sir Arthur and Julian Mendoza were in a taxi on the way to the General's house in Sloane Square.

"Who's talking about running away?" replied Julian smoothly. "All I said was that your son's a little young to be so far from his father, and I thought you ought to pay him a visit."

"He's with relatives in Scotland," snapped the General. "I can rely on them to look after him."

"Relatives! So that's the kind of father you are. The poor child idolises you. He's probably eating his heart out with loneliness."

"I miss the boy. I'd like to see him. But that's not what's worrying you, Mendoza. You want me out of the way in case Flannery tries to revenge himself on me for breaking up his gang."

"Supposing I do? The job you set out to do is completed.

You've cleaned up the Stadium. There's nothing cowardly in withdrawing from the scene for a while until the police get some evidence against Flannery and lodge him behind the bars."

"I'll think about it," said the General grudgingly.

The taxi stopped, and the driver reached back and opened the door. Sir Arthur and Julian alighted. Handing the driver half-a-crown, the General started to ascend his front steps, fumbling in his trouser pocket for his keys. About to follow, Julian noticed a car idling along beside the kerb. There was a woman at the steering-wheel, a man in the rear seat. The man was leaning forward, with something black in his hand.

Julian threw himself at the General and gripped his knees in a flying tackle, bringing him down on the steps with a thud.

A flash of orange flame. A sharp report.

Something clipped the reporter above the ear and he lost consciousness for a moment.

He came to, to find the General sitting on the steps beside him, nursing a bruised knee and a skinned nose.

"What the devil were you playing at?" demanded Sir Arthur testily.

Julian stood up and looked warily to right and left. The car was gone. "Someone took a pot shot at you from a car. Didn't you hear the bang?"

"The only bang I heard was when my nose hit the steps. I say—"

Leaning forward, the General stared anxiously at Julian. "You're hurt! There's blood trickling down your face."

"Perhaps you'll go to Scotland now," said Julian. "If not for your own sake, at least for mine. The next bullet I intercept on your behalf might be the last."

"My dear fellow, I'm fearfully sorry. Come in and I'll 'phone for a doctor."

"It's only a scratch," said Julian. "I'm a collector of that sort of souvenir. I can't stop now. I've something rather urgent to say to Mr. Flannery."

It was the gang leader in person who opened the door to Julian at the flat in Dean Street.

"This is an unexpected pleasure," said Flannery, opening the door wider. "Come in. We're having a little party. Poker and a drink or two."

Julian limped into the sitting-room. Mary and Big Annie were sitting at the table with cards in their hands. The rest of the pack lay on the green baize tabletop.

Julian looked at Little Pete, lying on the couch in a drunken stupor. Going to the table, he sorted out some cards: the ace of diamonds, the king of clubs, the queen of spades, the jack of hearts and the spade three.

"That's a good hand," he said, showing it to Big Annie.

"Sure," she said, smiling and nodding, "it's a swell hand."

"A fat lot you know about poker," retorted Julian, throwing the cards down. Turning to Mary Flannery, he said: "What do you need to beat a full house?"

Mary stared at him in silence.

"Little Pete's too drunk to see straight," said Julian. "Neither of the women knows the first thing about poker. With whom have you been playing, Flannery? Yourself?"

"Maybe it wasn't poker," said Flannery, without batting an eyelash. "Maybe it was some other game. I forget. Anyway, we've been playing cards for the past two hours."

"That's your story and you're sticking to it? Alright. There's just one thing I want to say. If the shot you fired at the General tonight had killed him, it's possible that this half-witted alibi of yours would have deceived the law. But the law wouldn't have been all you'd have had to reckon with. I couldn't sentence you to death with a black cap and all the trimmings, or string you up with a hempen rope—but there are more ways than one of destroying rats."

"Meaning?"

"Simply this: evidence or no evidence, if you kill the General, I'll attend to you personally."

"For a cripple," sneered Flannery, "you've got a lot to say. If it wasn't for your crocked leg—if we could fight on level terms—"

"That's easily arranged," said Julian.

He gave Flannery's right leg a kick that almost broke it.

With a scream of pain and rage, Flannery clutched his injured limb with both hands. "Alright, fellow-cripple," said Julian softly. "What about it?"

Half-demented with pain, Flannery snatched up a whisky bottle and hurled it at Julian's head. The reporter ducked and there was a crash as the projectile smashed on the wall. Taking a swift step forward, Julian sank one fist into Flannery's stomach and landed the other crisply, forcefully, on his chin. The first punch doubled up the gang leader, the second straightened him out. There was no need of a third. Flannery stumbled back against the card-table and took it over with him in his fall to the floor.

Julian turned to Mary Flannery. "So, he's dragged you down to his level? He's made you an accessory to an attempted murder. And I wasted my time begging you to leave him. Funny, wasn't it?"

She did not answer. The expression on her face was one Julian had seen before—on the corpse of a woman who had drowned herself.

In a whisky-soaked tenor, Little Pete chanted:

"Dove E quello tigre? Dove E quello tigre?" He had reached the Italian version of his variations on 'Tiger Rag' in seven languages.

Murder on the Night Express

With a clatter of milk bottles, to the shrill crescendo of a young servant-girls' voice tearing a popular song to pieces as she polished a door-knob, morning came to Dean Street. On the couch in Mary Flannery's sitting-room, Little Pete stirred and opened one eye. He shut it again quickly.

"I feel lousy," he muttered.

"Go to sleep again, poveretto," murmured Big Annie soothingly. "Sleep, angelo mio." "Where's Flannery?"

"He sleeps, the fat pig. He snores."

"What happened last night?"

"You got drunk. Flannery and his wife, they went to shoot the General. When they came back Flannery was cursing."

"He bungled it?"

"Si."

"I'll bet he's sore as hell at me."

"Do not think of it, my Petey. Go to sleep."

"That's a good idea," grunted Little Pete. "I feel lousy."

When he woke again it was almost noon and sunlight was streaming into the room. Mike Flannery was bending over him with a hard look on his face. Big Annie was watching the gang leader warily, ready to defend her lover if Flannery attacked him.

"Sorry about last night, Mike," said Little Pete humbly. "It was like this—"

"Skip it," retorted Flannery. "I've got something else on my mind. Go home and shave and put on a clean collar. We're leaving for Glasgow at 11.45 to-night."

"Why? What's up?"

"I went out for a walk a couple of hours ago, and who did I see in a taxi but the General's frosty-faced butler. On a hunch,

I haled another cab and followed him. He went to Euston and booked a first-class sleeper on the Night Scot. That means the General's going north—and we're going with him!"

"You're going to follow him clear to Scotland to bump him off?"

"Maybe we won't need to go all that way."

"If you're thinking of doin' it on the train, you're crazy."

"I've got an idea. It sounds a bit crackers so far, even to me, but perhaps I can work it out between now and tonight. Come back in good time for the train—sober!"

"If I was to be struck down this minute—"

"If there was any justice," said Flannery, "you would be."

*

11.29.

Sixteen minutes to go before the Night Scot steamed out of Euston.

In the wake of a porter carrying the General's two pigskin suitcases, Sir Arthur and Julian Mendoza weaved their way through the crowd on Platform 14, where the train was already waiting with smoke drifting lazily from its funnel. The porter led them into a first-class sleeping-car and along a carpeted corridor. He opened a door with a flourish, revealing a small compartment like a cabin for one on a liner, with a real bed. There was a washbasin with hot and cold water, a towel-rail, clothes-hanger, luggage-rack, hinged shelves and a full-length mirror. The walls were painted green and the rug and bedspread were to match. Always interested in creature comforts, Julian investigated the bed. It had a vi-spring mattress on a spring frame, with a hair mattress above.

"This is something like it," he said. "You ought to sleep like a top. Anything I can do for you before I go?"

"Nothing, thanks. You might keep an eye on things at the Stadium until I come back—which won't be long."

"I will. Well, so long. I've got to give my news-editor a ring."

Julian swung off the train and limped along the platform towards an exit. Glancing casually through the window of a third-class compartment, he saw Mike Flannery sitting inside. Turning back, he looked again and recognised the other occupants of the compartment—Little Pete, Mary Flannery and Big Annie Verucci. Flannery saw Julian staring in and he waved his hand.

Not far from Julian was a hand-truck piled high with luggage. Using a trunk as a table, the reporter scribbled a message for his news-editor. While he was thus engaged a woman brushed past him, hurrying to the exit. She looked vaguely familiar, but he could not quite place her. He handed a porter a coin and the pencilled message and asked him to wire the latter immediately.

Boarding the train again, he knocked on the door of the General's compartment. After a short delay it was opened by Sir Arthur, who had already undressed for bed. "I thought you'd gone."

"I've decided to stay with you."

"You mean you're coming to Scotland on this train?"

"In this very compartment."

"But why?"

"Flannery's on the train."

"Oh," said the General, his eyes narrowing.

"Precisely," said Julian.

He opened the window and put his head out, keeping an eye on the section of the train where Flannery and his companions were sitting.

Less than a minute before the train was due to leave, a peculiar-looking woman sprinted up the platform with a small case in her hand. She was of the type of middle-aged spinster which finds satisfaction in aping the male sex. Her mustard-yellow travelling suit was of shaggy tweed and she wore brown brogue shoes, thick woollen stockings, a masculine collar and tie and a felt hat. When she passed him, Julian noticed something that struck him as oddly incongruous; although everything about her suggested a contempt for feminine follies, her fingernails were long and pointed and lacquered bright red.

The guard waved his flag and blew his whistle. Steam hissed and curled beneath the footplate of the locomotive. The whole length of the train shuddered as the engine strained at it. The platform receded quickly as the Night Scot gathered speed.

Sir Arthur climbed into bed and lay smoking with his eyes on the ceiling. Julian lit his pipe and sat cross-legged on a suitcase. Neither was inclined for conversation. Both were wondering why Mike Flannery was on the train.

About an hour and a half after the train left Euston there was a knock at the door. Julian answered it. Little Pete was standing in the corridor. Stepping out, Julian closed the door of the General's compartment behind him.

"Well?" he said unpleasantly.

"Flannery wants to talk to you."

For a moment Julian hesitated, then: "Alright," he snapped. "You lead the way."

They passed through two corridor carriages. Halfway along the third, Little Pete stopped at the door of a compartment which had the blinds drawn. "In here," he said.

"You go first," retorted Julian, "and raise those blinds."

"You're too trusting," grinned Little Pete, "that's your trouble."

He went into the compartment and raised the blinds. Julian looked in through the glass. Flannery and Big Annie were facing each other in the window seats. Mary Flannery was sitting beside the door. The other seats were empty. A label on the window proclaimed that the compartment was entirely reserved for 'Mr. Flannery and party.' Julian went in and dropped into a corner seat facing Mary Flannery. "'The Rat's Nest' would be a good name for this compartment," he said.

Reddening, Mary Flannery avoided his gaze. Suddenly she rose and went out. Julian was sufficiently suspicious-minded to watch which way she went; it was the opposite direction to that which led to the first-class sleeping-car.

"She don't like you," leered Little Pete, taking the seat Mary Flannery had vacated.

"I wouldn't feel flattered if she did," Julian replied, "considering the kind of vermin she does like."

Flannery looked annoyed, but he forced a smile. "Have a drink?" he suggested, producing a bottle.

"Not with you. Get down to brass-tacks, Flannery. What are you doing on this train?"

"I'll tell you the truth—"

"When you begin like that, I know there's a lie coming."

"Nice polite bloke, ain't you, Mendoza?" said Flannery, with an edge to his voice.

"What are you doing on this train?"

"I happened to find out—never mind how—that the General was going north. I wanted a talk to him, to see if we couldn't declare a truce, so I thought I'd make the trip, too."

"Now tell me the one about The Three Bears."

"Think I'm kidding you? You're wrong. I know when I'm beaten. The gang's broken up. The boys are in jail. I'm broke."

"What do you want the General to do about it?"

"I want him to leave me alone, that's all. I'm quitting the racket and taking on a new line altogether and I want to be sure the General and that gang of his won't keep worrying me."

"You're lying, Flannery. You're not going to so much trouble merely to ask the General a question you could answer yourself. You know perfectly well he won't bother you if you don't bother him. There's something behind all this."

Out of the corner of his eye Julian saw the mannish woman in mustard-yellow tweed going along the corridor towards the first-class sleeper.

"You've got a suspicious mind, Mendoza," said Flannery. "I give you my word I only want to be friends with the old boy."

"That's why you took a shot at him the other night. You know better than to imagine for a moment that the General would be friends with one of your sort. What kind of friends do you mean? The kind you were with Nick Rossi?"

"Alright," said Flannery angrily, "have it your own way. I've told you the straight truth, but don't believe it if you don't want to."

"If you ever told the straight truth, Mike, you wouldn't believe your ears. Here's a tip: keep away from the General on the train and off it. I'll be with him as long as you're anywhere near, and at the first move you make that I don't like there'll be trouble."

Julian was puzzled as he went out of the compartment. The conversation with Flannery had not made sense. What was it all about? What was behind it?

He was passing through the first of the two carriages between the sleeping-car and Flannery's compartment when someone bumped into him and almost knocked him down. It was the middle-aged woman in mustard-yellow. She hurried on without stopping.

In the sleeping-car another woman was screaming herself into hysteria. Standing in the corridor in nightgown and silk wrap, she had her mouth wide open and one long noise was coming from it. A group of passengers in night attire were clustered round her, trying to find out what was the matter. A sleeping-car attendant was vainly offering her a glass of water.

Julian took it from him and dashed the contents in her face. She gulped and spluttered and opened her mouth to yell some more. Taking her by the shoulders, Julian shook her into silence. "Don't be such a fool. What's wrong?"

"In there," she stammered, pointing to the door of the General's compartment.

Drawing in his breath sharply, Julian opened the door. For a moment he stood on the threshold, his fingers tightening on the door-knob until the knuckles showed white. The others were jostling at his back, trying to see under his arm and over his shoulder.

Feeling suddenly tired and weak, Julian limped to the bed. The General was lying half in and half out of it, his eyes open and staring, his arms spread as though he were crucified. On the breast of his pyjama jacket was a red patch which might have been mistaken for a scarlet handkerchief protruding from a pocket, but for the fact that it was growing bigger every moment. Julian felt the General's still pulse, but that was hardly necessary. The gaping wound above his heart left no room for doubt that he was dead.

The sleeping-car attendant put up a shaky hand to pull the communication-cord.

"Don't do that," said Julian sharply, grasping his arm. "If you stop the train the person who did this will escape. We're travelling at seventy miles an hour. The murderer can't get off the train."

The woman who had been screaming pushed her way through the little crowd of white-faced passengers.

"I saw her leaving the compartment," she stammered. "The— the woman who did this. She was dressed in tweeds—almost like a man—yellow tweeds and a collar and tie. She came out of this compartment with a knife in her hand—it was red and dripping. Oh, my God! I almost died with fright!"

"You hear that?" said Julian to the sleeping-car attendant. "Fetch the guard. We've got to find that woman."

While the train roared north at seventy miles an hour, Julian, the guard, and two sleeping-car attendants searched it from end to end. They questioned every passenger and examined every corner big enough to hold a human being, but they did not find the woman in mustard-yellow tweeds. From the moment she bumped into Julian when hurrying away from the first-class sleeper, no one had seen her. She had vanished off the train, utterly and completely.

At Rugby, the first stop, the police were called in and the sleeping-car was detached from the rest of the train. Julian had a word with the inspector in charge—they had met before, on the occasion of a local murder trial—which resulted in the official detaining Flannery and his wife, Little Pete and Big Annie, as well as the passengers who had been present when the murder was discovered.

It seemed obvious that the only way the missing woman could have left the train was by jumping out on to the line. If she did that, she must be lying dead or seriously injured on the permanent way. Squads of railwaymen and police were assigned to search the line for several miles. One of them found the long knife with which the murder was committed—the handle had been wiped clean—but no trace of the woman was discovered.

In the early morning, after several hours of questioning, Flannery and his companions were released, and they hired a car to take them back to London. As he watched them walking out of the police station, Julian ground his teeth. Flannery was behind the murder; of that he was certain: he had inveigled Julian out of the way while it was committed; but his guilt could not be proved until the middle-aged spinster who actually wielded the knife was found.

Dead tired, Julian stretched himself with a yawn. His eyes were heavy from lack of sleep. The table at which he sat was littered with scribbled sheets of paper, and the ashtray overflowed with spent matches and tobacco ash. He had returned to London thirty-six hours ago after a long conference at Rugby between Scotland Yard officials and the local police, which left the murder as much of a mystery as ever. Since then, for a day and a half on end, he had tried to work out in his mind the way in which the murderess had left the Night Scot.

He had scrawled pages of theories, none of them even remotely possible. How had she done it? How? How? How? It was impossible, it couldn't be done. And yet, it had been done. Before the murder the woman in tweeds had been on the train, there were a score of witnesses to that. She had been seen leaving the General's compartment with the blood-stained knife in her hand and five minutes later she had disappeared, vanished off the train, at seventy miles an hour. She had not jumped out or her mangled body would have been found on the line. It was the most fantastic problem with which Julian had ever been faced.

Flannery was behind the killing, of course; but how had it been done? What had happened to the woman after she bumped into Julian in the corridor? Where had she gone? How had she left the train?

It was like one of those illusions' magicians do on the stage.

Julian stared into space, thinking. In his mind's eye he kept seeing the gloved fingers of Mary Flannery tying themselves in knots during the police questioning of her and the other witnesses at Rugby. Her gloved fingers…What on earth had they to do with the disappearance of the mannish spinster?

He rammed his hat on his head and shrugged himself into his overcoat. With his empty pipe between his teeth, he went out of the quiet house in which he lodged. Night had fallen, the second since the one which had been Sir Arthur's last.

A few minutes later he climbed the stairs of the rickety old building in which Mary Flannery lived, and knocked at the door. There was no answer. He knocked again. Still no answer. He was fumbling for his key-ring, intending to admit himself by means of the picklock which he always carried, when the door suddenly opened and Mary stood on the threshold.

"Where's Flannery?" he asked.

"I don't know. I haven't seen him all day."

Without awaiting an invitation, he walked in. Finding the living-room in darkness, he switched on the light. When Mary Flannery followed him, he gripped her wrist and held it so that he could see the back of her hand. There was a bright red polish on the fingernails, which were long and pointed.

"That's all I wanted to know," said Julian, in a cold, hard voice. "This is the hand that held the knife with which the General was murdered."

Deathly pale, Mary Flannery stared at him in silence.

"You're a good actress," he said harshly. "Your make-up was excellent but for one thing—you forgot to clean the polish off your nails. If you'd stopped to think, you'd have realised that a woman of the type you were portraying would never have coloured nails. That sort of thing would be too effeminate for her."

"I—I don't know what you mean."

"Oh, yes, you do. Shall I tell you how you did it? After you boarded the train with Flannery, Little Pete and Big Annie, you made a few changes in your appearance—just sufficient to prevent your being recognised at a casual glance as Mary Flannery—and went back down the platform. In a dressing-room

in the station you put on the mannish get-up—the tweed cos-
tume, the woollen stockings, the brown brogue shoes, the felt
hat—of the character you were to portray. You made up your
face and did your hair in keeping with the character. You forgot
the nails—that was the point that let you down.

"In the role of the middle-aged mannish spinster, you bought
another ticket and returned to the train, carrying your own
clothes in a small case. In the compartment Mike Flannery
had reserved you pulled down the blinds and changed back
into your own clothes and identity. When Little Pete brought
me to the compartment to talk to Flannery you rose and went
out. In a lavatory you resumed the mannish get-up. Going to
the General's compartment, you stabbed him.

"I rather imagine that on leaving it you went out of your way
to be seen with the knife in your hand. That would be part of the
plan. You wanted definitely to establish the guilt of the mannish
spinster, for in a few minutes she was going to cease to exist. Hurrying into a lavatory, you changed back into Mary Flannery again.
All that remained of the woman who killed the General was in
the small bag you carried when you got off the train at Rugby."

"You'll never prove all this," she said, in a shaken tone.

"I'm going to have a try. If I can—and I think I can—it
means the end of Flannery. As instigator of the murder and an
accessory, he'll hang."

One of Mary's long, white hands flew to her throat. He could
see what she was thinking—that, if he proved his theory, the
hangman's noose would be her end, too.

"I warned you to leave him. I told you what the end would
be. Why, in God's name, did you let him make you do it?"

"Even if"—her voice trembled—"even if what you accuse
me of is—is true, Mike had nothing to do with it. He—he
didn't—know—"

Julian turned on his heel.

"Where are you going?" she asked.

"To Scotland Yard. I'm sorry for you, but I'm a lot sorrier for the General's little boy. I'm going to give the law first chance at Flannery. If the law fails—" He limped out of the flat, slamming the door behind him.

Mary Flannery ran and opened the door that led to her bedroom. "Mike!" she cried. "Oh, Mike—"

Her husband stood in the doorway, a horrible grin twisting his features.

"Mike! Don't look at me like that! It isn't my fault that—Mike!"

Limping down the stairs, Julian felt a queer pain, as though cold fingers were tightening on his heart. Halting, he stood in the silent darkness, strangely disturbed and uneasy. For no sound reason of which he could think, he retraced his steps and knocked again on the door of the flat. Nothing stirred.

"Oh, hell," he said, and turned away.

He turned back again and gazed at the closed door. Feeling like a fool, he produced his keyring and used the burglar's tool to pick the lock. Pushing open the door, he went into the sitting-room, which was again in darkness.

"Mary," he said—he had a curious feeling that she was in the room.

There was no answer. Reaching out, he switched on the light. He drew in his breath sharply.

She was lying on the rug before the fire, the handle of a knife protruding from her neck. She was still alive, but only just alive. Julian knelt down and put an arm under her head. Her eyes flickered open and she stared up dully into his face. The spark of life was deserting her rapidly.

"Who did it? Flannery?"

"No," she managed to gasp. "I—I—myself—"

She was trying to say that she had committed suicide, her last brave lie in defence of the worthless rogue she had married. Her hand crawled shakily, painfully, up her chest and the fingers groped about until they found the handle of the knife. They clutched it convulsively. Julian realised what she was doing. With her own fingerprints she was covering those of her slayer. In the act, she gave a sigh and died.

Rising, Julian crossed the floor quietly to the closed door of the bedroom. Opening the door, he looked into the snake-like eyes of Little Pete. The gangster had a gun in each hand. Beside him stood Mike Flannery.

"Always pushin' in where you're not wanted, Mendoza," said Little Pete in a quiet voice. A voice that dripped venom. A voice with murder in it.

"Still sticking to Flannery?" asked Julian scornfully. "You're a fool. For this murder and the murder of the General he'll hang—and you'll hang with him."

"Mary killed herself," said Flannery hoarsely. "She told you so. If she killed the General, I didn't have anything to do with it. She told you that as well."

"She wasn't a good liar," said Julian sadly.

"That will be all from you," snarled Little Pete, prodding him with one of the guns. "Turn round and walk to the door. I'll be right behind you, so watch your step."

The gangsters had the whip hand. Julian had no option but to obey. They marshalled him down the stairs and out into Dean Street. Little Pete drew abreast of Julian, holding a gun at his side.

"This way," he growled, and they turned into a deserted alley.

"Shall I let him have it here, Mike?" whispered Little Pete.

"No. We'll take him out to the country and dump his body in a ditch."

Flannery's saloon car was standing in the alley. With the muzzle of the automatic pressed against his spine, Julian climbed into the rear seat. Little Pete settled beside him with both guns handy. Flannery slid his huge bulk in behind the steering-wheel.

In half an hour they were speeding through thinning outer suburbs. A little later there were open fields on either side of the car. Julian said something below his breath.

"What was that crack?" demanded Little Pete.

"Poetry," said Julian, almost casually. "A line came into my head: 'I have a rendezvous with Death…'"

"A rondyvoo. That's a date, ain't it? You certainly have. In about three minutes."

Julian turned his head and looked out of the rear window.

"Eyes front," snapped Little Pete, prodding him. Settling back, Julian chuckled softly.

"What's so funny?" asked Little Pete.

"We shot across that last cross-road without slowing down. That comes under the heading of dangerous driving—and there's a police car coming up behind."

Little Pete made the fatal error of turning his head to look back. Before he realised that the road behind was deserted, Julian punched him hard between neck and chin. The gangster sagged limply against the upholstery and his guns clattered to the floor. Mike Flannery looked back quickly and took in the situation at a glance. Removing his foot from the accelerator, he held the steering wheel steady with one hand and lashed at Julian with a jack-handle held in the other.

For fear of receiving a knock-out blow if he bent his head, Julian dared not stoop to pick up the guns. He grasped Flannery by the neck with both hands. Tugging with all his might, he dragged him clear of the driving seat, almost into the rear of the car.

Wobbling crazily from one side of the road to the other, the car ended by dashing into a low stone wall at a bend.

Out of a clamouring void, Julian returned to consciousness with a splitting headache and a bleeding scalp. He put up a hand and touched the floorboards of the car. It had somersaulted when the crash came and come down wrong side up. He was lying on the inner side of the roof.

He groped about until he found a jagged hole where one of the side windows should be. It was a tight fit, but he put his head through and managed to drag his body after it. He lay panting on the ground, every gasping breath tearing his lungs with pain. Not far off an indignant owl hooted.

Stumbling to his feet, he turned a grim eye on the wrecked car. Not much of a car now.

He walked round the wreckage and found Little Pete. The gangster was very dead. He had been thrown head first through the windscreen and the glass had done terrible things to his face and neck. A few yards farther on lay the two automatics, within a foot of each other.

Julian put one in his pocket. With the other in his hand, he limped in search of Flannery. He found him crawling over the smashed wall on his hands and knees. There was no fight left in the big gangster. He surrendered hastily when Julian poked a gun under his nose.

"I've got nothing to worry about," he said, half to himself, "nothing at all. You can't prove a thing against me, not a damned thing. At the trial the judge will be forced to dismiss me for lack of evidence."

Turning things over in his mind, Julian realised that Flannery was probably right.

"There isn't going to be a trial," he said. "I shot you after the smash. We had a fight and I shot you in self-defence."

Staring at him, Flannery began slowly to back away.

"You're crazy. There was no fight. I surrendered."

"That was a mistake. We'll have to do it all over again?"

"You can't do it, Mendoza. It—it would be murder."

"That's a laugh, coming from you."

Holding one gun in his hand, Julian took the other from his pocket and tossed it on to the bank at the side of the road.

"Pick it up," he said.

"No. I won't touch it. I—"

"Pick it up. If you don't, I'll shoot you where you stand and put the gun in your hand afterwards."

Flannery threw himself on the bank and snatched up the automatic. His hand was shaking and the bullet he fired at Julian chipped some bark off a tree on the other side of the road.

Before the report died away, Julian took careful aim at Flannery's head. After he pulled the trigger, he dropped the weapon and sat down on the bank, feeling sick and giddy. He did not look to see if his bullet had found its target. He was too good a shot to have missed at such close range.

THE END

HANGING'S TOO GOOD

The S.O.S.

"...two parts of Bacardi rum...one part of rye whisky...one part of ginger ale...two parts of Bacardi rum..."

"You said Bacardi rum, sir?"

"I'm saying it again. It's the second two parts, Charley, that get action."

"Yes, sir," said Charley, "I should think they would."

But for Julian Mendoza and the barman, the bar at Giovanni's was deserted. The barman looked doubtfully at the array of bottles—a score of them—from each of which he had poured a quantity into a cocktail shaker at Julian's orders. He glanced, even more dubiously, at the contents of the shaker. "You're not going to drink this, sir? It'll eat away your insides. Don't you think you ought to go home? I'll call you a taxi."

"You can call me anything you like," said Julian thickly, "but I'm not going home. The fact is, you think I'm drunk. And the truth of the matter is, you're right. I've been drunk for quite a time. How long would you say I'd been drunk, Charley?"

"Well, sir, you'd a heavy load on when you came in here. If it had been anyone else, I'd have refused to serve 'em. Knowing all the places that don't bother about licensing hours must be a big help to you, sir."

"I got drunk to forget something," said Julian. "And now I'm in trouble. I've forgotten what it was I got drunk to forget."

The bell of the telephone behind the bar rang shrilly. Charley answered it. He offered the receiver to Julian. "For you, Mr. Mendoza."

"I'm not here. I'm in China."

Charley said into the mouthpiece: "He's not here, he's in China," and hung up.

The telephone made a noise like an Italian washerwoman who has been offered a deadly insult. Charley lifted the receiver again and listened for a moment. His eyes grew round.

"That's no way to talk," he said severely. "You ought to be ashamed of yourself, using language like that. Alright, I'll tell him. But I think he's still in China."

He placed the instrument on the bar. "It's your news-editor, Mr. Mendoza."

Julian took the receiver. "Go way," he said, into the mouthpiece.

"Where have you been since Tuesday?" demanded an irate voice in his ear.

"Charley," said Julian, pushing aside the telephone, "how long ago was Tuesday?"

"Two days, sir."

"Then two days is how long I've been drunk."

Charley was listening to the telephone again. "He says you're a worthless, boozing tramp, Mr. Mendoza," he reported.

"Tell him I'm coming over to knock his block off as soon as I've had another drink."

"You'd better go at once, sir. You might forget."

"I won't forget. That's my trouble. I've got a memory like a nagging wife. It never lets me forget anything."

Shrugging his shoulders, the barman put the telephone back on its stand. He looked at the clock and sighed. It was long after midnight. The big front doors of the restaurant were locked for the night. The scrubbing-women were on their hands and knees on the marble floor of the grill-room. The band had gone home, the waiters had gone home, in a few minutes even the dishwashers would be going home. He, Charley, ought to have locked up the bar and left twenty-minutes ago. Instead, he had to stand talking to a drunken crime reporter who didn't know when he'd had enough.

Anyone but Julian Mendoza would have been forcibly ejected long ago. But Julian was a privileged character. He had once helped the boss out of a particularly nasty mess and the boss's orders were that when Julian came into the restaurant the employees were to behave as though the place belonged to him.

There was a strict rule that after seven o'clock in the evening only those in evening dress might enter Giovanni's. But Julian was not in evening dress. His large, muscular frame was clad in a shapeless lounge suit which looked as though it had been bought in the unredeemed-pledge department of a pawnshop. His battered felt hat would have disgraced a self-respecting scarecrow. On his chin was a three-day growth of stubble.

Julian was not a habitual drunkard, but when one of his moods of depression came upon him he fought it with a bout of hard drinking which made ordinary drunkenness seem almost temperate. For sixteen years he had lived on excitement, look- ing for trouble all over the world, and excitement was still the breath of life to him. His crippled right leg, mauled by a lion in West Africa four years before, kept him from the wild, roving existence he had led since he ran away from home at the age of seventeen; and when civilisation paled and his duties as crime reporter for the *London Morning World* grew monotonous, his hunger for excitement drove him to the bottle for forgetfulness.

He took out his pipe and began to fill it with tarry black tobacco. Charley wrinkled his nose. He knew that tobacco. It stank like something unmentionable in polite society.

"I don't think your memory's so hot, Mr. Mendoza," he said. "Didn't you just tell me you'd forgotten what it was you got drunk to forget?"

Julian stared across the bar at Charley. His eyes were haggard. "I hoped I had," he replied, in a dry, harsh voice, "but I haven't. It's at the back of my mind all the time. On Tuesday morning,

Charley, a man was hanged by the neck until he was dead."

"I read about it in the paper."

"I hanged that man, Charley. Oh, I didn't put the rope around his neck; I didn't spring the trap; but it was my evidence that got him convicted."

"You've no reason to feel bad about it, Mr. Mendoza. You were only doing your duty as a citizen."

"Duty!" Julian spat out the word. "I wasn't thinking of duty when I tracked the poor beggar down. I wanted a story for my paper."

"He was a murderer. He deserved to die."

"Yes, he was a murderer. He deserved to die. But he didn't deserve to die squirming on air at the end of a rope. No one deserves to die like that, not even the lowest thing that crawls, far less a man. Think of it, Charley. Imagine it happening to you. You don't like the thought, do you? They gave him three weeks to picture it in his mind. Three weeks in which to sweat with fear. And then they led him out and strung him up. Maybe you think I'm a sentimental fool, maybe you think it's the drink talking, but when I think of that poor bastard standing on the trap and realise that I put him there—"

"You're forgetting the poor bastard he murdered," said Charley.

"He murdered in white-hot anger—but they hanged him in cold blood. They led him out and strung him up with no more ceremony that if he'd been a bundle of washing."

"There's got to be a death penalty for murder," remarked Charlie unemotionally, "otherwise we wouldn't none of us be safe."

Someone started rattling the locked doors of the restaurant. Charley waited for a time, hoping that whoever was there would go away, but the rattling went on and on. With a sigh, the barman crossed the darkened dance-floor, unlocked the doors and peered out. When he returned a young man in a smart blue overcoat was with him. The young man handed an envelope to Julian.

"The Boss sent me down with this," he said.

"Have a drink?" suggested Julian.

"What a question!" retorted the young man. "Mine's a lager," he added, to Charley.

The barman said something short and blasphemous; but he poured the drink.

"Better read it," said the young man, to Julian. "The boss is in one hell of a temper."

The envelope contained a second sealed envelope, addressed to Julian, care of the *Morning World*; and a half-sheet of note-paper on which a few words were pencilled in the handwriting of Julian's news-editor. The news-editor's message was pithy and to the point: "If you don't report to me in ten minutes, you're fired. The enclosed envelope came for you two days ago."

Julian crumpled the note into a ball and dropped it on the floor. He tore open the other envelope. The brief letter inside read as follows:

DEAR MR. MENDOZA,

SIR, I WOULD LIKE TO SEE YOU AS SOON AS CONVENIENT TO YOU. I HAVE FOUND OUT SOMETHING THAT LOOKS BAD TO ME AND I AM VERY WORRIED ABOUT IT. CAN'T SAY WHAT, IN A LETTER, BUT BELIEVE ME WOULD BE GRATEFUL FOR YOUR ADVICE.

YRS. RESPECTFULLY,

DANIEL RIORDAN

Staring at the shakily-written letter, Julian for the first time regretted the spree that had prevented him from receiving it two days before. Old Dan Riordan was not the man to make a fuss about nothing. If he was worried it was certain that he had something to be worried about.

Dan was seventy and had seen a lot of life. He had seen Death, too, and faced it unflinchingly. Puny and undersized, he had spirit enough for ten men. One side of his face was puckered and red from a burn suffered in rescuing a woman and two children from a burning building; and, although he could not swim, he had once dived into the Thames to save a drowning boy. The heart of a giant in the body of a dwarf—that was Daniel Riordan.

"Look, Mr. Mendoza," said Charley plaintively, with another glance at the clock, "I've got a home to go to."

"Alright, Charlie, I'm leaving. I'm going to drop in on a friend."

"This is no time for paying calls, Mr. Mendoza. He'll be in bed."

"That's where you're wrong," said Julian. "He's a night watchman."

"Wait a minute, Medoza!" protested the young man in the blue overcoat. "What'll I tell the Boss?"

"Tell him if he fires me just once more, I'll quit."

In spite of his crippled leg and the prodigious quantity he had drunk, Julian hardly wavered as he walked to the employees' exit. Charley the barman looked after him admiringly. Anyone else with that load, he reflected, would be fit only for a straitjacket in a home for alcoholics.

When Mendoza Failed

At the far end of an alley which leads out of the Clerkenwell Road the huge warehouse of the Lambert Jewellery Manufacturing Company raised its sprawling bulk against a purple sky. The night was dark, and the alley, paved with uneven cobblestones, was as gloomy and uninviting as a corridor leading to hell. Here and there muddy pools from the previous day's rain gleamed darkly.

Picking his way between the puddles, Julian remembered that the last time he had done so his path had been lighted by a street lamp halfway down the alley. Tonight, the street lamp was not lit. That fact might have an innocent explanation, but it made him uneasy.

A youth in a soiled raincoat, with a greasy cap pulled low on his forehead, came out of the shadows. He was thin and pale and in his left hand he held an unlit cigarette. The other hand was in his pocket.

"Got a match on you?" he drawled.

Julian said: "No."

There was a full box in the reporter's pocket; but he always said 'no' when asked for a match by a stranger in a dark and deserted spot. Possibly he was unduly cautious, but he knew the match gag, a favourite trick of the holdup man. It works like this; you ask your victim for a match and while his hands are occupied in fumbling through his pockets you know him out with a punch on the jaw or a blow on the back of the head. Perhaps all the thin youth in the raincoat wanted was a light for his cigarette—but perhaps it wasn't. Julian was taking no chances.

Julian started to move on but the youth blocked his path. He was trembling slightly. "You can't go down there," he said.

"Why not?"

"This is why not."

The youth brought his right hand up. It held a revolver with a silencer attached. With the barrel of it he prodded Julian in the ribs. "Drop your walking stick and move over there against the wall," he ordered.

His voice was unsteady—but not with fear.

You can't argue with a gun. The reporter obeyed in silence. He wavered a little as he went where he was told to go. He was still very drunk. The youth leaned nearer to him, warily, watchfully, and peered into his face.

"You're as tight as hell," he said. It seemed to please him.

"Certainly, I'm tight," mumbled Julian. "Why not?"

"If it suits you, it suits me. Be a good boy and stand still against the wall and you won't get hurt. If you try any funny tricks, I'll shoot you in the belly."

He meant what he said, Julian had no doubt of that. This boy would have no qualms about shooting—and shooting to kill. They leaned against the wall, close enough to touch each other; and the mouth of the revolver pressed hard against the pit of Julian's stomach. It had a sobering effect on the reporter. His brain was clearing, becoming icily sharp.

They were in the shadows and the only light was the faint glow from the street lamps of the Clerkenwell Road, fifty yards away. Out of the corners of his eyes Julian studied his captor's face. It was deadly white and twitching. Beads of sweat stood out on it. The hand that held the gun was shaking ever so slightly. Suddenly Julian realised the truth about the youth in the raincoat; he was a snowbird, an addict to heroin or cocaine. And a gunman who is a snowbird will kill as readily as not. His keyed-up nerves get a thrill out of killing. He may be as cowardly as a rabbit—and usually is—when the effects of the drug wear off, but while they last, he is as dangerous as dynamite—and as ready to explode at a touch.

So, Julian stood very still. To move would be the equivalent of committing suicide and the reporter was fond of life. The Snowbird watched him narrowly. Julian could have groaned aloud. At the end of the alley, in the warehouse, was Old Dan Riordan—his friend. God only knew what was happening in the warehouse and to Old Dan while Julian stood against the wall with his hands up and the mouth of a gun in his stomach.

The Snowbird's ears were cocked; he was listening for something. Listening. Waiting. It came at last—the muffled roar of an explosion. So muffled that it came to them quite faintly from the bottom of the alley and certainly would not be heard fifty yards farther on. The Snowbird turned his head for a fraction of a second and the movement gave Julian his chance. It was a slim chance, but he took it.

He dropped his hand on the revolver and gripped the cartridge cylinder. If he gripped it tightly enough, he knew, the trigger could not be pulled, because the cylinder would not revolve. It was a good trick if he could do it. Certain death if he couldn't. In a panic, the Snowbird tried to shoot, but he was too late. Julian held the cylinder grimly. His life depended on it.

With his free hand he hit the Snowbird on the chin. All his strength went into the blow—he wanted it to hurt—and it smashed the youth's head back against the wall. Without a sound the Snowbird slid unconscious to the ground. Julian would have been willing to bet that he would not stir for an hour.

The reporter was still holding the revolver by the cylinder. With a sigh of relief, he put it in his pocket. There was an empty feeling in the pit of his stomach, but he preferred that to having a hole in it.

From the end of the alley came the sound of a powerful engine starting. Julian moved cautiously in the direction of the sound. As he drew nearer, he discerned the dim outline of a large car, standing without lights at the door of the warehouse. A dark figure ran out and sprang into the car, which came toward Julian, accelerating rapidly in low gear. As it drew level with the reporter it slowed down and a man put his head and shoulders out of the nearside window and called in a husky whisper: "Eddie! Where the devil are you?"

Julian stepped onto the running-board with the silenced revolver in his hand. There were two men in the car.

"Eddie's had an accident," he said grimly. "Put your hands up, both of you."

The driver uttered a startled oath. The car wobbled. And then, something hard and heavy—a tyre lever, or the butt of an automatic hard pistol—struck Julian viciously across the face, and he fell in a heap on the cobblestones. The car roared on up the alley, the occupants preferring to make their getaway rather than to linger and discover what had happened to their lookout man.

Dazed and bleeding, Julian groped until he found the revolver, which had slipped from his grasp when he fell. Raising himself on an elbow, he fired at one of the rear tyres of the car, which was turning the corner into the Clerkenwell Road. The tyre burst with a loud report and the back of the car swung round, hitting a wall with a crash that must have been heard half a mile away.

Staggering up, the reporter hurried towards the wreck at a stumbling run, his crippled right leg dragging on the cobblestones. Before he reached it the two men sprang out, one of them carrying a large black bag. Julian fired again, but the shot missed both men and the night swallowed them up.

The Snowbird was still lying where he had dropped—he would not move from there of his own volition for some time to come. Replacing the silenced revolver in his pocket, Julian picked up his walking-stick and limped towards the warehouse.

It was the back door of the place that opened to the alley; the principal entrance was on the other side of the building, on a main thoroughfare. The door stood open. Julian went in, and found himself in a long, dark passage. He fumbled for and found the light switch and pressed it. A naked electric-light bulb sharply illuminated the passage, but revealed nothing that seemed out of place.

"Dan!" he cried, "Dan Riordan! Where are you?"

His voice rang through the empty building, and was echoed back to him with a hollow, mocking intonation. He shouted again, but there was still no answer. He went through the ground floor of the building, turning on lights whenever he came to them.

It was in a large furnished as a private office that he found Daniel Riordan. A safe which stood in a corner had been blown open. The explosion had twisted the heavy steel door and wrenched it off its hinges. The inner doors of the safe stood open, the drawers were lying on the floor, torn papers were strewn all round them; but Julian had no eyes for these things.

As a crime reporter, sudden death was Julian Mendoza's business. Every day he was in contact with it in every gruesome shape and form. Only by schooling himself to be unsentimental about it had he prevented it souring his whole existence. But he could not be unsentimental about the room corpse that lay beneath a desk in the middle of the room.

The corpse of a puny old man with white hair, shrivelled hands. Shrunken throat… The corpse of Old Dan Riordan, who had carried the heart of a giant in the body of a dwarf, who had over and over again risked his life gladly for the sake of another, who had never in his long life been more than a night watchman, poorly paid and overworked—and never less than a hero.

There were tears in Julian's eyes and a pain like a knife-thrust in his heart as he knelt beside the crumpled, pathetic little body. He had no need to touch Old Dan's pulse to know that he was dead. A savage blow had crushed the old man's skull. One shrivelled hand was outstretched, as though Dan had been reaching for something when he was struck down. Perhaps the telephone on the desk above him was the thing for which he had been reaching. It would be like Old Dan to die in a hopeless attempt to do his duty.

"Did you have a feeling that something like this was going to happen?" said Julian, in a hoarse croak. "Was that why you wrote to me? There was something worrying you. You wanted me to come to you. And I failed you."

To the end of his life failing Old Dan Riordan was to be something for which Julian could never forgive himself. Had he only received the old man's letter in time, this might not have happened. But he was drunk—and the letter had lain on his desk at the office until it was too late.

Julian did not ask himself then how the night watchman could have known that the safe in the warehouse was to be robbed; or why the old man had not warned his employer or the police instead of writing to his newspaper reporter friend. Those were questions Julian was later to ask himself, but for the time being he was too heartsick to think of them.

When he stood up, there was a fierce light in his eyes and his mouth was grim. One thing at least he could do for Old Dan; he could track down the slayers and see that they got their deserts. This was one crime for which hanging was too good.

The shrill blasts of a whistle shattered the silence. A policeman patrolling his beat had found the wrecked car at the mouth of the alley and the unconscious form which lay half-way up it.

Julian lifted the telephone. "Whitehall 1212," he said. His

throat was so dry that it was an effort to bring the words out.

Police cars were parked along the Clerkenwell Road on either side of the entrance to the alley, and two uniformed constables stood between them, with orders to let no unauthorised person pass. They were keeping out reporters from most of the London dailies; which suited Julian Mendoza, for he was already in, and too important a witness to be put out.

After ringing up Scotland Yard, Julian had telephoned his newspaper. News was sacred to Julian, as it is to every good reporter. The murder of his friend had hit him like a physical blow, but his sorrow did not permit him to let hot news grow stale.

The Snowbird had been carried, unconscious, into the warehouse. The police surgeon knelt and took the youth's wrist between long, thin fingers.

"If you'd hit him just a little harder, Mendoza," he remarked grimly, "he'd never waken in this world again."

"Bring him round long enough to talk," retorted Julian bitterly, "and he can kick the bucket immediately after, for all I care."

Inspector Howells, who had come from Scotland Yard to take charge of the case, was engaged in taking a statement from Mr. Samuel Lambert, the managing director of the jewellery manufacturing company.

Mr. Lambert was a walking advertisement of the dangers of good living. He was soft and white and fat, like a well-fed slug. Fat bulged his cheeks and brows so that his little dark eyes were almost hidden between two puffy folds—they looked like raisins in a suet pudding. His stomach ballooned out from his thighs to his chest, his bald head was as round as a butterball. On a finger of one of his flabby hands gleamed a large diamond; and he wore its twin in his silk tie.

Although he had been called out of bed at one in the morning, Mr. Lambert had taken time to dress with care before driving to the scene of the crime. His patent-leather shoes were spotless and shining; his Ascot tie had been faultlessly arranged round his high wing-collar. These things suggested that Mr. Lambert had taken the news of the robbery with fortitude and calm—but there was nothing calm about him as he stood beside his mangled safe.

His voice was shrill and petulant. The backs of his hands and his dome-like forehead were moist with sweat.

"What do we pay police for, I'd like to know, if outrages like this can happen?" he wailed plaintively.

"You say that fifteen thousand pounds worth of uncut diamonds was missing?" said Inspector Howells patiently.

"Fifteen thousand pounds worth of diamonds—and five thousand pounds in cash! And our insurance doesn't cover the money! You've got to get it back, do you hear? I can't afford a loss like that."

"Is it your custom to keep so much cash in the safe?"

"No. This was an exceptional occasion. I intended to cross to Holland to buy stones tomorrow and some of the dealers I do business with prefer to be paid in cash."

"H'm. It could hardly have been mere chance that made the thieves pick tonight for the robbery. They must have had inside information about the cash on hand."

"Who could have told them?"

"That remains to be seen," said Inspector Howells. "Could you identify the diamonds?"

"I might, although uncut diamonds are not easy to identify. But if you don't get them back quickly the thieves will get someone to cut and polish them—and once they're cut, I'll have no way of telling whether they're mine or not."

"You said the money was in five-pound notes. Have you the numbers?"

"I wrote them down on a slip of paper."

"Where is the paper?"

Mr. Lambert looked foolish. He licked his lips. "I—I wrapped it round one of the bundles of notes and secured it with a rubber band."

"That's great," said Inspector Howells. "That's just fine. All we've got to do is catch the safe-breakers. If they've still got the paper, we'll be able to check the numbers of the notes—if they've still got the notes."

"You've got to catch them!" groaned Mr. Lambert. "The diamond trade has not been good for years. This loss is more than I can stand."

"You keep whining about your diamonds and your money," snapped Julian Mendoza suddenly, "but I haven't heard you say a word about the poor devil who was killed protecting them."

Mr. Lambert blinked up at him nervously. A tear trickled down his podgy cheek.

"I can't bear to think of it. Poor old Riordan! He had been with us for twenty years. If I've said nothing about him, it's because I'm trying to keep my mind off his terrible end. Murder… It's too shocking for words! The very thought of blood always makes me sick."

"You've got blood on your hands," retorted Julian.

For a moment it seemed that Mr. Lambert was going to fall over in a faint. He stared down in horror at his hands. They were white and fleshy—and spotlessly clean.

"What do you mean?" he muttered hoarsely.

"I mean that it was criminal to leave a feeble old man in sole charge of a fortune. What could he do against desperate killers?—only put up the weak resistance that resulted in his death."

"He—he shouldn't have resisted. The odds were too great. I should have understood that."

"If you've employed Old Dan for twenty years, you ought

to know that he'd do his duty if it cost every drop of blood in his body."

"We—we wanted him to retire. He said he couldn't afford to."

"You could have given him a pension."

"We can't afford to pension our employees. He was a bachelor. He should have saved for his old age."

"How much did you pay him?" asked Julian, bitingly.

"Thirty-five shillings a week until a few years ago—and then, since he was not so fit for his work, we reduced his wages by ten shillings."

"You mean, when he got his old-age pension you knocked the amount of it off his wages!"

"How dare you speak to me like that?" gasped Mr. Lambert, showing spirit for the first time. Inspector, must I stand here to be insulted?"

"I'd hate to be you, Lambert," said Julian remorselessly. "You've got a small fortune in diamonds on your finger and in your tie—but the blood of Old Dan Riordan is on your soul."

"Stop that! Stop it! I can't bear it. You're driving me mad. How was I to know this would happen?"

"That's enough, Mendoza," said Inspector Howells sternly. "You're supposed to be a reporter, not a street-corner evangelist."

Julian shrugged his shoulders. He was shaking with the force of his emotion. To steady himself he pulled out his foul, blackened briar and lit it.

"After all," he murmured, half to himself, "nothing I can say will bring Old Dan back to life. There's only one thing I can do now; find the killers and see that they get what's coming to them."

"Mendoza!" said Inspector Howells sharply. "If you know something about this—something you haven't told me—it is your duty—"

Julian thought of the note Old Dan Riodan had sent him,

but he said nothing about it.

"Duty be damned!" He spat out the words. "This isn't just another murder. That poor broken thing"—he pointed to the battered corpse—"was my friend. Find the men who killed him, if you can. If I find them first there won't be much for you to cart away."

In a silence so tense that it was almost audible the reporter and the police inspector glared at each other. They were old friends; and old enemies. Old allies; and old rivals. They worked always toward the same end; Justice—but often their paths were widely separated. Inspector Howells worked in accordance with official rules and regulations, but Julian made his own rules as he went along. More often than not the reporter made hay of the Law when he was on the trail of a law-breaker.

" Watch your step, Mendoza!" said the Inspector, in a tone that was all the more ominous because it was quiet. "If I catch you taking the law into your own hands, you'll pay for it, exactly like any other criminal!"

"If you catch me," replied Julian, with a smile in which there was no humour.

The tension was broken by the divisional-surgeon, who came to tell them that the Snowbird had at last opened his eyes.

The Snowbird was still very weak, but his first word was a curse. "I've got nothing to say!" he snarled up at Inspector Howells. "I ain't talking, see?" He groaned. His fingers gingerly explored the lump on the back of his head "God! My head aches. I'd like five minutes alone with the bastard who hit me."

"That would suit me too," said Julian Mendoza.

"Name?" asked the desk-sergeant at Old Street Police Station. He dipped his pen in the ink, shook a drop off it, and poised it above a charge-sheet.

"Find out!" snarled the Snowbird.

The desk-sergeant who had the pink, benign countenance of a bishop, looked reprovingly over the top of his spectacles. "One of the tough kind?" he said, amiably. "All right, Sonny. Don't you worry. We'll find out alright."

"Search him, then bring him in here," grunted Inspector Howells, opening the door of an office which lead out of the charge-room.

Two other police officials and Julian Mendoza followed the inspector into the office. Howells sat down at a desk in the middle of the room and placed on the blotter the silenced revolver which Julian had given him. The others grouped themselves about the room. In a few minutes the Snowbird was brought in and pushed into a chair. All that had been found on him were cigarettes, matches, a little silver and a slip of white paper—which, Julian noted, was of the size and shape that is used to wrap up a 'shot' of cocaine.

The Snowbird sneered at the faces all round him. He looked as vicious as a cobra and yet futile and weak. Weakness, depravity, were written in his furtive little eyes, on his slack mouth, his receding chin.

"You're wasting your time. I won't talk. Why don't you put me in a cell so I can get a night's rest?"

"You'll be in a cell soon enough—and you'll stay in it long enough to get sick of it," said Inspector Howells. "It is my duty to warn you—"

"That anything I say will be used against me. I know all that. That's why I've got nothing to say."

"If you think you can beat this rap, you're wrong. Perhaps you don't know it yet, but your pals killed the night watchman at the warehouse. That makes it a hanging job for all of you."

The Snowbird was shaking as though with ague; but his eyes were defiant. "I tell you; I've got nothing to say."

"Too loyal to squeal on your pals, eh? But they weren't too loyal to run out and leave you."

"I ain't got no pals."

"Don't tell me that. You were the look-out for the safe-breakers who robbed the warehouse."

"That's what you say."

"It's what the jury will say. Even if we don't catch your pals you'll still hang for murder."

For the first time the Snowbird's braggadocio deserted him. "Supposing I was the look-out? I ain't admitting nothing, but just supposing. How was I to know the inside blokes would croak the old watchman?"

"You won't get away with an argument like that. The law says that when several men embark on a crime together each is equally responsible for the actions of any one of them. Besides"—Inspector Howells tapped the gun on the desk—"you were prepared for murder. You were carrying this. You almost shot a man with it."

The Snowbird twisted in his chair to glare at Julian. "I wish I'd blasted his guts through his backbone!"

"It's a little late to think of that," said Howells dryly. "Don't be a fool, man. It was your pals who did the killing—but if they get away it'll be you who'll pay for it."

"I've got nothing to say."

A plainclothes-man came into the room. Having just come on duty, he had not been present when the Snowbird was brought in.

"Hello, Eddie," he said, looking at the little degenerate, who snarled up at him.

"You lousy flatfoot!" sneered the Snowbird.

"Know this man?" asked Inspector Howells.

"I ought to. I lagged him for extortion a couple of years ago. His name's Eddie Niven. He's only about twenty-two or -three, but he's made quite a nice little criminal record for himself in the time he's had at his disposal. Old Borstalian, aren't you, Eddie? I believe it was three years he spent in that academy for delinquent youths. He learned a lot there, too. When he came out, he specialised in extortion with menaces, and earned himself a couple of short rests at Pentonville."

"Where does he live?"

"I don't know. He moves so often. He used to live with his sister Margaret. She's on the square. Works in an estate agency. They're orphans, and she's done all she could to make a man of him. I told her years ago she was wasting her time. It would take a ruddy miracle to make a man of a rat like Eddie."

The Snowbird worked his jaws until he had gathered a mouthful of saliva, then he spat it at the plainclothesman. The detective raised his fist to hit the little degenerate on the jaw but, with a tight smile, dropped it again without striking.

"Do you know where the sister lives?" asked Inspector Howells.

"She has a flat in Guildford Street. I don't know the number, but I could find the house."

"Then go there and see if you can discover anything about Niven's associates."

After the plainclothes-man had left the room, Julian Mendoza went over to Inspector Howells and whispered in his ear:

"I know how to make Niven talk."

Inspector Howells glanced up suspiciously at the reporter. "I can imagine," he said grimly. "Your two fists and Niven in a locked room together. Nothing doing, Mendoza. If the Commissioner saw one mark on him—apart from those you've already made—I'd be thrown off the Force before I could draw my breath."

"This is simpler than that. Niven is a dope addict. He's coked up now and full of false courage, but when the effect of his last 'shot' wears off he'll go almost crazy from the reaction. He'll sell his soul, then, for a pinch of snow. Put him in a cell all by himself for a few hours. When his nerves start clamouring for dope, he'll spill all he knows."

Considering the suggestion, Inspector Howells bit his lip. He shook his head.

"It's a nice variation of the Third Degree, but I can't do it. When he starts shouting for dope, I'll have to call the divisional-surgeon, and if he really needs a drug, he'll get it."

"Have it your own way," said Julian harshly. "If it were up to me, I'd sweat the names of his confederates out of him before he was twenty-four hours older."

"It's a pity, in a way, that it isn't up to you, Mendoza," replied the inspector soberly. "But the C.I.D. can't work that way. I'm forbidden by strict regulations from putting any kind of pressure on him. If he won't talk, I'll have to find his accomplices by routine methods."

"Which means pulling in every known safe-cracker in London until you find the right ones—if you ever do. And, if Niven never talks, how are you going to know they're the right ones, when you've got them? I didn't get a close enough look to know them again—and the only man who did is a corpse."

The grave face of Inspector Howells was haggard and weary. He sighed. "Oh, for God's sake, Mendoza, shut up and leave me alone," he growled. "My job's tough enough without you making it sound tougher."

Eddie Niven was growing restless. "What are we waiting for?" he grumbled. "Why don't you take me down and lock me in a cell? You'll get nothing out of me, even if you chew the rag all night. Maybe you think my sister will soften me up if she comes and cries over me. If you do, you're crazy. Oh, she'll cry, all right. She'll boo and blubber all over the place.

But you won't get any change out of that. She's been turning on the waterworks ever since I can remember. It don't make no difference to me. I'm used to it."

A station constable put his head into the room.

"There's a young lady—" he began, but the young lady did not wait to be announced. She came in with a rush, as abruptly as though she had been kicked in. Correctly worn, her clothes would have been smart; but she had thrown them on anyhow in a frantic hurry. Her hat was a jaunty brown felt with an orange feather, and in crushing it on her head she had broken the feather. It looked funny—the kind of funny that brings a lump to your throat instead of a laugh to your lips.

Perhaps she was pretty, perhaps she was plain. It was not easy to tell. Her face had frozen in lines of stark dismay. It was drained of colour. She was not crying. There was a dry, chilled look in her eyes which said that she was far beyond the help of tears.

She said: "Oh, Eddie." That was all. Only two words—but they spoke volumes. They were filled with the heartache of years of broken promises, of being lied to, of always being let down.

It was the Snowbird who wept. The tears rolled down his cheeks as though they were being wrung out of a sponge. They were stage tears. He wanted his sister's pity; he needed her help; and he was putting on a show for her benefit.

"They're framing me, Marge!" he wept. "I'm innocent, I swear I am. They've got no evidence against me. They're trying to cook up a case because they can't find the blokes who really did the job."

Margaret Niven shook her head. "No, Eddie, they aren't framing you. I believed that story the first time and the second time, I even tried to believe it the third time; but it isn't true—it never was true. There's no need to lie to me, Eddie. You know I'll stick to you whatever you've done."

The Snowbird twisted in his chair and buried his face in his hands, his whole body shaking convulsively. Great gulping sobs shuddered in his throat. They seemed to be tearing him apart. The sounds made his sister look as though she were being burned alive.

"What is it this time?" she asked, trying pitifully to keep her voice steady. No one spoke.

Margaret Niven's tortured eyes travelled from the shaking form of her brother to the grave faces of the police officers and the reporter.

"What has he done? The detective who came to my flat wouldn't tell me. He didn't want me to come here, but I couldn't stop away."

Eddie Niven fell to his knees on the floor, grovelling at her feet, clawing at her frantically. "They're pinning a murder rap on me. I didn't do it; I swear to God I didn't. They've been trying to sweat a confession out of me. They're framing me, I tell you, framing me!"

"Murder! Eddie! No, it can't be true." She stared in horror at the police officers. "Eddie wouldn't commit a murder. It isn't in him. Oh, I know he's weak. There's a streak in him which makes him lie and cheat and thieve—but he wouldn't kill. He couldn't."

The policemen and the reporter exchanged awkward glances. No one wanted to be the one who answered.

"He is charged with being an accessory to murder," replied Inspector Howells at last. "The evidence is fairly conclusive."

"They'll hang me!" wailed the Snowbird, tugging at his sister's skirt. "I'm innocent, but I'll hang! My God! I don't want to die!" Margaret Niven's hand flew to her throat. In her mind she was picturing a dangling rope, a cringing wretch being dragged to the scaffold.

"No…no…They shan't do that to you. They shan't. It would be too cruel."

Her eyes fell on the revolver that lay on the desk. In one incredibly swift movement she snatched it up and backed to the door.

"Don't any of you move. If you do, I'll shoot. Come here, Eddie."

The Snowbird scrambled up and joined her, his tears swiftly dried. "Give me the gun. I'll put paid to a couple of these bastards."

"If you touch the gun, Eddie, I'll shoot you. Get behind me."

Inspector Howells had half-risen in his chair. Inwardly he was cursing himself for having left the revolver in sight. He had kept a careful eye on the Snowbird, lest he should try to grab it, but it had not occurred to him to be wary of the girl. The other police officers were tensed to spring, but uncertain when to make the move. None of them was armed. Julian Mendoza leaned against a wall, his hands in plain view. He had an idea that it would be wise to keep perfectly still.

"Don't be a fool, girl," said the inspector irritably. "Put down the gun. You're only making matters worse for your brother and yourself."

"You shan't hang my brother if I can help it."

"Stop this play-acting and drop the gun. You wouldn't dare use it."

While he spoke Inspector Howells was edging forward.

"If you make one more move, I'll fire," said Margaret Niven unsteadily. "I mean it."

"She does mean it, Howells," said Julian quietly.

And she did. None of them could look at her eyes without knowing that she would shoot unhesitatingly if they tried to crowd her. The very thought of harming a fellow-human would be repugnant to her; but she would do it, nevertheless. They all stood still. No one wanted to risk attacking her in the hope that her first bullet would not hit a vital spot.

"You're mad, girl," said Inspector Howells in an exasperated tone. "You're laying yourself open to a serious charge, and all to no purpose. You can't possibly get away."

"No, they can't get away," said Julian. "But I shouldn't try to stop them at the moment, if I were you."

The inspector realised what Julian meant. The girl would not shoot unless she was pressed—but if the Snowbird grew desperate and grabbed the gun, nothing was more certain than that murder would be done. A killer at heart, the Snowbird was itching to feel his fingers tightening on a trigger. Howells dropped into his chair and took a cigarette from a packet which lay on the desk. This, he reflected bitterly, was probably going to cost him his job and his pension. There was no sense in becoming so worked up that it cost a life as well.

"You may get as far as the charge-room," he remarked, in a matter-of-fact voice. "You may even get as far as the street. But there's only one finish to this, Miss Niven. You'll wind up in a cell, you'll be no earthly good to your brother. There's one thing more I must tell you. Firearms are kept at every police station in case of emergency. If you walk out of that door with your brother those firearms will be issued—and the first armed policeman who encounters you with that gun in your hand will shoot you down without hesitation."

"Open the door, Eddie," said Margaret Niven.

Her brother obeyed.

The girl put out her hand, touched the electric-light switch and plunged the room in darkness. She pushed her brother out and slammed the door behind them.

In the dark the police officers blundered against each other, and precious seconds were lost before one of them managed to grope his way to the door and wrench it open. They pounded out, shouting at the top of their voices.

Julian limped across the room and turned on the light. He was alone. He poked his head out of the office and saw that the charge-room was also empty. Outside motor-car engines were roaring, voices were bawling orders, police whistles were blowing his furiously…

Julian lifted the telephone and dialled his newspaper's number. A story as good as this must be dished up piping hot. He had almost finished dictating his account to a *Morning World* telephonist when Inspector Howells tramped back into the room. There was a scowl on his face, and he snatched the telephone as though he wanted to bat the reporter on the head with it. He dialled Whitehall 1212.

"They got away in a police car that was parked outside," he informed Julian in a sulphurous growl. "They won't go far. I've got two carloads of armed policemen right behind them!"

When he was connected with Scotland Yard the inspector asked for the Wireless Room and dictated a message to be relayed immediately by radio to every Squad, Q, and patrol car. In a matter of minutes police cars from all over London would be closing in on the fugitives. Five minutes passed: Inspector Howells paced the floor. Ten minutes; his frown grew blacker, his stride jerkier, his fingers began to tie themselves in knots. And then the telephone rang. The inspector snatched it up. He listened for a few moments, barked an order and slammed down the receiver.

"They've got the car they escaped in," he almost wailed. "One of the pursuing cars crowded it into the kerb. Niven and his sister jumped out—and the damned fools let them get away!"

Julian felt an irresistible yearning to go home to bed. He was dog-tired, he had not been to bed for the duration of his two-day spree; and his head was throbbing from the smash across the smash across the face he had received two hours before. A glass of water which he had taken a few minutes ago was stirring up the alcohol in his stomach and making him drunk again. Home. Bed. The thought of them was good.

"There's one thing you haven't told me," growled the inspector. "How it came to pass that you were in that alley at the time the safe-burglary was committed."

"Old Dan was a friend of mine. I often dropped in on him for a chat late at night."

"I see." There was a sarcastic inflexion in the inspector's tone. "It was a mere coincidence that you happened to drop in on your old friend at the psychological moment?"

"Yes," yawned Julian. "A mere coincidence."

The Empty Warehouse

At four o'clock the following afternoon an appetising aroma preceded Mrs. MacDougal up the stairs from her basement kitchen as she ascended carrying a laden tray. An aroma enticingly suggestive of steaming coffee, hot buttered toast, kidneys-and-bacon and fat brown sausages, it would have been almost enough to make a corpse climb up eagerly out of his grave.

A widow of sixty, Mrs. MacDougal had the small sleek head, the lean active body, the alert bright eyes and perky air of a sparrow. Her work-worn hands and nails were scrupulously clean, if unmanicured, and the honest soap and water which she vigorously applied to her face night and morning had not robbed her thin cheeks of their apple-redness. There were firm, almost hard lines at the corners of her mouth, the legacy of thirty years of coping with the whims and vagaries of boarders.

She had a foot on the first step of the stairs leading to the upper floor when the telephone in the hall rang shrilly. Muttering impatiently, she went to answer it.

"He's no' in…No, I dinna ken when he'll be in. I'm no' a mind-reader…Aye, I'll gie him the message. And will ye be guid enough tae contain yersel in patience until he calls ye back? I hae mair to dae than run up and doon stairs answerin' the 'phone!"

With that she banged the receiver back on its hook. At the other end of the wire the managing-editor of the London *Morning World* fumed with impatience, but that meant less than nothing to Mrs. MacDougal. She knew that sleep and food were the most important things in the world, and until her lodger had had sufficient of both anyone who rang up for him would receive the same answer, even if the impatient telephoner was the Prime Minister of England or the Archbishop of Canterbury.

Lifting the tray, she continued placidly up the stairs. A door on the upper landing opened and Julian Mendoza appeared, rubbing the sleep out of his eyes. In an ancient green dressing-gown, in pyjamas which had shrunk in the wash, with tousled hair and a three-day growth of beard, he looked more than ever like a scarecrow.

"I thought I heard the 'phone ringing," he yawned, stretching himself.

"Maybe ye did," said his landlady complacently. "It hasna stopped ringing since eight o'clock this mornin'."

"It wasn't someone for me, I suppose?" asked Julian suspiciously. He knew Mrs. MacDougal of old.

"Maybe it was and maybe it wasna," retorted Mrs. MacDougal, coming straight for him with the tray so that he was forced to retreat into his bedroom. "Get back into bed and eat your breakfast."

With the tray held in front of her like a snow-plough, she pursued him across the room, planting it on his lap when he sat on the edge of the bed.

"What's the time?" mumbled Julian, through a mouthful of sausage. "I've got to be out at eleven sharp."

"Then you're just five hours late," snapped Mrs. MacDougal, taking the studs out of his soiled shirt and rummaging in a drawer for a fresh one.

"You haven't let me sleep all day?"

"Eat your breakfast."

Putting down the tray, Julian threw off his dressing gown. "Leave the room, like a good soul. I've got to dress. I've got to telephone. I've got to look at a paper. There are a thousand things I've got to do."

"And the first," said Mrs. MacDougal grimly, "is to finish your breakfast. I'll no' leave the room till ye dae it, so it's nae use fumblin' with the cord of your pyjamas. Ye havena the nerve tae tak' them off wi' me lookin' at you. Will ye eat it yersel—or must I feed ye?"

"I'll eat it," said Julian bitterly. He knew when he was beaten. "—you meddling old cat!" he added.

It was not until the plates were bare that Mrs. MacDougal left him alone to dress. "Scotland Yard rang up for ye five times this mornin'," she said, as she left the room, "and your editor rang up eight times. They said it was verra urgent."

Julian's pyjamas were off as soon as the door closed.

"Where the devil have you been?" demanded the managing editor of the *Morning World* when Julian at last reached a telephone. "I've been trying to find you all day."

"Never mind that. What's new?"

"Nothing much. The story you turned in early this morning covers all the developments to date. Niven and his sister are still at large, although the police are scouring London for them. It's a great story, Mendoza. Come in and see me about it as quickly as you can."

"I can't I'm going to be busy."

"Busy doing what? If you're going on the booze again—"

"That's the idea. I'll save it for later."

"What are you going to be doing that's so urgent you can't come and see me?"

"I'm going to find Niven and his sister," replied Julian, hanging up.

Turning he found Mrs. MacDougal at his elbow.

"You were talking aboot the couple in the headlines this mornin'," she said. Her eyes were shining; murder and romance were her favourite reading. "And how dae ye expect tae find them when the whole police force canna?"

His eyes narrowed, Julian said slowly: "They had to find

a hiding-place quickly, for the cops were close behind them. Niven wouldn't be able to find his pals, for they, not knowing whether he'd squealed or not, would keep away from any haunt he knew about. The girl wouldn't take her brother to any of her own friends, for her friends are respectable and they'd feel it their duty to give him up. If you worked in an estate-agent's office—as the girl did—and you wanted to hide, where would be the first place you'd thing of?"

"An empty house!" breathed Mrs. MacDougal.

"Exactly. An empty house. One you knew about through your work."

*

In gilt lettering across the estate-agency's ground-floor window ran the legend:

SPECIALISTS IN FACTORY PROPERTIES.

So, the hideout would not be an empty house; it more probably would be an untenanted factory.

A young man who wore a shabby tweed jacket with the waistcoat and trousers of a smart blue suit was leaning on the inner side of the counter, scribbling aimlessly on a blotter, his worried eyes staring into vacancy. He was paler than one would have expected, for his broad shoulders and lean waist suggested that, outside the office, athletics were his main interest. He plied had a fresh, pleasant-looking face, perhaps a little too earnest in expression. A nice, respectable young man—some fond mother's devoted only son.

When Julian attracted his attention, he did his best to look alert; but there was obviously trouble, grave trouble, on his mind.

"Factory property, sir? What kind of factory property?"

He eyed Julian up and down, looking doubtful at sight of the reporter's shabby old greatcoat and his God-forsaken hat.

"I want something in the Bethnal Green area."

It had been at Bethnal Green that Margaret Niven and her brother had abandoned the police car and taken to foot.

The name of the district rang a bell in the clerk's mind. He stared at Julian with open mouth.

"Bethnal Green," he repeated. "That's funny."

"Have a good laugh," said Julian. "And then run through your books and see if you've a factory to let in that neighbourhood."

The clerk looked dizzy. He ran a trembling hand over his crisp brown hair. "I—I— Excuse me. I don't feel very well."

An older man came from a desk at the rear of the office. "You'd better go and sit down, George. I'll attend to this gentleman."

After the young clerk had walked unsteadily away, the older one said apologetically to Julian: "You must excuse our Mr. Norris. He's a bit upset. Had a nasty shock. He walks out with a young lady who works here, and she hasn't come to the office today. It says in the paper that she's wanted by the police. Too bad. A nice, quiet girl she always seemed…but you can't tell, nowadays, can you? What was it you wanted, sir? A factory in the Bethnal Green neighbourhood? If you'll wait a minute I'll just run through the books—"

He returned shortly with a typewritten list.

"These are all adjacent to Bethnal Green, sir. As you see, particulars of accommodation, power facilities, and rents are given in detail. Now, if there's anything here that interests you—"

"Are they vacant now? I must have immediate possession."

"Not all are vacant, sir. Some of them won't be until the end of the term. I'll tick off the ones that are."

He marked three. Julian folded the list and put it in his pocket. "I suppose these are absolutely all you have in that district?"

Noticing a look of hesitation in the other's eyes, Julian added:

"Confidentially, I want something with a very low rent. You haven't a property, I suppose, a little rundown and neglected, that—"

"Well, sir, there's one you could have for next to nothing, but I really can't recommend it. We seldom bother to mention it, as a matter of fact. It's been empty for years and is in a shocking state."

"It sounds like the very place," said Julian.

A three-storeyed building of crumbling brick, it stood in a yard cluttered with debris at the bottom of a dead end. The gloomy little houses—almost hovels—which lined the short street that led to it had been condemned by the local council. Awaiting demolition, they were as empty and forlorn as the factory itself. Urchins had smashed the glass of the street lamps and knocked out the windows of the scowling, deserted houses; and even the lower windows of the factory had jagged, gaping holes in them. The upper windows were boarded over.

As Julian warily crossed the yard, three huge rats ran from the shelter of some broken boxes and disappeared through a hole in the wall of the building. No wonder the estate agency seldom mentioned the place to applicants for factory premises! The look of it was enough to discourage the most hard-up prospective manufacturer; which was why Julian was greatly encouraged by it.

Up one side of the building ran a rusty iron fire-escape and the bottom section hung low enough to be grasped and pulled down by a tall man; but a second's thought made Julian reject the idea of using it to reach the upper floors. Even if the dilapidated contraption would bear his weight—which did not seem likely—he would cut too conspicuous a figure walking up it in broad daylight. He put his head through one of the shattered windows and looked about him. The ground floor was large and dusty and broken only by tall iron pillars and a network of rusty pulleys and dangling shafts. Everything was covered thickly with dirt and festooned with cobwebs, some of them like long lace curtains, which billowed slowly to and fro in the draught from the paneless windows. The floorboards were rotten, with here and there a great ragged hole in them.

As silently as possible, Julian drew himself over the window-ledge into the building. He picked his way across the sagging floor to a brick staircase against the far wall. There he paused and listened. Nothing stirred above. On tiptoe, he stole up the stairs.

The first upper storey was in the same decayed state as the ground floor. There was no hiding-place for any being larger than a rat. A hasty glance round and he went on up the stairs. On the top landing he was faced by three doors. He opened the first one cautiously. It led into a gloomy hole of a room, murky and stale-smelling, in which the only light came through the cracks between the boards that covered the window.

Julian stepped over the threshold. He heard a hoarse snarl, like that of a furious animal, and something hit him with terrific force on the head. As he dropped to his knees, stunned and almost unconscious, his dazed brain recorded the thought: "I've found the Snowbird."

It did not seem that finding Eddie Niven was going to do him any good. From behind the door the little jailbird darted with an iron bar in his hand and a snarl of hatred in his throat. Panting for blood, lusting to kill.

As Julian knelt in a dizzy stupor on the floor, another blow glanced off his skull and smashed numbingly on his right shoulder. He felt his senses slipping away; his body was too heavy a weight to be held up by his yielding thighs; he yearned to fall forward on his face and surrender to the black drowsiness that was washing over him. But to surrender was to die. To surrender was to be pounded into mangled oblivion by the raging beast who was raining savage blows on him.

"You dirty swine," panted the Snowbird. "I'll do for you."

Like an empty sack Julian dropped forward on his face.

With a fierce cry, the Snowbird threw himself forward,

battering, smashing, pounding with the iron bar in his hand. But the reporter's fading senses still held a spark of the will to live. He rolled over, knocking the Snowbird's legs from under him. For a while they lay, kicking and fighting, on the dusty floor together. The iron bar had dropped with a clatter, and was lost to both of them.

The Snowbird clawed like a maniac, His nails made bleeding furrows down Julian's face, raking off strips of skin from temple to chin. His knees jabbed piston-like into Julian's abdomen, making an aching void in the region of his vital organs. Julian's fingers groped blindly for the Snowbird's throat. They found it.

"Sweetheart," muttered Julian thickly.

He tightened his grasp and held on grimly. All his stunned brain was capable of knowing was that he must hold on…hold on…hold on…

The Snowbird became a dead weight across Julian's body. Still Julian's hands gripped the neck tightly, squeezing…squeezing… squeezing…

A voice in Julian's brain (it seemed to be coming from a great distance) said: "He isn't struggling any more. He's dead. You've killed him."

One part of Julian's brain said: "Good!"

It was a pleasant thought. And then, another part of his brain said: 'Not so good, you mustn't kill him. Not yet, He's got to talk." Julian released his grip. He rolled the limp body off him. He lay on the floor fighting back the giddiness that threatened him. He felt sick, weary, one vast ache from head to foot.

His lungs clamoured for air. Stumbling up, he staggered to the window and tried to push the boards away with his shaking fingers. They were nailed too tightly for that. On his hands and knees, he crawled about the floor until he found the iron bar. He used it to batter at the boards until three of them were sufficiently loose to prise off with his hands. For a long time, he stood at the window, gulping breath into his starving lungs. He was still only capable of thinking one thing at a time, and what he was thinking of at the moment was: air. Air—and then more air. When he was saner, he looked down at his hand. He was still holding the iron bar. Hairs from his own head, smears of blood from his own arteries, adhered to it. For no reason he could think of, that seemed funny. He put a hand to his face and brought it away sticky with blood.

Then he remembered the Snowbird. The little crook was lying very still where Julian had left him and his face was blue.

"Just my luck!" thought Julian. "He's dead."

Because it was bad thing for the Snowbird to be dead just yet, he dragged the limp form to the window and tried artificial respiration. Sweat was pouring down his face, making his raw wounds smart, before a sigh grumbled through between the Snowbird's lips. In the middle of the sigh the Snowbird's lungs drew in a trickle of air. Still unconscious, the Snowbird began, fitfully, to breathe.

That was good enough. The Snowbird wasn't going to die just yet: that was enough for the present. Julian had been sufficiently optimistic to bring a pair of regulation handcuffs. He fastened one cuff to Eddie Niven's limp wrist and the other to an iron bracket which was riveted to the wall.

Someone was coming up the stairs—someone who moved furtively. Julian could hear the scrape of show-leather on brick.

He crept out to the landing and peered down. A girl was stealing up, her eyes searching the shadows at the head of the stairs. It must be Margaret Niven, although it did not look like her. This girl was of Margaret Niven's height, but her hair was much darker and her clothes were not the ones in which Margaret Niven had escaped the night before.

She was ready for trouble. The revolver with which the police had been held up was clasped in her hand and pointing up the stairs. She was dressed for the street. Perhaps she had been out and, coming back, had looked up at the unboarded top window and realised that something was wrong. On her face was the expression Margaret Niven's face had worn the previous night—an expression which said that she would do anything, risk anything, for the Snowbird.

Crouching back, Julian waited. In exactly the same way, Eddie Niven had seen him coming up the stairs; and had waited for him, with the iron bar…

The girl reached the head of the stairs. Julian's empty hand chopped down, knocking the revolver out of her grasp.

With a stricken cry she stared up into his face. Between blood and sweat and bruises it must have been a horrible sight.

It was Margaret Niven, alright. She had made some changes in her appearance, rendering the police description of her a very poor fit. Her eyes flew to the revolver, but before she could reach it Julian picked it up and put it in his pocket. For a moment he thought she was going to fly blindly at his throat. "Let's not have any more fighting," said Julian flatly. "I'm sick of it."

Kneeling beside the motionless form of her brother, Margaret Niven put a small white hand on his clammy forehead. "What have you done to him? You've killed him!"

"No, thank God, I haven't. Not quite."

Slowly, Margaret Niven turned her head and stared up at Julian. She had the eyes of a soul in torment.

"Why thank God?" she asked, in a weary voice. "When all's said and done, he'd be better dead."

"He's got to talk," said Julian unemotionally.

"He won't talk. I think perhaps that's all the honour he's got…the thieves' code that won't let him betray his confederates."

"He'll talk, all right. I'll see to that."

"What are you going to do? You—you'll torture him?"

"I shan't lay a finger on him."

The girl stood up. She sighed. "Well, I've done what I could for him. It hasn't helped. It seems pretty futile now. Probably I should have let him face the music in the first place, but the thought of hanging…" A shiver ran through her slim body. "I suppose you're waiting for reinforcements before you take us both to prison?"

"There won't be any reinforcements," replied Julian. "And prison will have to wait."

"I don't understand."

"You think I'm a plainclothes detective. I'm not, I'm a newspaper reporter. What matters more, in this instance, is that I'm a friend of the man who was murdered. I want the names of the killers; and I don't think your brother would give that information to the police. The police methods aren't—shall we say?—sufficiently persuasive. That's why your brother isn't leaving here until he talks."

"But—you can't do that! It would be illegal."

"It was illegal for you to holdup a police station with a revolver, but you did it. It was illegal for your brother's confederates to murder Old Dan Riordan—but Old Dan is dead."

"I won't let you—"

"What can you do? You can't threaten to shoot me, because I've got the gun. It wouldn't be any good for you to attack me, for I'd have no gentlemanly scruples about giving you a sock on the jaw and chaining you to your brother. All you can do is run out and call a policeman. If you want to do that, I shan't stop you. But you won't. As long as your brother is my prisoner there's a chance he'll escape, but once he's back in the hands of the police, there's none. No, you won't call the cops—and there isn't another damned thing you can do."

In silence, Margaret Niven turned from him and walked to the window, every line of her body expressing defeat.

"Where had you been when I caught you tiptoeing up the stairs?" asked Julian.

"I'd been out to buy some food and—and—oh, some things we needed."

"You have nerve."

"The police were looking for a man and a woman, not a woman on her own," said Margaret Niven listlessly. "The only danger was while I was wearing the clothes I escaped in. Once I'd bought a different coat and hat, I was safe enough. I bought a bottle of dye, too, and touched up my hair in a rest-room at Selfridge's."

"What did you do with the food and things?"

"I left the parcels downstairs when I came up to see if something was wrong."

"I'll go and fetch them," said Julian, turning on his heel.

He had a reason for leaving the girl alone with her brother; he wanted her to make an attempt to open the handcuffs and find out, at the start, that she couldn't; he wanted to give her time to run over in her mind all the plans of escape she could think of—and to realise how hopeless they were.

A peculiar furry grey heap, almost round in shape, about two feet high and three feet wide, with long, thin, wriggling things like worms sticking out all over it, was squirming about on the bottom step of the brick staircase. Julian rapped his heel sharply on an upper step and the heap dissolved into a small army of rats. A dozen pairs of unwinking, beady eyes stared at him balefully; a dozen sets of sharp white teeth were bared. He took a step forward, and the rats scrambled away, spreading out fan-wise, darting for holes all over the rotting ground floor.

They had gnawed through the stout brown paper with which

Margaret Niven's parcels had been wrapped and made a large hole in a loaf of bread. Julian threw what remained of it out to the middle of the floor for the rats to finish at leisure. Most of the food—tinned stuff, boxes of biscuits, bottles of aerated water—they had been unable to get at.

Margaret Niven's handbag was lying to one side, a bit gnawed, but not much the worse. Julian opened it and examined the contents one by one. He found a small parcel with a chemist's label containing tubes of morphine tablets. There was also a hypodermic syringe and a doctor's prescription for morphia made out to 'Edward Norton', which presumably was one of the Snowbird's aliases. The reporter put tablets, syringe and prescription in his pocket and took out the revolver.

He started to climb the stairs with the tattered parcels in one arm. Making the disintegrating armful stay put while keeping one hand free for the revolver was tricky work; but he felt it wise to have the revolver ready for action. Before he reached the top landing he paused and said, calmly:

"If you're waiting up there, ready to bean me with something hard, you'd better think again. I'll shoot at sight—and I'm a good shot."

He heard the thump of something hard being dropped on the floor and the girl appeared, unarmed and crestfallen, at the head of the stairs.

"You're a funny girl," said Julian, dumping his burden higgledy-piggledy into her arms. "I don't suppose you'd hurt a fly to save yourself and yet you were all ready to bop me with a chunk of iron for the sake of that worthless brother of yours."

The girl did not answer. She carried the bundles into the room and laid them on the floor. Their torn condition made her eye Julian enquiringly.

"Rats," said Julian briefly.

The Snowbird had regained consciousness. He was groaning and trying to roll over but every time he tried, the arm that was manacled to the wall bracket pulled him back. He was too dazed to understand why he could not roll over. There was a silly look on his face, as if he did not know the answer to anything. His breathing was so guttural that it sounded more like snoring.

As soon as he was strong enough to have hysterics, he had hysterics.

In frantic haste Margaret Niven rummaged in her bag.

"If this is what you're looking for," remarked Julian, producing the morphine tablets, "you're wasting your time."

"Give them to me, please. Don't you see, he's got to have them? You don't think I'd have bought them if it wasn't vital for him to have them? He's really a hospital case. A doctor gave him the prescription some time ago; he knew that it's impossible for an addict to live without drugs."

"He'll get them when he talks," said Julian harshly.

Margaret stared at him in horror. "So that's what you're going to do?"

"Yes," replied Julian grimly, "that's what I'm going to do."

For a long time, the Snowbird screamed and raved. And then, exhausted, he lay sobbing on his back. After a while he began to curse and weep alternately. Night fell and the moon sailed into the patch of sky which was visible through the paneless, uncovered window and still he kept it up, screaming, raging, sobbing, cursing. In the dark room, with their nerves already on edge, it was horrible to hear. At times he sounded like a spoiled baby; at others, like a frenzied maniac; at others, like a trapped animal.

"Give me the names of your accomplices," said Julian steadily.

"I'll kill you for this!" shrieked the Snowbird.

"Don't be silly. You've had two chances already and you muffed both of them. You'd better forget about killing me and do some talking."

"I'll see you in hell first!"

"You'll talk," said Julian. "Sooner or later."

The Snowbird's next hysterical spell lasted longer than ever. It unbearably affected his sister, and she began to weep hysterically, too. She rushed at Julian, striking him wildly with her clenched fists. He drew back a little and gave her a smack on the face hard enough to bring her to her senses.

"One of us is enough. If we give way to our nerves, we'll all go barmy."

"You can't do this," she sobbed, more quietly. "It's too cruel."

"He's got to talk."

"He won't talk. Surely you can see he won't? You're not going to torture him all night? Oh, you can't be so cruel."

"No," said Julian soberly. "I thought I could, but I can't."

"Then you'll give him some morphia?"

"I can't do that, either."

"But, don't you see, he'll wear himself out carrying on like this."

"Are you willing to risk going out again?" asked Julian.

"If I must. But why?"

There were some candles among the things Margaret Niven had bought. Julian lit one and, by its guttering light, wrote a few words on a scrap of paper.

"Take this to a chemist," he said, handing the paper to her. "You're sure to find one open. It's something to make him sleep. Take an empty bottle with you and bring back some water."

With the candle in his hand to light the way, he escorted her downstairs and across the ground floor to a window. Rats scuttled under their feet, but Margaret did not cry out. Julian had a hand on her arm and he felt her trembling slightly, that was all.

"You're a brave girl," he murmured softly. He would have gone for the sedative himself, but she would probably have been driven mad if left she alone in the rat-ridden factory with the demented Snowbird. He waited at the window for her to return. She was gone fifteen minutes, and when at last she climbed in and Julian put out his hand to help her, he felt at the touch that her nerves were tauter than ever.

"I almost ran into a man my brother used to know," she explained breathlessly. "His name is Gort. I don't think he saw me. When I spotted him, I walked very fast to a corner and when I was round the corner I ran."

"Gort." Julian tried to remember whether he had ever heard of a safe-breaker of that name, but the more he thought the less the name meant to him. "Do you suppose he was one of your brother's accomplices last night?"

"I don't know. I only met him once with Eddie. I don't like the man—but, then, I never like Eddie's friends."

They went upstairs. The Snowbird lashed out with his feet

when Julian went near him. The reporter put a stop to that by sitting on the Snowbird's legs, but he was bitten twice before he succeeded in administering the sleeping-draught. It worked quickly. Utterly exhausted though he was, the Snowbird's last action before falling asleep was to try to kick Julian in the teeth when he stood up.

Foraging about, Julian found some old sacks. He draped two of them across the window to prevent the light of the candle being seen outside. He lifted the slumbering Snowbird in his arms while Margaret made her brother a bed of sacks.

"You'd better get some sleep, too," said Julian, when that was done. "You look all in. There are enough sacks to make beds for an army."

"I couldn't sleep."

"Care to try the sleeping-draught?"

"My God, no. As long as I live, I'll never touch a drug of any sort."

"Then what you need is fresh air. There's a fire-escape just outside the window. Let's go out for a breather."

Before they climbed through the window, Julian made sure that the rusty structure would bear their weight. They found that it led to a flat roof with a rampart three feet high. Going up, they climbed onto the roof and sat out of sight beneath the rampart. For a long time they sat in silence, looking at the round bright moon that sailed high across a clear blue sky. There were many stars, cold and brilliant.

Julian filled his pipe and lit it.

After a while, Margaret said with a shiver: "Life is strange, isn't it? When I was a little girl playing with a new baby brother, I thought him the most wonderful thing that ever happened. He had a little pink bald head and two tiny fists like…like crumpled rosebuds. There was nothing to show that he was going to grow up different from other children. Sometimes in the mornings Mother would let me wheel him out in his pram, and I'd be so proud I'd almost burst. When he was older, I tried to fight his battles for him. Perhaps that's where I failed him. It made him dependent on me. If I'd been more sensible, he wouldn't have grown up so weak and easily led."

"It's time you knew the truth," said Julian. "It isn't because he's weak and easily led that he's a crook. He's a crook because it isn't in him to be anything else. He's bad all through."

"People have been saying that all his life. From childhood he's been accused of beastly things—of lying, cheating, thieving—and I've stood up for him. How could I believe in the rottenness of my own brother? A brother so gentle and confiding as a boy. A brother who loved me." Her voice grew sharp with pain. "Or perhaps loving me was only a pose, too. It's hard, terribly hard, to accept, because—you see, I've built my life round him. If Eddie's bad to the core, I've nothing left."

"There are a lot of things in life."

"Not for me. All I have is Eddie. Take him away—and what remains? Nothing."

"There's a young man walking about in a daze because you're in trouble," said Julian, staring at the glowing bowl of his pipe. "Even when he tries hard to keep his mind on his work, his hand automatically scribbles your name on his blotter. 'Margaret. Marge. Margaret Niven. Margaret Norris…' I've seen the blotter."

"You mean George Norris," said Margaret, with a break in her voice. "Yes, George will be upset. But I've lost him, too. I'm wanted by the police. When they catch me, I'll be sent to prison. From now on respectable people won't have anything to do with me. And George is respectable. He runs his life in accordance with convention and the catechism. He's a sweet soul but he knows that jailbirds and decent people can't mix.

It may not be easy for him to shut me out of his heart, but he'll make no bones about shutting me out of his life. It won't occur to him for a moment that any other course is possible."

"If he throws you over because you're in trouble, you're better off without him."

"That's easy to say. Maybe it's true. But how does it help? Yesterday I had George and my job and my whole life in front of me. I've thrown all that away for Eddie."

"You'd do it again," said Julian uncomfortably—he could sense that she was perilously close to tears and if there was one thing he dreaded it was the tears of a woman.

"I probably would. But if Eddie's as bad as you say, what's the good of it all? What is there left for me?"

Julian had known it would happen and it did. She began to cry—dry, voiceless tears that shook her mercilessly from head to foot. Abhorring sentiments, he held out against them as long as he could and then he took her in his arms.

Like a child afraid of the dark, she clung to him desperately. He held her soft, warm body in his arms and for the first time realised that she was a beautiful girl, and not merely a pawn in a dangerous game. For the life of him he couldn't help it—he kissed her. Margaret did not resist. Her moist, warm mouth pressed hungrily on his with an almost hysterical eagerness. Julian said to himself: 'She's distraught, on the verge of collapse; it isn't fair to take advantage of her.' Easy to say—but to open his arms and let her go was more than he could do. Time stood still while they clung together in blind, delirious rapture.

And then, as suddenly as though he had been drenched with cold water, Julian returned to sanity. A hand was stealing down his side into his pocket.

He sat up abruptly and gripped Margaret's wrist. She was trying gingerly to withdraw the revolver.

"Nice girl," he said bitterly. "That was a good act you put on. You almost had me crying, too. And all you wanted was a chance to grab the gun!"

Even as he said it he realised that it was not true; that she had been carried away by emotion, exactly as he had been; and that the attempt to take the revolver had been an afterthought—the sort of afterthought, he reflected grimly, that he himself would probably have had if the circumstances had been reversed.

Margaret offered no defence. She did not tell him that for a moment she had almost been in love with him, or that now she hated him—although not so much as she hated herself.

*

The following day was the longest any of them had ever lived through. It began at daybreak, when the Snowbird opened his eyes and started to mutter incoherently. It dragged on to night-fall, punctuated by fits of wild shrieking, periods of maudlin weeping. None of them ate anything from the rising of the sun until it set.

To Julian Mendoza and Margaret Niven all the world had narrowed to the pile of dirty sacks on which the demented Snowbird lay. And still the Snowbird would not talk. He was being eaten alive by the craving for drugs…but he would not talk.

It was only by reminding himself constantly of Old Dan Riordan, done savagely to death, that Julian was able to steel himself to hold out against the Snowbird's nerve-wracking pleas. He longed to throw his hand in, to give the poor creature what he cried for: but, if he did, the Snowbird would never reveal the names of his accomplices.

To let the torture go on was Julian's only hope of discovering who killed his friend; and that was something he had to know, whatever happened. Time was becoming short. Sooner or later Inspector Howells would have the inspiration which had led Julian to the factory, and police would swarm through the littered yard below. Good-bye then, forever, to the reporter's chance of making the Snowbird talk.

"What are you going to do with him when he does talk?" asked Margaret, in the dusk of the evening.

The day had taken toll of her. She looked and spoke like an old woman.

"You ask that as though you were afraid I was going to kill him."

"I wouldn't put it past you. But I suppose you'll turn him over to the police and let the Law do it."

"When he talks," said Julian, "I'm going to unfasten the handcuffs and walk out of here and let you decide what to do with him. That's dead against my duty as a citizen, of course, but it's a little late to become particular about my duty. In any case, if I took him to the police, they'd hold me for trial for this little business. That would interfere with me going after the killers of Dan Riordan—and nothing on earth is going to interfere with that!"

The room was weirdly lit by candles stuck in bottles all-round the floor. Their wavering flames made grotesque patterns and shadows on the mildewed walls. Margaret Niven knelt on the floor beside her brother. "Did you hear that? If you talk, he'll let us go. Oh, Eddie, talk for my sake. I can't bear any more of this."

The Snowbird had sunk into listlessness. He stared up at her without speaking.

"Tell me, Eddie, tell me," she urged. "Who were the men inside the warehouse that night?"

The Snowbird shook his head.

"I've a hunch one of them was Gort," said Julian. "I hope to hell he didn't see you when you almost ran into him last night. He may have been prowling the neighbourhood in which you disappeared, looking for you."

"Gort!" The Snowbird started up. "I didn't say that! I didn't mention Gort's name!"

"But Gort was one of them," replied Julian grimly. "I can see it in your eyes. You may as well tell me the name of the other man and get it over with."

"Yes, Eddie," pleaded Margaret, "tell him and get it over with." A sigh escaped the Snowbird's ashen lips. Words came with it. "It was Mayo. Mayo…and Gort." The instant the words were out he reared up in a frenzy. "No! No! I was lying, trying to cheat you into letting me go. It wasn't Mayo and Gort. That was a lie. I haven't seen either of them for months."

"You weren't lying," said Julian quietly.

Tough As They Make 'Em!

"What's that?" cried Margaret suddenly.

Julian looked at her questioningly.

"I thought I heard a sound at the window," she gasped. "There it is again! No—it isn't at the window—it's on the stairs."

Crossing the room on tiptoe, Julian put his ear to the door. He heard a faint scratching which might have been made by a rat; but which could as easily be the scraping of feet on brick as they stole up the staircase. With his hand on the door-knob, Julian drew the revolver.

About to open the door, he thought better of it. If a furtive intruder was ascending the stairs, there was no saying how near he was. It was impossible to judge by the slight noise he was the making. He might be at the bottom or half-way up the top flight. In the latter case, if the intruder was an armed and desperate man, it would be suicide for Julian to step out onto the landing. Better to wait, with gun cocked, for the intruder to open the door…

Drawing back, Julian motioned Margaret against a wall. In the middle of the room, he stood waiting, with the mouth of the revolver pointing at the door. The scraping sounds came nearer…nearer…The Snowbird started whimpering with fear. Nearer. Nearer.

And, suddenly, the reporter drew in his breath with a hiss. He had thought of something: the Snowbird had two confederates; and his ears told him that only one a man was furtively ascending the stairs. Where was the other?

He remembered that when Margaret first heard the sounds, she thought they came from the window—

But he remembered it too late.

While he was wondering, his question was answered. Margaret screamed a warning. A hand came through the window and ripped away the sacking that covered it. A voice which rasped like a rusty file said: "Drop that gun!"

Julian spun on his heel, aiming the revolver at the window, but before he could fire, the Snowbird, still prone on the floor, hooked a foot round his ankle and tripped him up.

Hitting the floor with face, chest and knees almost simultaneously, Julian felt the revolver slipping from his grasp and heard it go skittering across the room. When he picked himself up a tall, thin man had climbed in through the window and a short, squat man was standing by the open door. Each had an automatic pistol in his right hand.

"Stand over there, against the wall," said the short, squat man, in a voice like a whisper through a foghorn. He sniffed noisily two or three times. He had a bad cold.

Without arguing, Julian joined Margaret against the wall, and the short, squat man came and stood beside them, with his automatic ready for business. The tall, thin man stooped, picked up the silenced revolver, flipped open the cylinder and counted the live cartridges. Uttering a satisfied grunt, he passed the revolver over to his right hand and put the automatic in his pocket. With unhurried steps he walked to where the Snowbird was lying.

"Gort!" whimpered the Snowbird. "Gort, old pal, for God's sake don't look at me like that. I didn't...I wouldn't...You don't think I..."

Its flesh the colour of putty, Gort's face had a sharpness, a hardness, that suggested an axe. The mouth was a thin slit, the eyes no more human than chips of chilled steel.

"I been crouched on that fire-escape, listening, for pretty near ten minutes," he said. "You dirty squealer!"

He raised his right hand and shot the Snowbird in the stomach. The sound that came from the silenced revolver was a muffed one like a cough. The cough was echoed by the Snowbird. That one choked gasp was all he uttered. His waxen face was twisted with unbearable pain.

"Eddie!" cried Margaret.

She ran across the room and knelt beside the dying youth, raising him in her arms, pillowing his slumping shoulders on her breast. The Snowbird was too far gone to know her. While she held him up, Gort leaned forward and shot the Snowbird in the head.

"Exit Eddie Niven," he said tonelessly. "He's dead, sister. Nursing him is a waste of time—and you ain't got much time to waste."

Margaret stood up and stared at the man. She said nothing, made no outcry; the ordeal she had been through during the previous forty-eight hours had wrung her dry of emotion. She only stared at him with wide, blank eyes, as though she, too, were dead.

Although he knew that to move meant death, Julian tensed himself to spring to her aid. The short, squat man dug his automatic into Julian's back.

"I wouldn't, if I was you," he said, with a sniff. As stiffly as a statue falling, Margaret dropped to the floor in a dead faint.

"It's better like that," said Gort, pointing the silenced revolver at her head. "She'll never know what hit her."

"I don't stand for that Gort," said Mayo hoarsely.

Gort stared in contemptuous amazement at his confederate.

"You turned yellow or something? There's a murder rap against us for the night watchman, ain't there? We'll get hemp neck-ties if we're caught. What difference does one more make?"

"I ain't yellow, only I don't stand for shooting no women."

"If you ain't yellow, you're crazy. She's seen our faces. She knows who we are. What's the matter with you? A woman can squawk as loud as a man, can't she?"

Cocking the revolver, Gort put it to Margaret's head.

"Shoot her," whispered Mayo, "and you and me are through, here and now."

"This is a nice time to go soft on me. There's only one way to keep a woman from talking. If we let her go, we'll swing, sure."

"I don't say let her go. We can take her with us and keep her hid until we blow the country."

"A hell of a long way we'll go with a woman on our hands!"

"Maybe she'd be useful, if the cops got too hot on our trail."

"As a hostage?" Gort considered the question. "It's an idea, at that. I'd rather rub her out—I'm a man that likes to make certain—but have it your own way. Only, don't start begging me not to croak the man."

"Hell," said Mayo, "we've got to croak the man."

Their voices were as unemotional as though drowning a litter of kittens were the subject of the discussion.

"I took care of Niven," said Gort, "you attend to this mug." He handed the silenced revolver to Mayo. "Do it with this, it don't make a noise."

"Get the girl out of here first," replied Mayo.

"What's the idea of that?"—the question was a sneer. "You squeamish about having her wake up and see you bumping off her boyfriend?"

"After I do the job, we'll want to make a getaway fast. I don't want to be lugging an unconscious girl down three flights of stairs when I'm taking it on the lam."

"Maybe you're right. I'll take her down now." Gort picked up Margaret and slung her over his shoulder. "Give me time to get to the car. I'll honk the horn once when I'm ready."

He looked at Julian. "Goodbye, mug," he said.

He took a flashlamp from his pocket, turned it on, and went out, carrying his burden effortlessly. Alone in the dimly-lit room with the sprawling corpse of the Snowbird, Julian and Mayo stood listening to the slowly receding footsteps.

"Move away from me a little," whispered Mayo hoarsely. "You're too near."

In silence, Julian obeyed. They faced each other, separated by three short paces. Mayo had a round, stolid-looking face, with a chunk of moustache on the upper lip. He resembled the type of respectable workman one sees in a public house bar of an evening with a pint beer mug in one hand and a clay pipe in the other. His face looked all wrong with a scowl; a broad grin would have come more naturally to it. It was a cold night, but sweat was pouring down his cheeks as profusely as though he were in a Turkish bath.

He wiped his nose with the cuff of his left sleeve. "I'm no killer," he said huskily. "I don't like this. It's just something I've got to do. I've got nothing against you, except that you know too much. It's your life or mine, so it's got to be yours. Maybe you think I don't mind doing it, but I do. I'm no killer. If I'd known what was going to happen the other night, I'd have passed up the job. On the level, I would. We didn't mean to kill the old watchman. It just happened. I was standing guard over him. Gort was drilling the safe. Suddenly the old fool makes a jump for the telephone. You wouldn't think anyone could be so daft. What could we do? We couldn't let him give the alarm. So Gort hit him with a crowbar. He hit him too hard. You can't take time to judge your blows when things are happening fast. You hit quick. The old man croaked. That made it murder. Funny how things happen. A man goes out to blow a safe and comes back a murderer."

Julian growled: "Why don't you stop talking and pull the trigger?"

Mayo looked hurt. "I've got to wait for the signal. I'm trying to explain how it was. I want you to understand that I'm not just a mad dog, killing for the fun of it. Fun!—my God!—it's anything but fun."

"You ought to have left the country two days ago."

"We're leaving, all right. But first we've got a score to settle—and some money to collect."

"A score to settle with whom?" asked Julian. "What money?"

"Never mind that. I'm telling you what I want to tell you, not what you want to know."

"You talk too much," said Julian. "When the time comes you won't have the nerve to shoot."

"I could see you thinking that. I could see it in your eyes. But you're wrong. I've only got to remember that it's your life or mine and I'll pull the trigger fast enough. It's something I've got to do, whether I like it or not. It's just as if I was one of a firing squad." He wiped his nose on his sleeve again. "When a firing squad shoots a man they bandage his eyes, so he won't see it coming. We ain't got time for that, but if you like to turn your back on me—"

"I'll take it looking at you."

"Maybe you think I won't have the nerve to look you in the eyes and shoot but don't count on that. This is something I've got to do. If it was your neck that was at stake, you'd shoot me. When it comes to living or dying, a man is a law to himself."

"Thanks, anyway, for sparing the girl."

"Hell," said Mayo. "I couldn't stand for shooting a woman."

The sound of a motor-horn floated up to them back a through the silent darkness. Mayo's eyes focused on a spot on Julian's waistcoat. His finger tightened on the trigger.

"Wait a minute," said Julian. "This wants more nerve than I've got. I'll take it in the back, after all."

He turned round. As he turned, he made a jump for the window.

Mayo fired and the bullet hit Julian in the shoulder, bowling him over.

He went through the window head first and felt his toes scraping the railings of the fire-escape as his body shot out into the air. He fell down…down…landing on the ground, three storeys below, with a thump that knocked him out.

A long time afterwards he regained consciousness.

It was still night and pitch-dark. He was lying in the yard outside the factory, and a stack of empty boxes had collapsed on top of him. Dully, he wondered why Mayo and Gort had not found him and finished him off. Perhaps they had looked and been unable to find him; perhaps they thought he was dead; perhaps they had taken alarm and fled: it didn't much matter. Julian was too badly hurt to care about anything except the bewildering fact that he was alive.

He was too sore to walk. But he could crawl.

On hands and knees, he groped and fumbled his way up the silent, empty street on which the factory was situated.

He lurched, filthy and ragged and bleeding, into an all-night restaurant in the next street. The woman behind the counter took one look at him and began to scream. With the last of his failing strength Julian lifted the receiver of a telephone which stood beside the cash register. He pushed the mouthpiece toward her. "Scream into that," he said. And then, he fainted.

The bed was soft and warm. He wanted to stay in it for ever. He pulled up the sheet, to keep the blankets from tickling his nose. It was a nice sheet. A clean, white, austere sheet. It felt good to his throbbing body. There was a smell about which was not so good. It was too sanitary a smell to be agreeable. Ether and disinfectant and starch were its principal ingredients.

"My God!" he said. "I'm in hospital."

"So, you've come round at last," said Inspector Howells.

Julian had not known that there was anyone near him. He pulled down the friendly sheet and looked at Howells over it, out of one eye. Quickly tiring of looking at Howells, he let the eye rove over his surroundings. He was in a green-walled private ward, with bars on the window and a nurse and a man in a navy-blue suit standing by the door.

"How do you feel?" asked Howells.

"I'd feel fine if you weren't here. Go away."

"I've been waiting three days for you to snap out of it and talk sense," said Howells. "I can't go away now."

"So that's how long I've been here? Three days?"

"This is the morning of the fourth. You've been delirious until now. Your ravings have been like a chunk out of the Arabian Nights. You've been through the mill, Mendoza."

"Did I mention any names?"

"None that were sufficiently coherent for me to catch. You can remedy that now."

"I don't know any names," said Julian, in a weary voice. "At least, none that matter."

"Don't be like that, Mendoza," retorted the inspector sternly. "We gathered sufficient from your ravings to realise that you know a lot. There was a trail of blood spots leading from the café in which you were found to the old factory. We found Niven's body in the factory. You've been rambling on about two men who shot Niven and took the girl away."

"Then I didn't dream it all."

"No, it wasn't a dream. Who were the two men, Mendoza?"

"I told you I don't know any names."

"That may be. But you must have seen their faces. I've got Rogue's Gallery of photographs here of every known safe-breaker in England. Take a look."

The inspector passed a score of photographs slowly one by one in front of Julian's eyes. He watched the reporter's face closely. Among them. was a photograph of Gort and one of Mayo, but Julian's expression remained perfectly blank. Gort and Mayo had the girl. If the police went after them, her life would be in danger.

"The safe-burglary was a professional job," said the inspector impatiently. "At least one of these men must have been in on it."

"I've never seen any of them before in my life."

Inspector Howells said something in a furious voice. The nurse came forward, full of prim and righteous indignation.

"You mustn't use language like that," she snapped. "He's still very weak."

"I'm not as weak as all that," said Julian. "Look, I can sit up."

"Goodness gracious me," cried the nurse in a panic. "Lie down at once or I'll call the doctor!"

Julian lay down again. "I only wanted to show you," he grumbled.

"Look here, Mendoza," said the inspector testily, "I've got to know who these two men were. The sooner you talk the better. It's no good saying you don't know them; I know better than that. You're playing some deep game of your own."

Snuggling under the sheet, Julian said firmly: "Go away."

"You'd better go," agreed the nurse, "you'll only upset him."

"I'll go," snapped Howells. "But I'll be back. I'm leaving a plainclothesman. He'll stay in the room beside you, Mendoza. You won't get away from me again until you talk!"

Julian lay very still under the sheet. After a while he put one eye out and saw the burly man in navy blue sitting beside the bed. There was no one else in sight.

"Inspector Howells gone?" asked Julian.

"Yes, sir," said the plainclothesman agreeably. "He's gone."

"Good! Then I can come out now."

"I wouldn't sit up, sir, if I was you."

"Maybe you wouldn't," replied Julian, painfully dragging himself into a more erect position. "Do you play chess?"

"Fairly well, sir."

"It's a pity I can't. But I can learn. See if you can find a board somewhere and we'll try."

"Oh, no, you don't, sir," said the plainclothesman pleasantly. "You don't catch me going out of the room on a fool's errand, giving you a chance to do a bunk. I'm staying right here. Orders are orders."

"All right," sighed Julian. "Bring out your notebook. We'll play noughts-and-crosses."

A long day trailed slowly to its close. The nurse came back several times and made Julian lie down. A doctor came, examined Julian's bandages, and said he was a remarkable specimen. Anyone else so badly knocked about, he remarked chattily, would now be reposing on a slab in the morgue: but not Julian; in a week or ten days Julian would be walking about again. Inspector Howells returned, worked himself into a frenzy over the reporter's unwillingness to answer questions, and departed, breathing fire. The night sister, coming on duty, popped in to ask Julian brightly how he felt this evening and looked vexed when he answered: "Lousy!"

The night was far advanced before Julian and the plain-clothesman were left alone again. In a plaintive tone, Julian asked for a glass of water. Although the bullet-wound in his shoulder had rendered his right arm almost useless, Julian took the glass in his right hand. He wanted his left hand free.

"I'm sorry to do this," he said.

"What, sir?" asked the plainclothesman, bending closer.

"This," said Julian. With his left hand he punched the man on the jaw. It was a good punch. It tore apart some of Julian's stitches and started his shoulder bleeding again; but it also did what it was meant to do. The plainclothesman's eyes rolled up and he fell across the bed. Climbing out of bed was agony, but Julian accomplished it. He coaxed off the unconscious man's trousers and jacket and managed, with great pain, to put them on over the hospital nightshirt. His left leg buckled under him twice, but he was used to that; it had not really been of much good to him for years. Leaving the plainclothesman to lie, in shirt and winter woollies, across the rumpled bed, he left the room, supporting himself by pushing against the wall with the flats of his hands. He found himself in a deserted ground-floor corridor.

There was no one about as he lurched and stumbled down the corridor to the main door of the building, but when he was within a yard of his goal a porter came out of a small glassed-in office.

"Good heavens, sir, you can't go out!"

"That's what you think," retorted Julian.

Pushing the man in the face, he lurched sideways to the door and fell down a flight of steps to the pavement. A taxi which was crawling along at the kerb pulled up sharply, and the driver leaned out and asked Julian if he was hurt.

Julian pulled himself up by the door handle. His weight wrenched the door open and he tumbled in. The hospital porter was running down the steps, shouting something. The taxi-driver opened the glass partition between him and his sprawling passenger and said:

"What's all this about, sir? Good God, it's Mr. Mendoza!"

"Get me out of here, quick," muttered Julian thickly.

"Yes, sir," replied the driver promptly. He let in his clutch with a jerk and the taxi jumped off its mark, leaving the hospital porter shouting impotently on the pavement.

"Where to, sir?" asked the driver, after he had taken three successive corners on two wheels. He added, in a troubled tone: "You're sure this is all right, Mr. Mendoza? You look like death warmed up."

"I'm all right. Take me home."

"Yes, sir."

When the taxi stopped at Mrs. MacDougal's house on the eastern fringe of Hyde Park, the driver opened the door and leaned in to help the reporter out. Julian shook his head.

"Go in and tell my landlady that I want a complete change of clothing, some money and a walking-stick as quickly as she can get them together. Hurry, man, hurry."

In a few minutes the taxi-driver returned with Mrs. Mac-Dougal. The elderly little Scotswoman had a bundle in her arms, but when she saw the condition her lodger was in, she refused to give it to him.

"You're comin' in tae bed this verra meenit!" she said flatly. "The driver will gie me a hand tae carry ye up the stairs."

"The police are after me," grunted Julian. "They'll be here any moment. They mustn't find me. There's something I've got to do. It's a matter of life and death."

The landlady and the taxi-driver stared at each other in

silence. They had each their own reasons for an unwavering loyalty to the reporter.

"Life an' death is right," said Mrs. MacDougal, with a catch in her voice. "It'll be your ain death, I'm thinkin."

With a savage gesture, she thrust clothes and walking-stick into the cab and handed Julian a wad of one-pound notes.

"Tak' the contrary b— wherever it is he wants tae go," she said to the driver.

At any other time, such language would have shocked her to the marrows.

"Giovanni's," said Julian.

"They're closed, sir. It's after midnight."

"The employees' entrance. Ask for Charley."

"Very good, sir."

Charley, the barman at Giovanni's, was locking up for the night when Julian and the taxi-driver, admitted by an open-mouthed dishwasher, came through the darkened restaurant. He groaned aloud when he saw who it was—he had been hoping for an early night—but when he realised that Julian was hurt his face clouded with anxiety.

"Mr. Mendoza! What's happened to you, sir? You look like a ruddy ghost."

"Don't talk so much," retorted Julian. "Help me on with these."

With a touching gentleness—the reporter said ironically that he was not sure which of them would make the best mother— the barman and the taxi-driver dressed Julian and propped him against the bar.

"What's it to be?" asked Charley (he knew that if the bona-fide ghost of Julian Mendoza ever walked into Giovanni's it would lose little time in calling for a drink).

"When you're flat on your back," said Julian, with a judicial frown, "the best lift-up is whisky. But I've got things to do which demand a clear head, so I daren't let myself go. I'll start with four double Scotches, and see how I feel about more."

He looked at the taxi-driver. "What's yours, George?"

"Mine's a beer, thanking you kindly," replied the driver, drawing the back of his hand across his mouth.

"Four double Scotches," said Charley. "One beer."

He glanced at the clock and sighed.

"How do you like your eggs?" asked Charley, at ten o'clock the following morning.

"Any way will do," grunted Julian Mendoza, "as long as there's plenty of them. I'm as ravenous as a wolf."

"The condemned man ate a hearty breakfast," said Charley. "You still look like a corpse to me, Mr. Mendoza."

"Looks aren't everything."

The reporter sat up and stretched himself, yawning widely. In the middle of stretching, he said: "Ouch!"

His wounded shoulder was getting its own back on him. He looked about him. Almost fully dressed, he was in bed in a small sunny room with a wallpaper of pink roses.

"Where am I?"

"I brought you home with me last night, Mr. Mendoza. Brought, did I say?—carried is the word. You were in a markedly liquid condition. One more drink and you'd have drowned. Me and George poured you up the stairs about two this morning. You kept telling me to call you early. I think you said you was to be Queen of the May."

"Well, this is early, all right," said Julian, screwing up his eyes to avoid the glare of the morning sun. "It's the earliest I've been awake for years."

He discovered that he was talking to himself. Charley had left the room. With a contented sigh, Julian curled himself like a cat, pulled the sheet over his head and went to sleep again. A second later—or so it seemed—Charley returned, followed by a plump, beaming young woman who carried a laden tray.

"This is the missus, Mr. Mendoza."

"It's a pleasure to meet you, sir," remarked Charley's wife pleasantly, setting the tray on Julian's lap. "From the things Charley says about you, you must be a wonderful man."

"She's confusing you with another gentleman," said Charley apologetically.

Half-a-dozen fried eggs, a dozen crisp bacon rashers, a mound of buttered toast… It looked a lot, but when Julian had finished there was a smear of yellow on one plate and nothing whatever on the others. At his fourth cup of coffee, he heaved a contented sigh.

"I'd stay in bed all day if I was you," said Charley earnestly. "You got enough wrong with you to keep a hospital in steady work for months."

"I've got to see a man about—about some dirty dogs. I'm beginning to see things, Charley, that I ought to have seen long ago."

"If you mean pink elephants, Mr. Mendoza, I've been wondering when you were going to start seeing 'em."

Julian said thoughtfully:

"Take the case of a man who suspects that his place of employment is about to be robbed and who doesn't warn his employer or the police."

"That's easy. He's in on the job."

"Not this man. This man was dead straight."

"Then I give up. It don't make sense."

"Supposing you found out, Charley, that Giovanni was stealing from his own till."

"You're delirious, Mr. Mendoza. The boss wouldn't rob himself."

"No, but he might rob his shareholders."

"That's different. I don't know just what I'd do, if I discovered something like that. It would take some thinking out. I've got a wife and kid. I wouldn't want to lose my job. I'd have to be dead sure before I made a move."

"Maybe you'd seek advice from someone you could trust."

"I expect I would. And if I was looking for someone to trust, Mr. Mendoza, I wouldn't look further than you—drunk or sober!"

A plump, golden-haired little girl ran into the room.

"Now, Caroline," said Charley fondly, "Mr. Mendoza doesn't want to be bothered with you."

But Caroline knew better. She climbed on to the bed. She pulled Julian's nose.

"How old are you?" she asked. "I'm four. Can you growl like a bear? Daddy can."

While Julian was growling like a bear, she pulled his head down to examine it closely, and was disappointed to find that his hair hadn't a hole in the middle, like Daddy's.

"And I thought you were tough, Mr. Mendoza!" said Charley disgustedly.

At the offices of the Lambert Jewellery Manufacturing Company a young woman with carmine fingernails patted her back hair languidly and said, in a superior tone: "Mr. Lambert is not here today. In any case, he sees no one without an appointment. If you care to tell me your business—"

With a disdainful air, she eyed Julian from head to foot. She plainly thought that Julian wanted to cadge old clothes from her employer. A shave, a shampoo, and a haircut had made the reporter look a shade less disreputable than before, but his appearance nevertheless suggested that he had come straight from the casual ward of a workhouse.

"If you hold it any higher, I'll pull it," said Julian pleasantly.

"Pull it? Pull what, may I ask?"

"Your nose. I've got to see Mr. Lambert without delay on a matter of vital importance, so climb down from your high horse and find out where he is."

For a moment he thought she was going to explode with a loud report. But, in spite of his shabby attire, Julian could always seem important when he wanted to and, although she glared at him angrily, the young woman was visibly impressed. "I—I'll see. What name, please?"

"Never mind the name. Tell him it's a matter of life and death—his own life or death."

With a lost look on her carefully made-up face, the young woman went to a telephone a few paces away and dialled a number. Watching closely, Julian made a mental note of the position on the dial of each of the holes into which her index finger poked. He had already ascertained that Mr. Lambert's private telephone was not listed in the directory. A few moments later the young woman returned to the counter. "Mr. Lambert is not at his flat. I really cannot say where he is to be found. If you care to leave a message…"

"Where is his flat?"

"I can't possibly tell you that."

"Never mind," said Julian. "I can find out for twopence."

Going to the nearest telephone booth, he placed twopence in the box and dialled exactly the same combination as the young woman had done. At the other end of the wire a voice that was only just masculine said: "Mayfair Arms Hotel."

"That's all I wanted to know," said Julian, pressing button B and getting his money back.

He took a taxi to the Mayfair Arms Hotel, a pretentious West End hostelry which specialised in luxury service flats. In answer to his first question, the dapper young reception clerk shook his marcelled head. "Mr. Lambert is not at home."

"Do you mean he isn't in—or simply that he's not receiving?"

"It really doesn't make much difference which," replied the young man with a coy smile. "He won't see anyone and he isn't taking telephone calls."

"Ring through to his flat and tell him I want to see him."

"Impossible. Quite impossible. He'd have my blood."

"How," said Julian smilingly, "would you like a sock on the nose?"

"What a divinely brutal question!" said the marcelled one, opening his eyes wide. "But you don't really mean it?"

"You'll find out in precisely ten seconds."

"Don't bother to count," said the young man, turning quickly to the switchboard. "What name shall I say?"

"Tell him…Gort," replied Julian, on a sudden inspiration. "Say I'm on my way up."

The young man looked thrilled all over when he turned back

from the switchboard. "Mr. Lambert doesn't seem eager to meet you, Mr. Gort. In fact, I think he fainted when I mentioned your name. At least, the line went dead right away."

"Splendid!" said Julian, making for the front door. "You're going the wrong way!" cried the young man, tremulous with excitement. "The lift is over there."

Without looking round, Julian continued through the revolving door. He limped along the street to a lane which ran down the side of the building. He limped down the lane to the back door of the hotel. Opposite the back door a smart two-seater car was parked, empty. Julian leaned against the wall and waited.

Before long the door opened and a fat little man came out in a frantic hurry. He was shaking like a mountainous jelly as he climbed into the car and kicked feverishly at the starter. When the car was moving away, Julian opened the near-side door and swung himself in. The fat little man gave a convulsive jump and the car swerved towards a wall.

"It isn't Gort," said Julian, steadying the steering wheel with one hand. "It's me."

Samuel Lambert put his foot on the brake and the car stopped with a jerk, its nose almost in the street. He took out a large silk handkerchief and mopped his perspiring brow. He looked like a terrified rabbit.

"I thought you'd make a bolt for it," remarked the reporter grimly, "if you heard that Gort was on his way up to see you."

"I—I d-don't know what you mean. G-get out of my car,"

"There's a policeman standing across the way. Call him over and have me put out."

They stared at each other; and the eyes of Samuel Lambert quickly looked away. In a shaking voice, he said: "I'm a busy man. I have a great deal to do."

"Alright," said Julian. "Where do we go first?"

"You—you can't go with me."

"That's where you're wrong. I'm going to stick to you like a brother. I'm looking for Gort and Mayo. They're looking for you. When they find you, I'll find them. It's as simple as that."

"I d-don't know what you're talking about. If you d-don't get out of my car at once I—I'll drive to the nearest police station and give you in charge."

"That suits me. What are we waiting for?"

Mr. Lambert put his foot on the clutch. He took it off again. His hands were trembling.

"We can't sit here all day," said Julian, after a lengthy pause. "You wouldn't want Gort to find you out in the open with no cover at hand. Let's go somewhere. You think of a place. Where were you going when I joined you?"

"I—I'm not going there if you're with me."

"Please yourself. It doesn't much matter. Wherever you go Gort will find you sooner or later."

"I—I don't know who this Gort is, you keep talking about."

"You're a wicked liar. The mere sound of his name sent you scuttling like a rabbit down the backstairs of your hotel. You can't bluff me, Lambert. I know too much. Old Dan Riordan smelled a rat a couple of days before he was murdered. You were the rat. I don't know what made him suspect the dirty game you were planning to play—but that doesn't matter.

"After the burglary and murder, you were summoned to the warehouse. It was one in the morning, and you were supposed to have been called out of bed to hear the shocking news that your safe had been cracked and your watchman killed; but you turned up faultlessly dressed. I should have spotted the significance of that fact at the time. You hadn't been to bed; you knew the safe was to be cracked; you were waiting for the news.

"That night I had an idea I'd seen you before, but I couldn't remember where. When I had time to think it over, I remembered. You're an honoured patron of a society that befriends ex-convicts, aren't you? It would be through the society that you got in touch with Mayo and Gort. The other night I had the pleasure of meeting your friend Mayo. He said that before he and Gort leave the country they have a score to settle, some money to collect. It's easy to figure that one out. You must have double-crossed them. Arranged with them to crack your company's safe—and pinched the swag yourself a few hours earlier.

"A nice little scheme, Mr. Bloody Lambert. The diamonds and the cash for you, a night's work without pay for Mayo and Gort—and your shareholders left holding the bag. Mayo and Gort would squeal when they were caught—but by that time you'd be out of the country with the boodle. Where have you hidden it, by the way? In a safe deposit box, I expect."

While Julian hissed all this into his ear, Lambert slumped lower and lower behind the steering wheel. Tears of self-pity were rolling down his podgy cheeks.

"I never dreamed they'd kill the watchman. He was so old, so feeble, I felt sure he wouldn't resist."

"He was old and feeble," repeated Julian fiercely; "but game as hell. You're as guilty as anyone of his murder. It's going to give me exquisite pleasure, Lambert, to see you hanged."

"Don't!" Lambert almost screamed, covering both ears with his hands. "I can't bear it!"

"Maybe you won't hang. Maybe Gort and Mayo will take care of you."

"They're d-desperate men. You won't let them..."

"Let them? I'll help them!"

It occurred to Mr. Lambert that sitting about in the open at such a time was most unwise. Either Gort or Mayo, or both, might come prowling down the lane, and that was not a nice thought, to Mr. Lambert, at least. He put the car in gear and drove shakily out of the lane.

"I—I have a house up the river," he mumbled. "I've been trying for days to pluck up courage to go there, but I—I was afraid to leave the hotel."

"It'll be as good a rendezvous as any," replied Julian.

For a quarter of a mile the two-seater had bumped over a rutted country road, between hedges of hawthorn, without passing a single human dwelling. It swung off the road, through tall, wrought-iron gates, and hummed smoothly along a wide gravel drive, flanked by stately poplars, bowing like graceful ladies in the wind. The house came in sight round a bend; low, white, rambling, with a tile roof of many colours, blue, green, wine-red, grey and orange, all mellowed by suns and rains to a mottled copper. The diamond-paned leaded windows winked in the afternoon sun.

Beyond the house a shaven lawn sloped to the sluggish river. Moored to a wooden landing-stage was a powerful-looking motor launch.

"Nice place you have here," remarked Julian.

"I only rent it. The lease is about to expire."

"Just as well. You won't be needing it any longer."

Samuel Lambert looked at Julian with haggard eyes that twitched and blinked in an ashen-grey face. "I wish you'd stop that," he groaned plaintively.

When it came to entering the house, he stood back to let Julian go first. The reporter smiled at that. He knew what was in the other's mind. It was just possible that Mayo and Gort had been here and rigged up a trap inside and, if so, Mr. Lambert did not want to be the one who stepped into it. The reporter went in warily, but saw nothing suspicious about the large lounge hall in which he found himself. There was not a sound to be heard. The place was as hushed and still as a country graveyard.

The fat face of Samuel Lambert peered with nervous caution round the door.

"I haven't found any bombs," said Julian reassuringly.

His flabby body wobbling in a most undignified manner, Lambert pushed past the reporter, ran clumsily across the lounge and went through a door in the far wall. Such haste looked ominous. Julian hurriedly followed, but his left foot slipped on the polished floor and, by the time he had righted himself and hobbled across the lounge, Lambert came back with a double-barrelled shotgun in his hands.

He stared at Julian with a frightened yet menacing gleam in his eyes. The gun was pointed at the reporter. Fired at close range it would make a hole in him big enough to put a football in.

"Don't be a damned fool," said Julian calmly. "What would you do with the body? I'm too big to be lugged about by a fat little slacker like you." "

"I—I didn't fetch the gun to shoot you. I fetched it in case Gort comes."

"Maybe so. But after you'd fetched it, you certainly had the idea of using it on me to start with. Forget it. It's a rotten idea."

"I won't shoot you," whispered Lambert jerkily, "if you keep your distance. Walk in front of me into the kitchen. I have a job for you."

The job was to fasten the shutters of all the ground-floor windows. They went from room to room, and Lambert stood behind Julian with the shotgun at the ready while the reporter wrestled with the clumsy wooden barriers. When they returned to the lounge, Lambert motioned with the gun toward a staircase near the front door. Julian took a pace or two forward, but found that his fleshy shadow was not following. Looking round, he saw Lambert staring in consternation at a picture which hung above the fireplace. It was slightly out of plumb.

"Take down that picture," said Lambert hoarsely.

Julian took it down. Behind it was a wall safe, the door of

which was ajar. The reporter looked at Lambert, whose face had turned a sickly green.

"You weren't fool enough to leave the plunder in a sardine tin like that? A good cracksman could open it with a penknife."

"There was n-nothing in the safe." Lambert's eyes were bulging with terror.

"But it proves that Gort's been here? And, since he failed to find what he came for, he may still be here. By God!"—Julian laughed loudly—"it'll be a good joke if you've gone to all this trouble to shut yourself in the house with him."

Lambert was gaping at the staircase. Footsteps could be heard crossing the landing above. They were coming toward the head of the stairs. Shaking with fright, Lambert put the shotgun to his shoulder and aimed at the spot where the approaching person would first come into view. The pressure of his finger on the trigger made the knuckle-bone show white through the taut skin.

In a split second a booming report would roar out a message of death…

A pair of silk-clad legs appeared at the top of the stairs.

With an inarticulate cry Julian threw himself forward in a Rugby tackle, bringing Lambert crashing to the floor. The shotgun clattered against a wall.

"That's fine," said a chilling voice from the upper landing. "Don't try to rise, either of you, or I'll put a bullet through your ugly heads."

There followed the sound of several pairs of feet descending the stairs and crossing the polished oak floor. "Alright," said the voice, "you can stand up now. Rise slowly and don't make no funny moves."

Julian rose, taking care to keep both hands in plain view. A few paces from him Margaret Niven was standing, with Gort and Mayo close behind her. The girl tried to smile gamely but it was a pitiful attempt. The two cracksmen had automatic pistols in their hands; and looked ready to use them.

"You was supposed to have bumped off this mug!" said Gort, to his partner.

"How was I to know a bullet wouldn't kill him?" grumbled Mayo. His cold in the head was worse than ever.

"A bullet will kill him, all right. Wait a bit and you'll see." Gort uttered a laugh that was void of mirth. "I thought you'd find a way to get the shotgun out of Lambert's hands," he said, to Julian; "if I sent the girl down first. Kind of sweet on her, ain't you? Too bad you ain't going to live long enough to do anything about it."

While he spoke he ran his hands over Julian's clothes and made sure that the reporter was unarmed. The last feeble dregs of spirit had oozed out of Lambert, who continued to lie, quaking with fear, on the floor.

"I said, get up!" growled Gort, kicking him in the ribs.

The fat man whimpered and lay still. With an oath, Gort reached down and jerked him to his feet. Holding his quivering victim's lapels by one hand, Gort struck him three vicious blows across the face with the barrel of his automatic.

"You rat!" hissed the cracksman, pushing Lambert into a chair. "I've got a mind to knock you off here and now. There was to be five thousand pounds in cash in the safe, was there? You didn't want none of it because you was taking the diamonds as your share. You double-crossing bastard, there wasn't five pence in the safe, not five pence. Thought you could hog it all, did you; and leave us to take the rap for a twenty-thousand-quid robbery and a murder?"

"You—you oughn't to have killed the watchman," whined Lambert. "Murder wasn't in the plan."

"Tell me what I oughtn't to have done!" snarled Gort, hitting him again with the gun. "Was it in the plan for you to empty the safe beforehand and leave nothing but old papers for us? Talk, you old bastard—and talk fast. What did you do with the swag? Where is it? Speak up, or I'll break your head in."

"It—it's in a safe deposit vault in Fetter Lane."

"You wouldn't have it handy, would you?" said Gort, hitting him again.

Mayo sneezed. "You'll kill the bastard," he remarked, unemotionally.

"That suits me. It's the kind of fun I like, beating to death a fat swine like this—and taking my time about it."

"Have your fun. But don't croak him until he tells us how to get the stuff from the safe deposit vault."

"Talk, rat, talk," rasped Gort in Lambert's ear. "How do we get the stuff?"

"T-there are t-two k-keys to every safe d-deposit b-box," wept Lambert. Big tears were chasing each other down his podgy cheeks. "The v-vault c-company k-keeps one and the c-client k-keeps the other. When a c-client wants to open his b-box he p-p-produces his k-key and an official b-brings out the co-company's k-key—it t-takes both k-keys to open the b-box."

"Where's your key?"

"If I t-tell you, how do I know you w-won't k-k-kill me?"

"You don't know," said Gort, rapping him on the head. "Where is it?"

Blinking with terror, Lambert fumbled in a waistcoat pocket. After much groping he succeeded in producing a keyring, but his trembling fingers were unequal to the task of detaching the right key. Impatiently, Gort broke the chain to which the ring was attached and found the safe deposit key for himself.

"You and your safe deposits," he growled, hitting Lambert. "Why couldn't you hide the stuff where it would be easy to get at?"

"I could go—" began Lambert hoarsely, eagerly.

"Sure, you could go. And we could trust you to come back, I don't think."

"One of you could go with me."

"And you'd start hollering bloody murder the first copper we saw. Shut up and let me think."

"It's too risky for either of us to go," croaked Mayo huskily. He wiped his moist nose on his sleeve.

"Do you think I don't know it?" retorted Gort. "Keep an eye on these mugs while I work something out."

Lighting a cigarette, he paced the floor. On one of his perambulations, he came upon the shotgun, and picking it up, tucked it under his arm. Suddenly, he stopped short and stared at Julian. "You came here looking for us," he said slowly. "Why didn't you bring the cops? No—don't tell me. I can figure it out for myself. We had the girl; you're sweet on her; you didn't want anything to happen to her; you knew there would be fireworks if you brought the cops…

"Well, we've still got the girl." He put the mouth of the shotgun to Margaret Niven's ear. "Know what would happen if I pulled the trigger? It would blow her bloody head off. You don't like the idea; I can see it in your eyes. Alright. You're the little lad who's going to take the key and fetch the stuff. And you'd better come back alone and unarmed. If I don't like the look of things when you return, I'll put this gun to your girl's head and pull the trigger."

"And if I bring back the stuff without trying any tricks," said Julian steadily, "what then?"

"Mayo and me will make our getaway, leaving you and the girl here, tied up. You won't be tied so tightly that you can't work yourself free in a few hours."

He was lying. Julian could tell that he was lying. Gort had

no intention of letting any of them live to testify against him.

"Alright," said Julian, "I'll go. I'll need a letter of authority to open the box."

"Write one," said Gort, to Lambert. The fat man was too cowed to argue.

Julian drove to London in Lambert's car. In an outlying suburb he left the car at a garage and took a taxi, for he was too conspicuous a figure in the open two-seater; and by this time the police must be looking for him in earnest. Obtaining that for which he had come was simple: he presented letter and key at the offices of the safe deposit company; and walked out of the building four minutes later carrying a fortune in uncut diamonds and five-pound notes in a black leather bag.

Climbing into the taxi, he made himself as small as possible; drew his hat down over his eyes, turned his coat collar up to his chin. He was round the corner from the heart of Newspaperland and he had no wish to be seen. Through the speaking-tube he instructed the taxi-driver to take him to the office of a certain estate agency. On arriving there he sent the driver in to ask George Norris to come out to speak to him.

In a few moments the staid-looking young man in smart blue trousers and shabby tweed coat from whom Julian had asked for particulars of factories to let four or five days before crossed the pavement and peered, with a bewildered air, into the car.

In an urgent whisper, Julian said: "I've no time to waste. Exactly how much does Margaret Niven mean to you?"

The young man's eyes almost popped out of his head. In a startled tone, he replied: "She means everything in the world to me. Do you know where she is?"

"Don't ask questions. Simply answer mine. Would you risk your life to save hers?"

George Norris drew a deep breath. "I would," he said firmly.

"Even if the chances against you were ten to one?"

"I'd rather die with her than go on living without her."

"You're sure of that?"

"Good God, man!" groaned Norris. "I've been through hell since she disappeared. I've had time to realise that my life means nothing without her. Where is she?"

"Get your hat and coat," replied Julian curtly.

In ten seconds flat, George Norris was climbing into the taxi in his shirtsleeves with his hat in one hand and the jacket of the blue suit in the other. While the taxi weaved through traffic, Julian spoke to him in urgent whispers.

The next halt was at a shop where conjuring tricks and other novelties were sold. Julian went in. When he returned, he handed something to Norris, who put it in his pocket. The taxi dropped them at the garage in which Julian had left Lambert's car and they went on from there in the two-seater.

At the wrought-iron gates of Samuel Lambert's house up the river, Julian stopped the car and climbed out. He went up the drive alone. Mayo and Gort met him at the door. Gort was carrying the shotgun.

"Where's the car?" demanded Gort. He ran his hands over Julian's clothes, to make sure that the reporter was still unarmed.

"Did you get the stuff?" asked Mayo.

"What happened? Why did you come back on foot?"

"Did they smell a rat?"

"The car is outside in the road," replied Julian calmly. "I came in on foot because I didn't want you to get the wind up and start shooting when you saw someone sitting beside me."

"Someone sitting beside you," repeated Gort, in a voice that dripped icicles. "What are you trying to put over on us? If you've squawked to the dicks—"

"Don't get excited," said Julian. "He isn't a policeman. He's a clerk from the safe deposit company. They wouldn't let me take the stuff unless he came along to make sure that everything is all right. All he wants is Lambert's signature to a receipt."

"I'll give him a receipt," snarled Gort. He patted the shotgun and added: "With this."

"Don't be a fool," said Julian. "You can't expect twenty thousand pounds in diamonds and cash to be handed over without formalities. This young clerk has to ring up his company and assure them that everything is all right. If he doesn't, they'll become windy, and the place will be swarming with police before you can turn round."

"Come inside," said Gort.

Julian walked into the lounge, with the shotgun nudging him in the back. Margaret and Lambert were gagged and tied to chairs. "You'll have to set them free," he said calmly. "The safe deposit company's clerk won't like the look of this at all."

"Alright, you untie them," said Gort.

Julian obeyed. When he released Lambert, Gort walked forward and took the fat man by the lapels. "Look," he said grimly, "there's a mug outside with a receipt for you to sign. When he comes in, sign it. No fuss. No backchat. Just sign it."

"I'll sign it," whimpered Lambert tremulously.

"You'd better."

"His face don't look so good," said Mayo.

"He got those bruises falling downstairs," said Gort. "That's what you say when he comes in, Lambert. 'I'm sorry to bring you all the way out here,' you'll say; 'but I had a nasty fall and I don't feel so good.' Say it with a smile."

"This mug will have to be good and simple to swallow that yarn," said Mayo.

"If he swallows it long enough to 'phone the okay to his company that's all I want."

Gort helped Lambert up and almost carried him to a chair at a desk which stood at one end of the lounge. The fat man fell into the chair and sat there like a stuffed dummy.

"You can be reading a book," said Gort to Margaret, "and try to look like you was enjoying it."

He pushed her into an easy chair, took a volume at random from a well-filled bookcase, and tossed it into her lap.

"We'll have these open," he added, walking to the French windows. "It's a nice day. They'll look more natural open."

Hiding the shotgun behind a curtain, he stood with his back to it. One hand was in his pocket. "I've got my automatic handy," he said grimly, "and I can reach the shotgun without any trouble. I'm going to stand right here watching you all, and at the first funny move there'll be hell to pay. You"—this to Julian—"stand back against the wall. That's better. Alright, Mayo, go out and bring this clerk in. Put your gun away—but keep your hand on it."

There was tense silence in the large, sunny lounge while Mayo was gone. In a few minutes he returned leading George Norris, who carried the black bag. Julian was relieved that Margaret did not look up from her book, for she might have given the game away by crying out in surprise when she recognised Norris.

Gort looked meaningfully at Lambert, who gulped and said, with a sickly grin: "I'm sorry to bring you all the way out here, but I—I had a nasty fall, and I don't feel well enough to go up to town."

"That's perfectly all right, sir," said Norris, placing the bag on the desk. He was pale but composed.

At the sound of his voice Margaret looked up with an incredulous frown. She did not cry out. She simply gaped at him.

"I have a receipt form for you to sign, sir," said Norris, fumbling in his pockets. He brought out what seemed to be a perfectly innocent fountain pen.

Julian tensed himself. The pen was a trick one.

Mayo was standing close behind the young man, with his hand in the pocket that contained his automatic.

Norris turned suddenly and, aiming the pen at Mayo's face, squirted a stream of ammonia into his eyes. Without waiting to see whether the ammonia had taken effect, the young man darted to Margaret and dragged her into a corner that was sheltered by a bookcase.

As the ammonia left the nozzle of the trick pen, Julian threw himself forward. Mayo roared with pain and clapped one hand to his burning eyes. The other came out of his pocket, holding the automatic. Before he could use it, Julian snatched it out of his grasp.

"You bastard," said Gort. He fired at Julian through his pocket. The bullet hit the reporter in the chest and knocked him back against the wall.

Julian put one hand to his chest. Blood trickled through between his fingers. He slid helplessly down the wall and landed with a thump in a sitting position on the floor. The hand in which he held the gun felt as heavy as lead, but somehow, he brought it up and aimed the automatic at Gort.

With a fixed grin on his face, Gort fired again.

Both shots roared at once. Gort's bullet thudded into the wall an inch above Julian's head. Julian's found a billet between the cracksman's eyes.

For an instant Gort seemed to rise on his toes, then he toppled forward and fell on his face on the floor.

After the crashing reports there was a deathly hush in the room. It only lasted for a few seconds. Grabbing the bag which contained diamonds and money, Lambert made a dash for the open French windows. Mayo staggered after him, tears streaming from his eyes.

The fat little man dived through the French windows and ran frantically across the lawn toward the motor-launch that was moored to the landing-stage. Snatching up the shotgun which was hidden behind the curtain, Mayo put it to his shoulder and pulled one trigger. A charge of buckshot hit Lambert in the head, sheering away the roof of his skull as a knife might take the top off an egg. He turned a somersault and landed on the ground in a clumsy heap. The bag flew up in the air and came down within a yard of his body. It burst open, scattering five-pound notes and uncut diamonds over the lawn.

For a moment Mayo stood quite still, looking at the lawn. Julian raised the automatic, ready to fire if Mayo turned round. But he did not turn round. Bending down, he put his ear to the mouth of the shotgun and pulled the second trigger.

*

"Margaret has fainted," said George Norris, coming over to Julian. He looked as though in another moment he, too, would faint.

"Get her…out of here…as quickly…as you…can," gasped Julian painfully. "If she's…here…when the…police come…they'll…arrest…her…for helping…brother… escape."

"Where shall I take her?"

"How…should…I know? She's…your…problem. You'll both…have to…start again…in a place where you're…not known. Take Lambert's…car. Make…for…a…a railway sta-tion. If you…need money…help yourself. Plenty of money… on the lawn…"

"But what about you? You need a doctor."

"Get to…hell…out of here," said Julian in feeble anger.

After they had gone, he lay for a long time with his eyes

shut. It hurt to breathe. His breath came in guttural grunts. Painfully, slowly, he crawled to the desk and groped about until his numbed fingers found the telephone. They dragged it over the edge and it fell on the floor beside him.

"Number, please," said the girl at the exchange brightly.

Julian tried to speak. The words would not come.

"Number, please," said the girl again.

There was still no answer. Julian had fainted.

When the operator tired of saying:

"Number please," she sent for the supervisor, who listened to the grunts that were coming over the wire and put in an urgent call to the local police station.

THE END

THE WAR MAKERS

A Bomb and a Lodger

" And then," said Mr. Ginsberg shakily, "there was a big bang."

"I believe you," said the police inspector. "It must have been a devil of a bang."

They stood on the first-floor landing of a house in Whitechapel, looking up at the sky through a ragged hole in the roof. The stairs which had led to the attic were gone and so was most of the top of the house. Through a gaping rip in the plastered wall the laths showed like unfleshed ribs. Mr. Ginsberg's head was swathed in bandages; his knuckles were skinned and bloody; his clothes white with plaster.

The helmeted head of a policeman appeared in the hole in the roof. His face was very white. He climbed down a builder's ladder to the landing, holding on with one hand. In the other hand he held a boot. The boot contained a human foot, attached to some inches of ankle and shin.

"Found this behind the chimney stack, sir," reported the policeman, looking as if he were about to be sick.

"Put it with the rest," said the inspector, his eyes avoiding the grisly object.

The policeman placed his find on a tarpaulin on which already lay some fingers and a bit of bone to which skin and hair adhered; all that was mortal of Mr. Ginsberg's lodger; the remains of a man in whose arms a homemade bomb had exploded.

"He was always talking about blowing up the men who make wars," said Mr. Ginsberg weakly. "He said you had to kill them to save the world."

"You ought to have done something about it," snapped the police inspector. "You ought to have reported him at the police station."

"How should I know he was serious? I'm a tailor not a detective. I thought he was crazy. I thought it was all talk. He used to make speeches at Hyde Park about blowing up the men who make wars. None of the people who heard him reported him to the police. They just thought he was crazy. How was anyone to know he meant it?"

"You're sure no one else was in the house when it happened?"

"No one but me," said Mr. Ginsberg sadly. "Maybe you think I'd have been here if I'd known what was going to happen."

Hearing dragging footsteps behind him, the inspector turned his head and saw a battered felt hat and an impressive pair of shoulders appearing round the bend of the stairs. They belonged to a tall, shabbily clad man, ascending as rapidly as a crippled right leg would allow. A puff of acrid smoke drifted up in front of him. The inspector made a wry face. He knew that rank tobacco. He knew the man who was smoking it. There was only one person in his circle of acquaintances who could—or would—have smoked it.

"Mendoza," he growled. "How did you get in? I gave orders no reporters were to be admitted."

"I told the cop at the door that I live here," replied Julian cheerfully. "I expect he thought no one would claim to live in a dump like this if it wasn't true."

The inspector coughed. "Put out that charcoal burner. Isn't it enough that the place has been blown up without gassing it out as well?"

The crime reporter's eyes fell on the exhibits that lay on the tarpaulin. His lined face grew pale. This was death at its ugliest. He took of his stained felt hat. "How many casualties?"

"Only one, unless you count the crack on the head the landlord got."

"How did it happen?"

"That's what I'm finding out. The inspector turned to Mr. Ginsberg. "Go on with your story."

"Beginning at the beginning," added Julian, "for the benefit of those who came in late."

His tone was flippant, but his eyes were sad. It was not disrespect for the dead that made him speak lightly, but respect for his own sanity. Sudden death was his business. Every day he was in contact with it, in every gruesome form. By schooling himself to be unsentimental about it he prevented it from poisoning his existence.

"He was always raving about the men who make wars," said Mr. Ginsberg. "If you'd heard him, you'd have said he was crazy, same as I did. He'd got bees in his belfry about war. His lungs was in shreds from being gassed a couple of times in the last war and he lived on a pension from the guv'mint. He looked like he was dying on his feet—no, he looked like he was dead. Like a ghost, he looked.

"Most days he stayed in his room, making smells, but sometimes he would go out and come back with a parcel. They was always little parcels, with chemists' labels on 'em. One day, kind of joking, I said to him: 'Mister, what do you do with all that chemistry stuff?' and he said to me: 'I'm making bombs to blow up the men who make wars'."

"If he was making smells in his room all day you ought to have known he was up to no good," said the inspector angrily.

Mr. Ginsberg spread his hands. "What's a smell?" he asked indignantly. "Can you ask it questions? Can you take its fingerprints? You can't tell nothing from a smell. All my lodgers make smells. The things they cook stink like something you positively wouldn't believe. Am I a bloodhound? Should I sniff under their doors to find out what they're up to?"

"Dropping this fascinating subject for the moment," said Julian, "let's get on with what happened."

"I've got a cold in the head," said Mr. Ginsberg. He paused and looked startled. He sniffed two or three times and shook his head in a wondering way. "That's funny. I ain't got it no more. The explosion must have scared it out of me. Anyway, this afternoon I had it. A cold in the head what I wouldn't wish on my worst enemy."

"You interest me strangely," said Julian patiently. "We must have a long chat about your cold in the head one day. Meanwhile, let's get back to the hole in the roof and how it got there."

"That's what I'm telling you," retorted Mr. Ginsberg with some asperity. "My cold in the head is part of it. If I hadn't had it, I wouldn't have left my shop and come upstairs for a handkerchief. If I hadn't come upstairs for a handkerchief, I wouldn't have met him coming down. So, if I hadn't had a cold in the head—"

"You win," said Julian. "What happened when you met him on the stairs?"

"He was carrying a brown paper parcel, tied up with string. I could see an address written on it and it was stamped, so he must have been going out to the post. I said: 'Hello, Mister, going out?' He hadn't noticed me and my voice startled him. He was always a nervous feller, jumpy like a kitten. He tripped and fell. There was big bang and something hit me on the head. Oi, what a wallop! When I came to, he was gone—blown to bits— and so was the top of the house—blown clean up to the sky!"

"What was his name?" asked Julian.

"I don't know. I just called him Mister."

"You didn't know the name of your own lodger?" demanded the police inspector.

"I got eight lodgers," said Mr. Ginsberg wearily, "and maybe

I know the names of three of 'em. If they pay me every Monday, ain't that enough? If they don't pay me, out they go. What would I want with names?"

"If he had a disabled soldier's pension," said Julian to the inspector, "the Ministry of Pensions will be able to tell you all about him. From my point of view his name doesn't matter. An unknown soldier, shattered by the last war, half-mad and dying, who wanted to end wars by blowing up the men who make them and who only succeeded in blowing up himself—that's my story. Worth about half a column. If we knew for whom he meant the bomb, it would be worth half the front page."

Mr. Ginsberg ran after Julian as the reporter limped downstairs.

"Mister!" he called. "Mister!"

Julian halted. "Yes?"

"That suit, Mister," said the tailor, regarding Julian's baggy clothes with shocked eyes. "It looks like you got it from a pawnshop. Now, I can make for you a beautiful suit so cheap you positively wouldn't believe—"

"Your own clothes don't look so smart," smiled Julian. "What's this?" He plucked something from a tear in Mr. Ginsberg's waistcoat.

"I don't know, Mister," said the tailor impatiently. "Wallpaper, maybe. I got thrown about so much by the explosion, it's a wonder I got a stitch left on me. About this suit—"

The reporter was not listening. He was looking at the object in his hand, part of the debris that had rained on Mr. Ginsberg after the explosion. It was a small piece of wrapping paper, and written on it in ink were some words that could only be part of an address:

HEAD,

   TON SQUARE,

 N, W.8.

Julian's heart skipped a beat. Could this be part of the paper in which the bomb had been wrapped? It seemed too good to be true, but it was just possible. Mr. Ginsberg was still talking but the reporter paid no attention to him. With his find in his hand, he hurried out of the

House and through the drab streets of Whitechapel to the nearest post office. There he borrowed a street directory and worked his way through a section that embraced the W.8. postal district: all the squares ending in 'ton'; all the residents whose names ended in 'head.'

It took him twenty minutes to find the name and address he was seeking:

PROFESSOR HENRY COOPER LOCHHEAD,
29, ELVISTON SQUARE,
KENSINGTON, W.8.

Julian remembered having seen Professor Lochhead once at a dinner given to distinguished scientists. A little old man with the face of a rabbit, long white hair and myopic blue eyes that blinked nervously from behind thick-lensed spectacles. As harmless an old man, to all appearances, as ever breathed. What had he to do with the making of wars?

Oh, it was absurd. The scrap of paper could not have any connection with the bomb. Even a fanatical maniac could not have intended so sinister a parcel for so mild an old man. And yet— Investigating the unlikely, the impossible, even the preposterous, was part of Julian's job. Putting the scrap of paper in an inner pocket, he boarded a passing bus.

Girl in a Hurry

A quiet square of tall grey houses with a garden in the middle. Dusk was creeping into the square, and the street lamps were not lit. At the kerb in front of one of the houses a smart two-seater car stood empty, its engine running in defiance of Regulations 11 and 71 of the Road Traffic Act. Walking round the square, ticking off the numbers of the houses, Julian noticed that a policeman standing within fifty feet of the stationary car was paying no attention to the fact that the engine was illegally in motion. He was a very young policeman.

No.26. No.27. No.28. The two-seater was in front of No.29, the residence of Professor Henry Cooper Lochhead. As Julian approached it the front door opened and a girl shot down the steps as suddenly as though she had been kicked down them. In a headlong rush she crossed the pavement and sprang into the driving seat of the waiting car. In the open doorway of the house appeared a manservant in livery. Waving his arms, he bawled at the top of his voice: "Stop thief! Stop thief!"

He sprinted towards the car, but it sped away before he could reach it. More people came out of the house. They shouted wildly: "Stop that car!"

The policeman appeared to be asleep on his feet.

In spite of his crippled leg Julian could move with incredible speed. As the car swung passed him, he swung onto the running board and clung there, holding tightly to the nearside door. The shouts of 'Stop thief!' from behind were gaining in volume.

"They mean you, Lady," said Julian pleasantly. "You don't look like a thief but, nowadays, it isn't easy to tell. Pull in to the kerb and we'll find out."

The girl was steering with one hand. The other was groping

about on the floor. It came up holding a tyre-lever. Without looking at him, she gave Julian a backhand swipe on the head with it. Not a hard swipe. Just hard enough to knock him off the running-board. He landed with a thump in the road.

And then she made a fatal mistake.

She looked back to see if he was hurt. The off-side front wheel ran into a pothole and jerked the steering-wheel out of her hand. Swerving across the road, the car put its radiator halfway through some railings. The policeman came to life with a suddenness that was startling. The pace at which he sped to the wrecked car would not have disgraced a champion sprinter.

In falling, Julian had let his muscles relax—a trick he had learnt in his circus days—and almost as soon as he landed on his back, he was on his feet again, bruised and shaken but otherwise uninjured. He limped over to the car. The policeman was helping the girl out and asking her, in an anxious voice with a public-school accent, whether she was hurt. Her hat—a jaunty brown felt hat with an orange feather—was crushed over one eye. She straightened it.

"A bang on the head and a blow to my pride," she answered in a clear young voice, "that's the extent of the damage."

"Then we're almost quits," said Julian, leaning against the car. "They're my worst injuries, too. But I'm one up on you. I've a nasty bruise where I sit down."

"I hope it hurts," retorted the girl. "But for you I'd have got away."

She looked about her, as if hoping she might yet escape, but two other men were approaching at a run; the manservant and a young man in a smart grey suit. Shrugging her shoulders, the girl sat on the running-board and powdered her nose. It was a notably attractive little nose.

The grey-suited one panted up. He had a pale face and sleek yellow hair.

"Arrest that woman, officer!" She has stolen a valuable paper from Professor Lochhead."

"Calm yourself, Sydney," said the girl coolly. "I'm safe in the grip of the law." She glanced up at the policeman. "And a nice-looking bit of law, too."

The officer blushed.

"What have you done with it?" demanded Sydney furiously. "Where is it? Search her, officer."

"What, right here, with all those people watching from the windows?" said the girl, in a mock-modest tone."

"Joking won't help you," retorted Sydney angrily. "Take her back to the house, officer."

With another shrug of her slender shoulders, the girl rose and started walking along the pavement with the policeman at her side. The manservant followed at a discreet distance, but Sydney gripped the girl's arm officiously. She tried to shake him off, and he dug his fingers more tightly into elbow.

"I shouldn't do that if I were you," said Julian, just behind him, in a quiet but very firm tone. "She can't escape. There are too many of us."

"What business is it of yours?" snapped Sydney, turning his head to glare at the reporter. "Who are you?"

Julian replied softly. "I'm just the man who's going to give you one beautiful kick in the pants in half a second if you don't let go of her arm."

He looked alarmingly large, disconcertingly broad, and there was an unpleasant glitter in his eyes. Sydney relinquished his grip quickly.

They trooped up the steps to No.29, Elviston Square. Sydney tried to shut the door in the reporter's face, but Julian had expected something of the sort and his foot was in the way.

"I'm coming in," he said flatly. "If I'd minded my own

business she'd have escaped, so it's up to me to make sure that all this is on the level."

A tall, handsome woman in her middle thirties was standing in the hall. She had the hardest, most calculating eyes Julian had ever seen.

"Oh, Sybil!" she exclaimed. "How could you do this to him when you know how fond of you he is?"

Without answering, the girl walked straight past her into a room at the end of the hall. The others followed, all but the manservant, who closed the front door and withdrew. Professor Lochhead was sitting at a large desk in the middle of the room, which was furnished as a study. His heads buried in his thin hands. He looked crumpled and pathetic.

Looking at the girl, Julian saw her face brimming with tears. In that mood, she looked very lovely.

"I'm sorry," she said in a small voice.

The professor looked up. Behind the thick-lensed spectacles his eyes were wide with horror. More than ever, he resembled a likeable elderly rabbit.

"I trusted you. You were nearly the only person in the world I did trust."

"If I could only explain," said the girl. "It was for Eric's sake I did it. For Eric, who died so horribly. Oh, can't you understand? If he could come back, he'd say to you—he'd beg of you—"

"The manner of Eric's death has nothing whatever to do with it," replied the professor hoarsely. Between shock and emotion, he was almost at the breaking point. "I loved Eric, too, but sentiment cannot be allowed to interfere with my life's work—that is all-important. I could never have believed, Sybil, that you—" His voice broke. "I can't tell you what your action has done to me. Give me my paper and go. I am afraid I do not wish to see you again—ever."

"Think of humanity," urged the girl. "Think of the millions of boys who—"

"Give me my paper!"

The policeman had been silent until now. "Look here," he said, "what's this all about?"

"She stole a paper from my desk. An immensely valuable paper of national importance."

"Is this true, miss?"

"Of course, it is true!" cried Sydney. "She simply snatched it up and ran from the house."

"You'd better give it to me, miss," said the policeman, holding out his hand.

Meekly she took a long envelope from the neck of her dress and handed it to him.

"That is it," replied Professor Lochhead eagerly. "Give it to me."

"I'm afraid I shall have to take charge of it, sir. Evidence, you know."

"But I do not wish to charge her."

"Rather late to think of that, sir. She's already been taken into custody. You will be required to give evidence at the trial. After it is over, your property will be returned to you." Turning to the girl, the policeman added: "You'll have to come along with me, miss."

Julian was leaning indolently against a wall. Like most people with vast stores of energy to draw on, he liked to conserve it by relaxing as often as possible.

"Just a moment," he said quietly.

The policeman turned to stare at him. "Sir?"

"Is this your regular beat?"

"Certainly. Why?"

"You're a damned liar," said Julian, smiling. "The initial

letter on your shoulder is S. That's the initial of the Golder's Green division. If you were a local copper your shoulder initial would be F."

"I—I was transferred from Golder's Green quite recently."

"The devil you were," said Julian in the same conversational tone. "When a cop is transferred, he invariably changes his shoulder initial before going on duty. That's part of Police Regulations. You're not a cop!"

Swinging open the door, the bogus policeman tossed the envelope to the girl. "Here, Sybil—catch!" he cried. "Run for it! I'll hold them off."

It did not work out like that, however. Catching the envelope, the girl made for the door, but before she reached it her long, silk-clad legs became entangled with Julian's outthrust foot; she sprawled on the floor and the envelope slipped out of her fingers. The bogus policeman aimed a punch at Julian, a beautiful straight left. Julian ducked it and retaliated with a hook to the stomach which he had learned on the Barbary Coast of San Francisco. The pink drained out of the bogus policeman's face and he slumped against a wall, holding his abdomen with both hands.

Bending down unhurriedly, Julian picked up the envelope. He crossed the room without haste and gave it to Professor Lochhead.

"Better make sure the paper is inside. They'd brains enough to think of the policeman gag, so they may have prepared a dummy envelope."

With trembling hands, the professor ripped it open. A glance at the contents and he said shakily: "Yes, my paper is safe. I am indebted to you, sir, more than I can say. You have done me a great service. If there is ever anything I can do for you, you need only mention it."

The sleek-haired, pale-faced, smartly-dressed young man whom the girl called Sydney lifted the telephone receiver.

"Whitehall 1212. Hurry please."

"No, Sydney," said the professor wearily. "Not the police. I shall let them go."

The girl had picked herself up and was standing at the door with an arm round the bogus policeman, who looked far from well or happy.

"Go, both of you," said the professor. "And, Sybil, my house is closed to you from now on. I am bitterly disappointed in you."

Before she and the bogus policeman left the room, she turned to Julian and said, with a weak smile: "You're a fast worker. If you'd been on our side, we'd have got away with it."

There was no malice in her tone, and her smile was genuine. Julian liked her. She was a game loser.

After she was gone the professor said: "Perhaps you will accept some slight monetary reward. If, say, twenty pounds will be of use to you—"

He was eyeing Julian's baggy trousers and dusty shoes, which suggested that the wearer was perilously near destitution. Opening a drawer, he took out a chequebook.

"Thanks all the same," said Julian, "but I only muscled-in for the fun of it, and I'm still not sure whether I'm glad or sorry."

"What is your name? I should like to know to whom I am indebted."

"My name's Mendoza. I'm on the *Morning World*."

"Reporter!" exclaimed Sydney, as though it was another word for smallpox.

"Not a word of this in your newspaper, young man," said the professor hastily. "Not a word, I beg of you."

"Don't worry. I don't know enough about all this to make a coherent story of it, so unless you care to tell me the details—"

"No! No!" replied the professor jerkily. "I really have nothing to say, nothing whatever to say to a representative of the Press."

"Have it your own way; but there's one thing I really would like to know. Why would anyone want to blow you up?"

"Blow me up?"

"Yes. With a bomb."

"You're talking in riddles, young man. Blow me up with a bomb, indeed. What earthly reason would anyone have for doing such a thing?"

"That's what I asked you."

"Young man," said the professor, his eyes owlish behind the thick lenses, "are you a fool?"

"No more than most people."

"Then don't talk like one!"

It was beginning to get dark when Julian left the house. The girl and her male ally were trying to coax the two-seater from its resting-place among the twisted railings. Two errand-boys with gaping mouths were standing by in somnolent contemplation.

"You'd better get a move on," said Julian softly. "There may be a real copper along any minute."

"What do you think we're doing?" demanded the bogus policeman. "We've pushed and pulled and the blessed thing won't budge. If you think you can do and better—"

"That's easy," said Julian, picking up a tyre-lever. Thrusting it down the inside of a mudguard entangled in the railings he ripped the mudguard off in one piece. Pushing it through the railings onto the garden, he said to the girl:

"Start the engine and back her out."

The girl obeyed. There was a sound of tearing metal as the little car came backwards. The show over, the errand-boys shuffled off, apparently walking in their sleep.

"Thanks," said the bogus policeman as though the word choked him.

"Not bearing malice for that poke in the tummy?" said Julian. "You asked for it, you know."

The bogus policeman grinned feebly. "You handled me as if I were a novice. Hang it all, at school I was supposed to be pretty useful with my fists."

"In the school in which I was raised, you would be a novice. Better get rid of that uniform."

The youngster took off helmet and tunic and hid them in the dickey. Beneath the tunic he was wearing the jacket of a blue lounge suit which matched the trousers of the uniform. He climbed in beside the girl. Julian leaned on the door looking at them.

"You're a pair of nice kids, but you aren't cut out for crime. If you wanted that paper so badly you should have found a professional burglar to pinch it for you."

"No professional burglar could get near it," replied the girl. "Most of the time it's locked in a safe guaranteed uncrackable."

"If the paper's as precious as all that, how did you get close enough to snatch it and run?"

"I'm Professor Lochhead's daughter."

"I suppose you wouldn't know why anyone would want to blow him up—with a bomb?"

Sybil Lochhead's lovely face grew hard. "I can think of ten million good reasons. That paper is a passport to hell for the male youth of the world."

Julian opened the door of the car. "Move over, I'm coming with you. There's a story in this and I want it."

"You're a newspaper man?" she asked, as he crowded in beside them.

"Right in one. My name's Mendoza. I'm on the *Morning World*."

For a moment the girl said nothing. She sat staring at Julian, and her eyes were thoughtful. She let in the clutch with a jerk and the little car jumped forward. As it shot out of the square, taking the corner on two wheels, she said:

"The story is yours. We'll go somewhere for a drink and a sandwich, and I'll tell you all about it."

"Look out for that bus," said Julian grimly.

"Who's driving, you or me?" snapped Sybil. She cut incredible patterns in the traffic as calmly as a little girl scissoring paper dolls. "By the way, the boyfriend's name is Billy Menzies. He's the one person in the world who doesn't think I'm completely mad."

*

Over liver-sausage sandwiches and lager beer in a dimly lit, half-empty café, Sybil Lochhead said, in a faraway voice:

"It could begin almost anywhere, this story I'm going to tell you, but I'll begin it with the death of my brother Eric. That's going back to 1918, when I was three years old. At that time, it didn't mean much to me—death doesn't, to a child of three—but as I grew up it began to mean a lot. I had no other brothers or sisters, my mother had died when I was born; my father was always too engrossed in his research work to give me much of his time. There was a tremendous gap in my life which Eric could have filled, a need for affection and understanding that he might have supplied.

"He died in a mud-hole in France. He was only eighteen. That's young to die, isn't it? At eighteen, life ought to be just beginning. For him it was over. There was a gas attack and he had no gas mask."

"You don't know what it's like to be gassed, do you? I do. Not from personal experience. I spent an evening recently with a man who knew all about it. He had been gassed in the Great War. It didn't kill him. It left him a physical wreck."

"Who was that man?" asked Julian suddenly.

"I don't know his name. He lived in some hovel in Whitechapel. Billy and I were walking in Hyde Park one Sunday afternoon and this man was speaking from a soapbox. He was talking about the horrors of war. He made you see them. He said the people of Great Britain and France and Germany hadn't wanted the last war. It was thrust on them, exactly as this one will be.

"After he came down from his soapbox, Billy and I made friends with him. We went to a teashop and had something to eat. Perhaps he was a little mad; I don't know. The way he put things sounded sane enough. He said if anyone had to die it ought to be the men responsible for wars. Kill them, he said, and you'd save the world. The politicians, the money grubbers, the dictators, the scientists who devised devilish new ways of killing. It was the last classification that hit home to me for my father comes under it. He has spent years working on a deadly poison gas."

"You didn't happen to tell this man about it?" asked Julian.

"I believe I did."

"I see." Julian understood now why the bomb that had blown its maker to bits had been addressed to Professor Lochhead. "Go on."

"This gas is infinitely more deadly than any used in warfare before. It could wipe out a trenchful of men without warning. Ordinary poison gas can be seen coming or smelt soon enough to enable a gas mask to be put on, but this gas is colourless and odourless. You breathe it in unsuspectingly and in breathing you die. Think what a weapon like that would mean in the hands of a power hungry for conquest."

"In the hands of our government," said Julian, "it might be a powerful argument for peace."

"Do you imagine for a moment that we could keep it to ourselves? With the spies of every great power doing their utmost to get hold of it? Next time we went to war we'd have to share it with our allies. In a later war they might be our enemies and use it against us. Even if we could keep it to ourselves, it would be a curse to the world in the long run. You can't benefit humanity by working out new ways to slaughter innocent people.

"No, however you look at it, my father's discovery makes war in the near future inevitable. I went to my father and begged him to suppress it. I don't live at home, by the way. Father married again a few years ago, and my stepmother and I disagreed from the start. You may have met her this evening. She was standing in the hall when I was marched back to the house in disgrace."

"A tall, handsome woman? She looked hard as nails."

"She is. Heaven knows what father sees in her—or what she sees in him for that matter. He's a decent sort at heart, but hardly the type you'd think would appeal to a good-looking woman half his age. However, that's beside the point. My father wouldn't listen to me when I begged him to destroy his formula. He argued, as you have done, that with the gas as a threat Great Britain could enforce peace. No new way of killing people has ever meant peace, but I couldn't make him see that. I decided to steal the formula and destroy it myself."

"What good would that have done?" objected Julian. "You could tear up the paper, but he's sure to have another copy."

"He hasn't. The paper I had in my possession this evening is the only copy."

"Then he could work it out again by going back over the processes that brought him to it."

"He couldn't do that, either. The element that makes the gas so much more potent than any other was discovered by accident. All the important part of the work has been done entirely on his own. He didn't even trust Sydney Lanham, his secretary and laboratory assistant. Destroy the formula and the secret of the gas would be lost."

Sybil heaved a sigh. "But for you," she said, "I should have got away with the formula. By now it would have been reduced to ashes."

"I suppose there is no doubt your father will offer it to the British Government?"

"He has already done so. The War Office is to test it secretly in a few days."

"Just why do you want me to print this story?"

"If human beings are to die like flies at some future date, they have a right to know about it. Tell them. Ask the mothers of the world if that is the end to which they reared their sons."

Billy Menzies caught the eye of a passing waiter. "Three more beers," he said. They were the first words he had uttered for a long time.

"If that's a sample of your conversation," said Julian, "I'd like to hear more of it."

*

Later that night, Julian sat at his desk in the reporter's room of the *Morning World*, tapping on a battered typewriter with one finger of each of his large hairy hands. He wrote of a half-mad derelict of the Great War who thought that for the good of the world the makers of wars must die; and of a girl who listened to him and was inspired to steal from her father the formula of the ghastliest means of dealing wholesale death the world has ever known. He told of how the girl inadvertently had inspired the derelict to prepare, for the purpose of killing her father, a bomb with which he had only succeeded in blowing up himself. At the end of the story, he asked if humanity really wanted bigger and better ways of wiping itself out.

He took it to the news editor who read it in engrossed silence.

"Well? What do you think of it?"

"It's great," said the news editor. "It's the biggest story you've ever done."

He tore the sheets of typescript into small pieces, piled them in an ashtray, and set a match to the pile.

"Write it again," he said in a flat, stale tone. "Only, this time, make it a couple of paragraphs about a man in Whitechapel who was experimenting with explosives and blew himself up. Never mind why he was experimenting with explosives—and leave out the girl, the professor, and the poison gas."

"What's the idea? You're scrapping the story of the year."

"The War Office wouldn't like it. In fact, a certain high official was on the 'phone an hour ago. It seems that after you left the professor's house the old boy looked out of a window and saw you getting into the car with his daughter. Fearing that she might open her little mouth too wide, he rang up the War Office. It isn't in the public interest for our readers to know the treat that's in store for them one sunny day."

"If the War Office think they can keep this new gas a secret," hissed Julian, "they're crazy. I know about it, the girl knows about it, the poor devil in Whitechapel knew about it. Heaven knows who else knows. I'll bet a month's pay half the spies in Europe are in the know—and plotting at this very minute to steal the blooming formula!"

"That's fine," said the news editor, turning back to his work. "Just fine. You'll be able to get me a red-hot spy story."

Late that night a murder was committed in a Liverpool slum, and Julian was dispatched by air to report it for his paper. After two long days and sleepless nights of hard work he was wired to proceed to Glasgow, where war had broken out between rival gangs of razor-slashers. Three days later he returned to London, haggard, unshaven, worn-out, all but asleep on his feet. After a warm bath he went to bed, hoping, in every tired muscle and aching sinew, to be allowed to stay there for twenty-four hours at least.

It was late the following afternoon before he telephoned his office to report.

"Where in blazes have you been?" demanded his news editor angrily.

"In bed," yawned Julian, stretching himself.

"Well, you can snap awake. I've a job for you."

"Give it to someone else. I'm heading for a Turkish bath."

"Can't be done. You've got to handle this. It's your spy story."

"Spy story?" Julian's mind was empty.

"Remember the professor's poison-gas formula? You said all the spies in Europe would be after it. Well, they are. In the past twenty-four hours the police have made surprise raids on houses all over London and taken into custody a number of aliens. In addition, two Russians were arrested last night attempting to land from a schooner off the Norfolk coast. Inspector Howells is bossing the show. He's a pal of yours, isn't he?"

"When I know something, he doesn't he's my closest pal. When it's the other way about you'd think I had an infectious disease."

"Well, see him at once and get him to talk."

Half an hour later Julian called at Scotland Yard, but

Inspector Howells was not there. He found him in a little pub round the corner, sitting on a high stool at an otherwise deserted bar. Julian perched himself on a neighbouring stool and rang for a barmaid. "Two double brandies," he ordered.

The Inspector's face twitched at the sound of this familiar voice. "Go away," he said, without looking round.

"Is that nice?" murmured Julian, squirting soda into one glass and pushing the other one nearer the C.I.D. man's elbow.

"Look," growled Howells, "I've got troubles. Make it some other time."

"Sure. Starting with Professor Lochhead's formula, you've got plenty of troubles. Not quite your sunny self today, are you? I know the symptoms; you've been on the carpet."

Inspector Howells drained the brandy neat at a gulp. "I've worked my head off for two solid days. We've pinched Germans, Russians, Japs, Italians, Greeks, trying to smuggle themselves into the country with every kind of passport under the sun. Known spies, all of 'em, and after the biggest coup of the year. I've been in a hundred stinking little cafés and questioned three times that many unsavoury scoundrels, and what has it got me? A whale of a carpeting, that's what. Something's going to break, Mendoza. Something big. I can feel it in the air. The higher-ups know it, they're like cats on hot bricks. Not one of the rogues we've picked up has let out a squeak."

"Tried Benny Shapiro?" asked Julian. His tone was casual. Too casual.

"Benny's been in Dartmoor for six months. He doesn't know a thing."

"Get him out on parole and he might turn up something. Benny has a lot of contacts. He gets around."

"I put it to him, more or less like that. Benny doesn't like jail, but he wouldn't listen. Whatever is about to break, Mendoza, is big enough to put the wind up even the toughest boys in London."

"To cause so much worry," said Julian thoughtfully, "the formula must still be in the dubious custody of Professor Lochhead."

"He's holding onto it until after the W.O. test," said Howells. "That's another headache. If I had my way, I'd guard the old boy's house with barbed wire and machine guns. But that might call the attention of the public to the fact that something's up, so all I'm allowed to do is keep a couple of plainclothes men in the square and hope for the best. I don't know what to turn to next."

"There's always the river," said Julian, rising and turning up his coat collar. "If I think of it, I'll send a wreath." Outside, Julian hailed a crawling taxi and gave the driver an address in Soho.

"Seen Angelo lately?" he asked the proprietor of the seedy café at which the taxi drew up.

The proprietor, a fleshy Italian with a sallow, inscrutable face and a curling black moustache like the handlebars of a bicycle, mopped his linoleum-topped counter with a filthy rag. "Angelo ain't been around for two-three days. Just lately the cops is too busy to suit Angelo. He likes it quieter."

"Where's he hanging out?"

"I wouldn't know."

"What about Rossi?"

"The cops shopped Rossi las' night," said the Italian indifferently. He sliced a thick chunk from the end of a sausage malodorous with garlic and munched it stolidly. "He told them straight they was wastin' their time. Funny thing about Rosso, get him in a copshop and he can't speak a word of English."

"Franky Manusco?"

"Franky took a trip to Ostend. He said the air around here is beginning to steenk."

"Maybe Franky knew what he was talking about," remarked

Julian, eyeing the garlic sausage with distaste. "You heard any-thing about a big job that's about to be pulled?"

"Me," said the Italian, shrugging his fat shoulders, "I don't never hear nothin'. I got good ears, like that. One is deaf and the other don't hear so good. Cup of tea?" he suggested, as a hint that the interview was over. He reached for a greasy pot.

"Heaven forbid," said Julian hastily. He went out to the waiting taxi.

"Commercial Road," he told the driver. "I'll tell you when to stop."

His destination was another café, this one with an inscription in Yiddish above the door. There was also an electric sign which said: 'M. Goldfarb. GOOD EATS.' Behind the counter laden with delicatessen stood a man with a long, pale, melancholy face and a body bent like a question mark.

"I'm looking for Maxie Steiner," said the reporter.

"Steiner? Steiner? Never heard of him."

"Think again. Take your time. There's no hurry."

Morris Goldfarb looked Julian up and down from battered hat to dusty shoes. He shook his head. "By me, this Steiner is a stranger."

"By me," said Julian agreeably, "you're a liar. I suppose you never heard of Maxie's sister Lena?"

"If I should be struck down this very minute, I never heard of either of them."

"If there was any justice," said Julian amiably, "you'd be struck down this minute, alright. You married Lena Steiner eighteen months ago. Maxie brought me to the wedding. One of the guests drank too much and got playful with a knife, and Maxie and I had to throw him out."

A great light broke over Goldfarb's enigmatic face. "I thought I seen you before. Between you and me, I had an idea you was a cop. You know how it is. For one reason and another, Maxie don't like cops. What would you want to see him about?"

"I have a job for him." Julian took a ten-pound note from his pocket and tore it in half. "My card," he said, giving one portion to the delicatessen proprietor. He tucked the other in a waistcoat pocket.

"I'll see he gets it right away, Mister," said Goldfarb, fondling the 'calling card' lovingly. "Take a seat at the table over there. I'll be back."

Taking off his apron, reaching for his coat, he poked his head through a gap in some curtains at the rear of the place and shouted: "Oi, Lena!"

A fat woman came clumping downstairs into the shop.

"You should look after the place for ten minutes," explained Goldfarb hurriedly. "I got to go out." He indicated Julian. "You remember this gent? He beat up Moise Cohen at our weddink. He beat him up good."

Mrs. Goldfarb showed a gold tooth in a smile and gave Julian a hand like a bunch of bananas. "Moise had it comin'," she said unemotionally. "No one but a vulgar shtunk would make monkey-shines with a knife at a weddink."

Her spouse went out. He was gone a little more than half an hour. When he returned, he made a fleeting and cryptic motion with an eyebrow and his wife silently plodded upstairs. In as heavy a silence, Goldfarb removed his coat and put on his apron. He stood behind the counter, expressionless of face, slicing onions with a long knife.

Julian said nothing. He lit his pipe. After a while, something stirred behind the curtains at the rear of the place. So small a sound, it might have been made by a mouse. But no mouse had made it. Goldfarb looked at Julian and made a brief motion with his head. "In there," he said quietly.

Julian rose and went.

Candidate for a Coffin

"You only got to have your throat cut once," whispered Maxie Steiner huskily. "Just once, that's all. Count me out, Mendoza. I'm no candidate for a coffin."

Dark, odorous and full of shadows, the back room at Goldfarb's. Heavy curtains shut it off from the shop and more curtains draped the far wall, covering a window and a door that led to a foul alley. The only light was from a flickering gas-jet that hung by a pipe from the ceiling, casting a murky, unearthly illumination on the faces of the two men who sat on rickety chairs at a scarred table in the middle of the room.

Maxie was little and thin, his principal characteristic an enormous nose with a definite twist to one side as though a giant hand had tweaked it before it was set. His furtive little eyes moved constantly in his grey face, like goldfish in a bowl. Hair prematurely white. Long, lean, nicotine-stained fingers that could not be still. On his colourless lips a perpetual smile that had no relation to mirth. Hat drawn down. Collar turned up. A frayed, unlit cigarette dangling from his mouth, the paper discoloured with moisture.

"There's fifty quid in this for you," said Julian persuasively.

"Make it a hundred and the answer's still 'No.'"

"And yet you look as if you were on the ribs."

"I am. Broke to the wide. Alright. A feller is broke, must he get his throat cut as well?"

"A hundred quid for nosing around a bit and finding out a thing or two. That's good pay."

"Did I say it wasn't?" The restless fingers tied themselves in knots. "All I ask is, what does a corpse want with money?"

"You've heard things already or you wouldn't be scared."

"For the other half of that ten-quid note," husked Maxie, "you can know as much as me. And that's the finish, see? I don't want to know no more, so don't go keepin' at me to help you."

Without a word Julian produced the remaining portion of the banknote and pushed it across the table. The nervous fingers snatched it up, crumpled it into a ball and stowed it out of sight quicker than a conjurer could have done.

"Four fellers are talkin', see," muttered Maxie Steiner hoarsely, "in a room at the top of a house that's supposed to be empty. I'm on the roof, listenin' through a skylight. Don't ask me what I'm doin' on the roof. That's another story. At first, I think these fellers are plannin' a steal, so I listen. There's money in knowin' things: sometimes you squeeze it out of the bloke you know things about; sometimes you get it from the cops for squeakin'. I never pass up a chance to listen when fellers is talkin' private. Soon I begin to wish I'd buttoned-up my ears. These are tough boys, see; just lookin' at them, you know they'd stick a knife in you without no second thought. And they ain't discussin' no penny-ante steal. They're talking in millions. They'd croak you for a dollar; and this is millions; so you see the spot I'm in, up there on that roof. There's a paper they're after and it's worth all the dough in the world. To get it, maybe they'll have to croak a dozen people, maybe more. That don't weight heavy on them; they talk it over as calmly as though it was kippers for breakfast. There's a Big Boy comin' over from the Continent to boss the show. They're waitin' for him. And if they're poison, he's dynamite. This was something I didn't want no part of, so I get out of there in a hurry."

"What's the name of the Big Boy?"

"That's somethin' I didn't hear."

The reporter looked searchingly at Maxie and the little man's eyes faced the keen scrutiny as steadily as they could face anything—which wasn't very steady. Julian had a feeling that Steiner was telling the truth. "Where is this house?"

"That's somethin' I ain't goin' to tell you. Little Maxie has a yen to go on livin'. I tell you the address, you go nosin' round the place, and these fellers nail you. They'd cut you up in little bits to make you tell what you know. You'd talk. You think you wouldn't, but you would. Anyone would. 'Maxie Steiner steered me here,' you'd say when they put on the pressure. Right then Maxie Steiner would be as good as dead."

The little man stood up. On feet so noiseless that they might have been carpeted, he stole to the curtained rear of the room.

"You sit there for a minute," he said, looking back, "then go out through the front."

"A hundred quid for the name of the Big Boy," said Julian urgently. "Just the name, Maxie, that's all."

The curtains quivered, a door opened and shut, and Maxie Steiner was gone.

With a disgruntled feeling and the unhappy certainty that he knew nothing out of which a good story could be constructed, Julian taxied back to the *Morning World* office and sat down at his desk. He put a sheet of clean white paper in his typewriter and scowled at it. He hadn't an earthly notion what to write. He made several false starts and many sheets of clean white paper, marred by odd lines of typing, fell crushed into the wastepaper basket.

"A girl 'phoned you several times today," said the young voice of the office-boy at his elbow. "She sounded cross as— Maybe you forgot a date with her. Huh?"

He handed Julian a slip of paper on which was scribbled: 'Phone Miss Sybil Lochhead'; and a Mayfair telephone number. Without a second glance, Julian thrust it into a pocket. He thought he knew what Miss Lochhead wanted; she would be impatient to know why the formula story had not appeared.

Well, he had plenty of worries without trying to explain things to an unreasonable young woman.

"If I were you, I'd make it up with her," said the boy, grinning. "Over the 'phone she sounded to me like a nice bit of stuff."

Julian aimed a slap at the youngster's head, and the office-boy ducked and made off, thumbing his nose.

The reporter turned back to his typewriter. For a while he sat staring, and chewing the stem of his pipe. In the end he tapped out a vague routine story which was probably identical with those which would appear the following morning in every London newspaper. He took it to the news editor, who read it through and bristled with disgust.

"Twenty quid a week, the cashier going bald over your expense sheets, and this is the best you can do. If all you want is practise in typing, why not try 'the quick brown fox jumped right over the lazy dog'?"

The following day was pretty much the same. More dingy cafés. More fruitless questioning. More noncommittal answers. Bleak eyes. Still tongues. Expressionless faces.

In the evening he returned wearily to the office once more. The office-boy told him that someone had rung up for him six times in an hour.

"That girl again?" said Julian dully.

"No; she only rang up once. I think she's gone off you. This was a man. Steiner, he said his name was."

"Did he leave a number?" asked Julian eagerly.

"No, he said he'd ring again. He's cruising round London in a taxi. He sounded crackers to me. Nice friends you've got, Mr. Mendoza."

Julian stood over his telephone, hag-ridden by impatience, until it rang again. When that happened, he snatched up the receiver in a hurry. "Mendoza speaking."

The voice that came to him from the other end of the wire was almost delirious with fear. "This is Maxie Steiner. I'm in a spot, Mendoza. You gotta help me."

"Where are you?"

"In a callbox near St. Paul's. I got a taxi waiting. I've had it hours, and I ain't got no dough, and the driver is talkin' abut callin' a cop. That's the least of my worries. There's a bloke hangin' about across the street. I think he's one of Them. Cripes, I'm in a mess—and it's all your fault."

Julian said crisply: "Tell your taximan to drive down Fleet Street and slow up at the World office. I'll join you there."

Hanging up, Julian pulled on his hat, grabbed his stick, limped downstairs in haste and waited. In a few minutes a taxi crept past the building and he glimpsed the pallid face and cringing figure of Maxie Steiner, crouched back as far as he could get. Crossing the pavement in two strides, Julian wrenched open the door and jumped in. The taxi-driver looked back over his shoulder.

"This bloke owes me a couple of quid," he said, without preliminary. "What abaht it?"

"Here"—Julian shoved some notes at the man—"keep driving round until I tell you to stop."

"Right, sir," said the driver, after one glance at the money.

Max Steiner whimpered: "I've been driving round until I'm sick and giddy. I'm scared to stop. They're after me, Mendoza."

"What happened?"

The frantic eye darted to the taxi-driver's solid back and from there to Julian's face. They told their own story. Steiner was scared to talk where a third pair of ears would overhear.

"Where do you want to go?" asked Julian impatiently. "There's a little pub across the river—"

"Think I'm crazy? If they're following, they'll cut my throat and yours, too, just as soon as they get us alone."

"What about the Yard, then? They couldn't get at you there."

"Nothin' doing. If I showed up my nose at the Yard the copper's start rememberin' things I'd rather they forget."

"If you know enough to make it worth their while, they'll forget what they know about you."

"I ain't goin' near no bloomin' Scotland Yard."

"Where then? Nino's? Poloni's? The Blue Spot?"

"I can't take a chance on none of those places. I'm a marked man, I tell you."

"What about your brother-in-law's place? After all, you've got to roost somewhere sooner or later."

"That's what scares me." Maxie hesitated. "O.K., we'll go to Morris. It ain't safe, nowhere is safe, but I got to get out of this perishin' cab sometime."

"Goldfarb's, in Commercial Road," said Julian, leaning over to speak to the driver. "Make it fast. I'll pay your fine if you're pinched."

"You won't get me my licence back if I lose it," grumbled the driver; but he trod heavily on the accelerator.

The taxi went through a red light without slowing down and took a turn at high speed. Julian kept looking back through the rear window.

"There's no one following," he said, after a while.

"That's what you think," quavered Maxie Steiner. "That's what you think."

When the vehicle drew up outside the delicatessen in Commercial Road, Maxie lowered his head and scuttled in like a startled crab, looking neither to right nor left. The reporter followed with less haste, and found Goldfarb gaping open-mouthed at the curtains at the back of his shop through which his brother-in-law had disappeared.

"What's put the wind up Maxie?" he gasped.

"Something's happened," replied Julian curtly. "Let no one else through."

The reporter went between the curtains into the back. Steiner was pacing the dusty boards like a caged animal, so desperate with fright that he was almost climbing the walls. Sheer funk stared from his jumping eyes. Sweat stood out in great drops on his pallid face. His bloodless lips were trembling, slavering. "Look out at the back," he whispered frantically. "Maybe someone's there."

Crossing the small room to the rear wall, Julian groped between the curtains until he found the handle of the door leading to the alley. Opening it, he walked out onto the muddy cobblestones and took a long look round. Save for a mangey prowling cat, investigating a fly-swarming dustbin, the alley was deserted. He retraced his steps and closed the door.

"How do you lock it?" he asked. "I can't find the key."

"There ain't no key," whimpered Maxie. "If you're in the know, you turn the doorknob left and right in a certain way and the door opens and you walk in. If you ain't in the know, you stop out."

The curtains partitioning off the shop parted and Goldfarb came in carrying a pot of coffee that smelled as strong as tar. He set it on a table and backed slowly towards the shop. His puzzled eyes were on his brother-in-law's grey face.

"What's up Maxie? What's up? You done something to bring the cops in on me?"

Maxie Steiner uttered a hysterical cackle. "No, I ain't bringin' the cops in on you. Maybe you'll wish it was the cops."

With a jerk of his head, Julian silently ordered the delicatessen proprietor out. Goldfarb went, his popping eyes never leaving Steiner's face until the curtains closed over him. Julian filled a cracked cup with the strong black coffee and gave it to the shivering little man.

"Drink this and pull yourself together."

"Easy to say," moaned Maxie, gulping the coffee. "Easy to say—but you don't know what I know. Got a fag on you?"

Julian handed him a yellow packet. Steiner's shaking hands fumbled until they closed on a cigarette, spilling the others on the floor. He tried to put it in his mouth. Broke it, cascading tobacco down his front. Threw it aside.

The reporter pushed him into a chair. "Alright, let's have the story."

"I got to thinkin' about what you said, see. Cripes, I thought, a hundred nicker, I could use dough like that. And all I had to do was listen a little. All I had to do—" Again that hysterical cackle. "Cripes, that's a laugh. You think I'm yellow. Alright, I'm yellow. You'll be, too, when I tell you."

His voice trailed off into silence, and he turned his head and stared, terror-stricken at the curtains behind him.

"There's someone there. I heard a sound."

To humour him, Julian went and looked, but no one was there.

"You're imagining things. Get on with the story."

"I went up on that roof again and peered through the skylight. Only one eye, see, I didn't want them to spot me. There was four or five fellers in the room. One of them I knew—he used to be in the Pinker Street Gang—the rest was strangers to me. The feller I knew is a hard customer, bad news at any time. They were talkin', and I listened. Cripes, I wish I never had. The Big Boy is comin' from the Continent and landin' in Yorkshire early tomorrow mornin'. And who do you think he is?"

"Who?" asked Julian tensely.

Maxie Steiner took a deep breath. "I get a hundred nicker for this." Cupidity showed through the funk in his eyes.

"Yes, you get a hundred quid."

"It's Spider Marcovicz."

Julian blinked. He had heard of Spider Marcovicz—who hadn't? Star executioner until he was marked for death and fled from his country in a hurry, leaving a bloodstained trail behind him. International spy. Infamous thug. Crook without conscience. A man who could claim to have spilled more blood, filled more cemeteries, than anyone on earth. If the Spider was landing in England tonight, all hell was due to break loose.

"One of them looked up and seen me," wailed Maxie Steiner. "I know he did. The feller I knew, he looked up and seen me listening. I got out of there in a hurry, but what good was that? They'd follow. You can bet they'd go after me."

"Where is Marcovicz landing?"

"He's landing—" Steiner's mouth hung open. He looked sick. He swayed on his chair. "He's landing—"

"You said that. Tell me where."

Slowly, so very, very slowly, Maxie Steiner folded in the middle and dropped forward across the table, sending cup and coffee pot crashing to the floor. Through the curtains and through the back of his chair protruded a long, razor-sharp blade. While Julian stared in morbid fascination, the blade withdrew.

A tall man in dark clothes came out from behind the curtains. His eyes were baleful and glittering; the eyes of a killer. He came at Julian swiftly, silently, his mouth no more than a slit in the middle of his face. He knew how to handle a knife. Julian could see that it was as much a part of him as his index finger. With the precision of an expert, his eyes sought and found Julian's jugular vein. One jab with the sharp point in that spot and it would be goodbye, Julian Mendoza!

The reporter flung himself out of the chair and across the room. The killer followed, weaving for an opening like a boxer. His lips drawn back; his yellow teeth bared. The knife poised ready to strike like lightning.

Julian threw up his fists; but that was only a sham; you couldn't punch as quickly as that knife could strike. For a brief instant, the killer's eyes darted to the raised fists; and that instant was sufficient. Julian buried the toe of his boot in the lowest part of the killer's stomach.

With an agonised grunt, the intruder double up and the knife fell from his paralysed fingers. For good measure, Julian struck him a vicious blow on the point of the chin. The killer's head snapped back as if it were on a hinge and he fell heavily to the floor.

Trembling and perspiring, Julian looked down at the wicked bloodstained knife.

"You so-and-so!" he breathed. "You dirty, misbegotten so-and-so."

A fat woman sobbed in the drab back room of a shady café; sobbing her heart out for the dirty little scoundrel who had been her brother, and who lay dead. Sorrow made the woman ludicrous; she was too fleshy for emotion; the tears running down her puffy cheeks cut winding streams through the caked powder. Her husband—bald, bent, apprehensive—stood close beside her, giving ineffectual pats to her flabby arm. An absurd, almost laughable couple; but none of the watchers felt like laughing.

Police cars were parked along Commercial Road on either side of the place, and two uniformed constables stood at the front, with orders to let no unauthorised person pass. The shop, back room and alley swarmed with plainclothes men—fingerprinting, measuring, photographing. A divisional surgeon, kneeling beside the prostrate form of the killer, looked up with an eyebrow raised expressively.

"He's still out cold. What did you hit him with, Mendoza? A paving-stone?"

"He's still breathing," said Julian unemotionally. "He'll live to be hanged."

"It's Slasher Strom," said Inspector Howells. "Used to be one of the Pinker Street crowd. Steiner worked with that bunch, too, at one time."

"That explains how Strom knew where to look for Steiner and how he knew the secret of opening the back door."

"This story Steiner told you. Do you think it was on the level? He wasn't leading you up the garden path?"

"Want do you think?" retorted Julian, pointing to the corpse. "Does that look as if he was playing games with me? Maxie was sweating blood. This was once he was on the level, if he never was before. I tell you; Spider Marcovicz is landing in England within the next few hours. Need I explain what that means?"

The Scotland Yard official grunted and shook his head. With a thunderous frown he paced the floor.

"You oughtn't to have hit the swine so hard," he complained. "He may not come round for hours. We won't have a chance to make him talk until it's too late."

"So, you think he'd talk if he were conscious?" scoffed Julian. "If you do, you're crazy. Take a look at this. I found it in the Slasher's pocket."

On the scarred table the reporter flattened a soiled sheet of paper on which a map was crudely drawn. A house, some outbuildings, fields, trees and paths, were roughly sketched in. Along the bottom ran two lines of close writing in the Russian language and in Russian script. Inspector Howells bent over the table, peering at the map in the vague light of the hissing gas-jet.

"If that isn't the spot where Marcovicz's plane will land," murmured Julian softly, "I'll eat my hat."

Howells threw up his hands. "Yes, but where is it? It might be anywhere."

"Steiner said Yorkshire."

"Yorkshire! The biggest county in England. That's a big help. That's a devil of a big help."

"Must I work out everything for you? What do you suppose that screed in Russian means? Get an expert linguist onto it—and maybe he'll be able to tell you just where the plane is coming in."

"That's almost too much to hope for—but it's worth trying."

"I'll come back to the Yard with you."

The shrewd eyes of Inspector Howells narrowed, and into them crept an evasive expression. He stroked his chin with a lean forefinger. "No, it wouldn't be a good idea for you to come back with me."

Julian shot out his jaw. "Oh? Why not?"

"Well—" The inspector fumbled for words. "Oh, confound it, use your common-sense, Mendoza. Things will be happening fast when I get back to the Yard. I'll have a thousand-and-one jobs to do, and the Assistant Commissioner at my elbow. You'd only be in the way."

"Take my information and cut me out. Is that it?"

The chill of an icy wind swept through the reporter's voice. "Not at all."

"What's on your mind, then? Do I come with you if and when you go after Marcovicz—or don't I?"

Inspector Howells sighed. "I suppose you'll have to come."

"That's better. So maybe I should accompany you to the Yard, after all, to be on hand when things start moving."

"No, that won't do. Go back to your office. I'll phone you."

"You're sure you'll phone me?"

"Haven't I promised? Go on, get out of here."

The reporter went back to the '*World*' office and wrote an account of the murder of Maxie Steiner, avoiding all mention of international spies and the poison-gas formula, and anything else that might embarrass or annoy the War Office. Reading the story, one would infer that the killing arose simply out of a difference of opinion between two members of a ruffian gang.

Having sent his copy to the newsroom he sat down to wait for the telephone call from Howells. He tried to contain himself in patience, but almost at once he jumped up again like a jack-in-the-box. He walked the floor, scratched his bushy hair. He chewed on his pipe-stem until it snapped. After twelve minutes of this, he telephoned Scotland Yard. Inspector Howells was there.

"Don't bother me now," Howells shouted irritably. "I'm up to my neck in it."

"Had the Russian translated yet?"

"Yes, it's been translated."

"Well, what does it say?"

"It's in code," Howells almost yelled. "It's gone to another expert to be deciphered. Get off the line. I'm busy."

Julian hung up. He dropped into the chair at his desk. Got up again. Walked across the room and looked out of the window, chewing his lip. Snail-slow, the seconds slithered away. After thirty seemingly endless minutes of marking time, Julian snatched up the telephone again.

"Inspector Howells cannot speak on the phone now, sir," said the detached voice of the Scotland Yard operator. "He's in conference."

Hands deep in his pockets, eyes straying constantly to the clock, a new pipe-stem leading a short and thankless life between his grinding teeth, Julian paced the worn linoleum of the reporter's room. In a few minutes he was ringing Whitehall 1212 again. This time, Inspector Howells spoke to him, mincing no words.

"—and another thing: if you ring again until I'm ready for you, I'll—I'll—"

"Your code expert is taking his time, isn't he?"

"He finished the job five minutes ago. You were right. We know the time and the place of Marcovicz's landing. We're getting in touch with the local police now. For Peter's sake, sit back and relax until I call you."

"You won't try any funny business? You really are going to take me with you?"

"You don't think I'd go back on my word?" said Inspector Howells indignantly.

Along the wire came a sharp click as he hung up.

Julian did not know what he thought. All he knew was that the time for action was drawing near. Things would be happening, fast and furiously, somewhere in Yorkshire in a few hours' time, and he wanted to be there. No use trying to wait for Howells to phone him. He couldn't do it. He simply couldn't keep still a second longer.

He was leaving the building by the employees' entrance when the doorkeeper put his head out of the cubicle and said:

"Young lady to see you, Mr. Mendoza. She's in the waiting room."

"She can stop there. I'm in a hurry."

"Oh, she can!" said the voice of Sybil Lochhead at his elbow. "Where have you been hiding the past week? I've tried to find you a dozen times."

Julian kept on walking. The girl was still at his side when he reached the end of Fetter Lane and turned into Fleet Street.

"What a broken reed you turned out to be," she said bitterly.

Julian did not answer. He was looking for a taxi. "You promised to print that story I gave you."

"I promised to write it. My news editor turned it down. The War Office didn't like it, so that was that. Now run along, I'm in a hurry."

"One would think you wanted to get rid of me."

"One would be right. I've work to do."

"If you're in such a hurry, I'll give you a lift. Hop in."

They had reached Sybil's car, parked in Fleet Street. She slid her trim figure behind the steering wheel and left the door invitingly open. Julian looked up and down for a taxi, but there was none in sight. With a sigh, he climbed in beside her.

"Where to?"

"Scotland Yard. And no exhibition of stunt driving, please. My nerves won't stand it today."

"You'll be sorry for those words, my fine-feathered friend."

And he was.

Before they reached the headquarters of the Metropolitan

Police, she did everything but stand the car on end. With another sigh—this time of relief—Julian opened the door. He slammed it again without getting out.

"Of all the double-crossing rats!" he breathed furiously. "Leaving me flat, is he? We'll see about that. Follow that car," he snapped, pointing to a long black Bentley that had come out of the gateway of New Scotland Yard.

Without a word, Sybil Lochhead obeyed. She asked no questions; she played no more hair-raising tricks, but for half an hour she kept her little car within fifty yards of the Bentley. At the end of that period the cars passed through Barnet and roared north. It was very dark now, and on the open road Sybil had to urge the two-seater to something over seventy miles an hour in order to keep the bobbing tail light of the Bentley in sight. In under twenty minutes they covered more than twenty-two miles.

"Looks as though we're making for Scotland," remarked Sybil chattily. "Remind me to pick up a toothbrush as the first stop."

Hunched in his seat, the reporter said nothing. In his mind he was giving Inspector Howells the tongue-lashing of a lifetime, and he was trying to think of any profane epithet he might not yet have used.

A corner rushed to meet them and Sybil steered round it without slackening speed. An instant later she braked so suddenly that Julian was thrown against the windscreen with a force that almost knocked him out. The little car skidded twenty feet, its tyres screaming on the concrete surface. It spun round dizzily and stopped, almost in the ditch, the radiator pointing in the direction from which it had come.

The impact with the windscreen had jammed Julian's hat down over his eyes. He wrenched it off and sat up. He saw the dark shape of the Bentley blocking the road and two burly figures walking towards the two-seater.

"You alright?" he said to Sybil, who was doubled-up between seat and floorboards.

"I'll never be the same again," she gasped.

Julian helped her up. She had a black eye and a skinned nose—but no broken bones.

The stern face of Inspector Howells stared into the car. Behind him stood another severe-looking officer in plainclothes.

"Perhaps you'll explain—" began Inspector Howells heavily. He broke off sharply and added: "I might have known it. Mendoza! Of course, it would be you."

"Next time you decide to stop," said Sybil bitterly, "you might put out your hand."

"I'm sorry, miss." Inspector Howells did not look in the least sorry; only very grim. "We noticed you following and had to find out why. Now I've seen your passenger, I know exactly why. You can turn round and go back again, Mendoza. I'm not having you on my tail tonight."

"You choice rat!" said Julian, his dark eyes glowing. "You—" Words failed him.

"Look, Mendoza, be reasonable."

"Sure, I'll be reasonable. As reasonable as you are; no more, no less. I know—I know you have a job to do, well, so have I. And I'm sticking with it. You just try to stop me. Go on, try!"

For a while they exchanged bleak stares, and at last the police officer beckoned with his head and walked to the side of the road. Climbing out of the car, Julian followed him.

"This is the biggest job of my life," said Inspector Howells in a low tone. "I had to leave you out. Use your head: how could I take a reporter on an errand like this? The Commissioner would have my scalp. If you keep trailing me, you'll gum up the works. Do that and I promise you, you'll get all the trouble you're looking for."

"But for me you'd never have got wind of this affair."

"I realise that and I'm grateful, but—"

"Don't be like that. I know what you're thinking. You're afraid of publicity. Well, I promise not to print a word of anything I see or hear tonight until you give me the O.K. Otherwise, you'll have to jail me to freeze me out."

"I could jail you, alright. Don't think I wouldn't."

"And what a stink that would raise."

"What about the girl?" said Howells dubiously.

"She won't follow. I'll see to that."

There was another long silence, and then: "Alright! Shake off the girl and you can come."

Julian walked back to the car. "This is where you make for home, sweetheart. I'm sorry! Thanks for the buggy ride."

"Think again!" Sybil retorted cheerfully. "I've come this far to please you. I'll go the rest of the way to suit myself."

"Like that, is it?"

"Just like that," said Sybil, enunciating every syllable distinctly. "And what can you do about it?"

Without answering Julian strolled to the front of the car and raised the bonnet. His hands worked swiftly inside. With a cry, Sybil jumped out and ran to him.

"What are you doing?"

"Only making sure that you stay put," he replied, pocketing her distributor-head.

"Why, you—" Sybil swung a small but workmanlike fist at his head. Blocking the punch, Julian picked her up and dumped her in the driving-seat of her car.

"See you later."

And then he was off down the road as fast as one sound leg and a crippled one would carry him. He climbed into the police Bentley.

"Let's go," he said.

*

The police car roared through the night. Inspector Howells lit a pipe with fingers that shook a little. The flame in his cupped hands cast a weird light on his eyes, nose and mouth.

"I hope you lads are armed," said Julian. "This is no picnic we're going on."

"Yes," said Inspector Howells quietly.

It was an ominous quietness. "Yes. We're armed."

The Bentley rushed on. At a crossroads more than 150 miles from London, a score of broad-shouldered country policemen were waiting. Their lips were set. Their eyes hard. Many of them carried rifles. All of them knew what they were there for, and the dangers involved. There was little time and less need for indirect speech. Half a dozen cars and police vans were drawn up along the roadside. The chief constable of the county, in coat and breeches of military cut, exchanged curt greeting with Inspector Howells. In the glare of powerful headlights, Howells and a little knot of the local men, studied the crude map.

"That'll be Moortop Farm," said a sergeant who had been a poacher as a lad and knew every inch of the countryside. He pointed to the roughly drawn building. "It's empty. Been derelict for years. No other building within miles. That ragged line to the left represents Five Acres Wood. There's the Boulder, over in the corner—a giant stone hillock on the edge of the place. If this ain't a wild-goose chase, the plane will land in Long Field, that's the only one sufficiently large and smooth."

"How far are we from this farm?"

"A good six miles."

Inspector Howells thumbed his chin. "Let's get going."

The men piled into cars and vans and the procession moved off. When it had gone less than four miles, the chief constable signalled for a halt. At the side of the road he conferred again with Inspector Howells.

"We'll go the rest of the way on foot, there are sure to be confederates on the spot. We'll spread out and close in on Long Field in a circle."

"Better make some arrangement for the cars to follow up, sir. We'll want all the light we can get when the time comes. The headlights will come in handy."

"We'll leave one man to each car, with orders to start moving slowly up to the farm after we've been gone half-an-hour. There's a good dirt road they can take."

Whispered orders. Tightening nerves. The party split into four groups, which moved off in different directions. As much as possible, the men walked on grass, for it was a matter of importance—of life and death—to reach their objective as noiselessly as possible. Julian accompanied Inspector Howells' squad, which was guided by the sergeant, who had been a poacher.

Dry leaves rustled as they advanced. Strange, spine-tingling shapes looked up out of the darkness, resolving themselves prosaically into posts and trees and mounds of stone. In the dark, leafless branches brushed their faces, seeming to pluck at them like dead fingers. Pitch-black night. Rutted paths. Uneven turf. Rocks to trip over. Holes to stumble into. Every moment the risk of breaking a leg. Their muscles aching with the unaccustomed strain of walking gingerly.

On! On! On!

The Metropolitan Police officials were perspiring and breathing harshly and cursing inwardly. In the lead, the local sergeant halted and crouched down, motioning for the others to do likewise. For what seemed an eternity, they knelt there, knee-joints complaining, hearts heavily pounding. The sergeant's head was on one side; he listened, as a bird might listen.

"Long Field is just over that rise," he whispered. "I can't hear a sound. The woods take that line"—he waved to the left with a large hand—"we'd better follow them. Keep to the grass verge and walk warily. The dry twigs snap like pistol shots.

On again, crouching this time, with back muscles protesting, getting their own back with jabs of pain.

Again, the local sergeant called a halt. "There's a car parked without lights on the edge of the woods, sir," he said in a whisper.

Inspector Howells hesitated. "See if you can find the chief constable and report to him," he muttered at last.

"Very good, sir."

The local sergeant disappeared into the darkness. The others stayed where they were. He told the inspector that the other squads had now moved up to their positions, which meant that Long Field was encircled by the police.

"Everything is dead quiet," he went on. "The only sign of life is the car I spotted over there. The chief constable wants us to move upon it with caution and apprehend the occupants, if any."

More whispered instructions, and Inspector Howell's party went gingerly forward, spreading out. Flashlights ready to switch on; revolvers cocked in large hands. At a given signal the men ran the last few yards that separated them from the parked car. They surrounded it, flooding it with light from their electric torches.

In the front seat of the car, two people blinked in the dazzling blade of light. One was clad in raincoat and trilby, the other in rich furs and a smart cloche hat with a veil. They had their arms round one another.

"For the love of Pete," said one of the policemen, "it's a spooning couple!"

Inspector Howells wrenched open one of the doors of the car. His light fell on silk-stockinged legs protruding from a pleated skirt and terminating in high-heeled shoes.

"What's the meaning of this?" demanded the man in raincoat and trilby. "Can't me and my young lady come up here for a quiet half-hour without a lot of Nosy Parkers breaking in on us?"

"I'm sorry," said Inspector Howells quietly. "My apologies to you, too, miss. The fact is, we are police officers and had reason to suspect that—"

"Police!" repeated the man sharply. "Look here, officer, we've done nothing wrong. Oh, perhaps we're trespassing, but the place has been empty for years, and me and my young lady come up here often to get away from everything. You can't arrest us for that."

"You don't mind if my men search your car?"

"Go ahead and search. I'm darned if I know what you expect to find."

The rain-coated individual and his fur-clad companion climbed out of the car, which the Scotland Yard men submitted to a brisk and efficient search. They found nothing of a suspicious nature."

"I suppose we can go now?" said the rain-coated one, climbing back behind the steering wheel. His companion settled by his side, lighting a gold-tipped cigarette with well-manicured hands.

"I'm afraid not," replied Howells firmly. "Perhaps you're as innocent as you look—and perhaps not. In any case, I must insist that you remain here for the present."

The sergeant, who had been a poacher, went down to the field to investigate. Spaced at regular intervals, he found a ring of landing flares, all ready to be lit. The ring extended in a circle completely round the field.

"Someone put them there," said Howells, out of earshot of the parked car. "Someone who intended to light them when the time came. And there was no one about when we got here except that man and woman."

"If it is a woman," said Julian.

"What's that?" asked the local sergeant sharply.

'That' was a steady drumming in the sky, the rhythmic beat of an aeroplane engine. For a while they stood stock-still, listening.

There was nothing to see; the aeroplane was showing no lights. The drumming became louder and louder as it approached, until at last it was directly overhead, and then faded by degrees as the aeroplane passed on and went north. A few minutes later the sound grew louder again; it came closer, closer, and was once more above their heads. This time it was of constant pitch; the aeroplane was flying in circles above them.

The two people in the parked car seemed to pay little attention to it.

"Someone's got to light the flares," said Inspector Howells. "I suppose we're elected."

He uttered a series of sharp commands, and several of the policemen started running down the field. A moment later the first of the flares spread a ragged light over its immediate vicinity. Another spluttered into flame, and another, and another, until the field was ringed with light. The police, who formed a human barricade beyond the flares, waited, tense and on edge.

The sound of the engine grew as the plane lost altitude in a series of downward swoops. Looking up, Julian saw the dark winged shape pass overhead in a sloping glide. It skimmed low over the flares nearest him and came down; bounced a little on the uneven surface and then came to a stop almost in the centre of the field.

In the murky night, Julian saw the pilot climb out, followed by another man. The passenger was tall and very thin. He wore a black hat with brim drawn down and a long black coat, with turned-up collar, that shrouded him almost to the heels. In one hand he gripped a violin case.

"Marcovicz!" said the reporter in a strained whisper. "Let me have a rifle, Howells, and I'll pick him off right here and now."

"The police can't work that way, Mendoza—and you know it."

"It's the way we'd better work when dealing with the Spider."

There was a commotion behind him.

One of the police left guarding the parked car had taken his eyes off the occupants for a moment while he watched the aeroplane gliding in. That moment was enough for the fur-coated one. A beautiful straight left—which established, at least, that the fur-coated one was no woman—landed on the policeman's jaw, knocking him out. Throwing the car door open, the female impersonator scrambled out and ran across the field, shouting something in a loud, hoarse voice.

Spider Marcovicz threw open his violin case, took something out, and dropped the case to the ground. Julian drew in his breath sharply. He had recognised the stubby object; it was a submachinegun. Marcovicz put it to his shoulder and flashes of orange flame stabbed the night air. The skirted running figure doubled forward, went head-over-heels in clumsy somersaults, landed in an awkward heap on the grass and lay still.

A whistle shrilled and the lights of the police-cars which had been brought up to surround the field came on. Like crossed swords the broad beams tangled from all directions, bathing in their brilliance the aeroplane and the two men who had landed from it.

"You can't get away, Marcovicz!" shouted a stentorian voice. "Throw down that gun and surrender."

With the submachinegun to his shoulder Marcovicz dropped on one knee. Pulling the trigger, he swung his body from the waist scattering lead in a half-circle at the rate of four hundred bullets a minute.

Crashing of glass—clanging of bullets on metal—shrill screams of men in agony.

Julian threw himself down as the spray of death was turned in his direction. Behind him a man coughed and died. For what seemed an eternity the death-dealing rattle continued.

All of a sudden there was silence.

Cautiously Julian raised his head. There was now a black gap in the ring of headlights like a toothless space in the gums of an old crone. And Spider Marcovicz was running toward the gap with the deadly weapon under his arm. At his heels ran the pilot of the aeroplane.

Jumping up the reporter looked for a gun. He found a rifle lying under the body of a man who would need it no longer. Taking hasty aim, he fired. The pilot threw up his hands and fell. Several others had the same idea as the reporter; there was a burst of rifle fire from various parts of the field. But Spider Marcovicz disappeared unhurt through the gap in the ring of lights.

From the direction in which he had vanished came the ghastly staccato stuttering of the submachinegun once more. It ceased and there was a roar as a motorcar engine sprang to life. Julian gritted his teeth. The swine was escaping in a police car. There was no way to stop him. It was impossible to fire blindly in the direction of the throbbing engine; there were ninety-nine chances to one that his shots would find the wrong billet.

At his elbow he heard the voice of Inspector Howells almost incoherent with horror. "I should have let you shoot! My heaven, I didn't realise what we were up against! I had no idea. I should have let you shoot him."

"Pull yourself together," snarled the reporter. "It's too late to worry about that now. Let's check up on the position and get after him as fast as we can."

There were fewer causalities than Julian at first had feared. The fur-clad individual—a man, of course—lay very dead in the middle of the field; the pilot lay, no less dead, fifty yards further on; and the man in raincoat and trilby was slumped over his steering-wheel with a hole through his head, behind the shattered windscreen of his parked car.

One policeman was dead and four others were wounded. Flying lead had put out of action the engines of three police cars. The thing that chiefly had to be dealt with was the shocked consternation of the policemen who had not been wounded. That such an incident could have taken place in England seemed to stun them into paralysed inactivity.

"You're dealing with a crook to whom human lives mean nothing!" hissed Julian to the chief constable, who was frozen with bewilderment. "He's after loot worth millions. There's nothing he won't do to get his hands on it. It's up to us to stop him before he gets any further."

The wounded men were loaded into a van and started on their journey to hospital. A car shot away to raise the alarm; in a matter of minutes the telephone and telegraph wires would be humming with the news of what had happened and the police of every county in England would be on the watch for Marcovicz.

Those policemen still fit for duty were loaded into the undamaged cars—this time with orders to shoot first and talk after— and the pursuit was on.

But it was fruitless.

No trace of Spider Marcovicz was found that night.

*

In the early morning Julian headed back to London with Inspector Howells in the Flying Squad Bentley.

Suddenly the reporter tugged at the driver's sleeve. "Pull up here," he said.

The man obeyed. Julian climbed out and crossed the road to Sybil Lochhead's smart two-seater which stood with its front wheels almost in the ditch. He looked right and left, but there was no sign of the girl. Returning to the Bentley, he put his head in at the front offside window.

"You go on without me," he said. "I'd better take Miss Lochhead's car back to London."

The Bentley drove off. Julian walked back to the two-seater, taking its distribution head from his pocket. He raised the bonnet and linked up the connections so that the little car would run. He had no sooner finished the job than he received a terrific kick in the seat of the trousers from a pointed toe. Without looking round, he knew that the donor was Miss Sybil Lochhead.

"That's for you," snapped her voice behind him. "You ugly brute!"

Julian turned. "I suppose I deserved it."

All of a sudden, Sybil was in tears. "I've been s-sitting here all n-night, and I'm ti-tired and p-practically f-frozen and—and it's all your f-fault. You're the m-most hateful m-man I've ever m-met."

With a handkerchief sufficiently large to have served as a tray cloth, Julian dried her eyes. He coaxed her into the car, and she started the engine. As the two-seater moved off, Sybil turned her head to give him another piece of her mind.

But Julian was fast asleep. As soon as he relaxed against the cushions he had dropped off.

A spiteful look came into Sybil's eyes. She applied the brake. The car stopped and for a moment she sat looking at Julian with a cross expression on her lovely face. And then her eyes softened. Taking the rug from the headrest, she spread it over the sleeping man.

Releasing the brake, she trod upon the accelerator and the little car went on, gathering speed rapidly.

*

The next forty-eight hours was a period of feverish activity for police forces all over England, and especially in the Metropolitan areas. Every alien of dubious reputation who could be traced was taken in for questioning. Houses all over London and in every provincial city were raided. All departments of the Criminal Investigation Department worked at full blast day and night.

And the net results—as far as the apprehension of Spider Marcovicz and his accomplices was concerned—were nil.

"Lovely morning, inspector."

Inspector Howells spun on his heels. "Mendoza! What the devil do you want?"

"I thought I'd join the party."

"You can think again. The test is to be held in secret. No newspapermen. You haven't a chance of being allowed to come."

"I'll see what my fairy godfather has to say about that," said Julian cheerfully.

It was the morning on which the War Office was to make an official test of the new poison gas. Outside Professor Lochhead's house in Elviston Square a Rolls-Royce saloon waited at the kerb. A foot or two behind it stood a powerful open Bentley—a Flying Squad car—with four burly men in it.

Julian went up the steps to the professor's front door, which stood open. Professor Lochhead was fussing about, supervising his secretary and his chauffeur, who were red in the face with their efforts to carry an iron box through the hall.

"Morning, Sydney," said Julian pleasantly.

The secretary, bent double with the strain, gave him a dirty look. Although they had only met once before, they heartily disliked each other. It was one of those intense mutual antagonisms that spring up in an instant and last a lifetime.

The professor had to peer closely at Julian before he recognised him. "I can't talk to you now, young man," he said in a flustered voice. "I am engaged on most important business."

"That's what I want to see you about. I'd like to witness the test of your gas."

"Impossible! Quite out of the question. No one is to attend except the War Office representatives, a number of police and military guards, and my assistant."

"I could be one of your assistants."

"No, no, I couldn't hear of it!"

"You said," Julian reminded him, "that if there was ever anything you could do for me—"

"Yes, yes; but what you ask is impossible. A representative of the Press could not on any account be permitted to attend."

"Then let me come in a purely private capacity. I won't write a line about the test until you give me permission. After all, you owe me something. But for me you'd have lost the formula."

"If you take my advice, sir," said Sydney Lanham, "you will not listen to this man. In my opinion, he is not to be trusted."

That settled it. Like many small men, Professor Lochhead had a large sense of his own importance.

"I didn't ask your opinion, Sydney," he snapped. "Be good enough to keep your mind on what you are doing." Turning to Julian, he added: "If you give me your word that no account of this morning's experiments will appear in your newspaper without my permission—"

"I'll give it willingly."

"Very well, you may come."

"Thanks Sydney," Julian whispered to the secretary who gave him a venomous glare.

With much panting and straining, the iron box was carried out and securely strapped to the luggage carrier of the Rolls-Royce. When the reporter took his seat in front with the chauffeur, Inspector Howells stared at him and scratched his head in astonishment, but made no comment. The professor and his secretary settled themselves in the rear seat. Leaning his head in through the window, Inspector Howells said:

"My men and I will go on in front in the Bentley, sir. It will be advisable for your chauffeur to keep close behind us. If you wish to get in touch with me during the run, signal with two sharp blasts of the horn. It isn't likely that anything untoward will happen while you are under police protection, but, in case of trouble, we're prepared. My men are armed with revolvers and ready to use them."

The War Office test was to be held on the bleak moors that stretch for miles on all sides of Princetown, where Dartmoor Prison is situated. The two cars weaved their way through the traffic of London, through the thinning suburbs; and settled down to a steady fifty miles an hour when open country was reached.

When they were nearly forty miles from London, Julian found that another vehicle had joined the procession. He spotted it in the driving-mirror; a large saloon car about a hundred yards in the rear. He watched it for a few minutes and saw that it neither gained on them nor dropped back.

"There's a car following us," he told the chauffeur. "Blow your horn to warn Inspector Howells."

The chauffeur gave no sign of having heard. He kept his eyes on the road in front. There was a tension in his grip on the steering wheel that made Julian eye him suspiciously. Leaning across, the reporter pressed the button of the electric horn twice. In the rear seat of the Bentley, Inspector Howells turned his head and looked back. The police car began to slow down.

They were approaching a side turning. Passing it, the police car came to a halt. Its driver put out a hand and waved the Rolls-Royce on.

At that moment a heavy truck shot out of the side road and stopped broadside-on across the main highway completely blocking it. A man sprang down from the driving seat and took to his heels. Before he had gone three yards the truck burst into flames.

It was as neat a trap as Julian had ever seen. The police car was on one side of the burning tuck, the Rolls-Royce and the pursuing car on the other.

"Don't stop," he ordered the chauffeur. "Take the turning and go like blazes."

This time the man heard—and obeyed. He spun the steering wheel, and the Rolls glided down the side road. Almost at once it began to slow down. The chauffeur kept his foot on the accelerator, but the engine did not respond. Its smooth purring died away. The car trickled slowly to a halt a hundred yards or so up the road.

"Engine trouble," mumbled the chauffeur. "We can't go any further."

"Engine trouble be damned," retorted Julian. "You switched off the ignition with your knee. I saw you."

The chauffeur's hand dropped to his side. It came up holding a revolver. He jabbed the weapon into Julian's stomach.

"Alright, I switched off the ignition. This is as far as we go, just the same."

Professor Lochhead uttered a startled gasp. "Parker! What are you doing? Have you gone mad?"

"Shut up and sit still!" snarled the chauffeur, "unless you want me to blast this man's guts through his backbone. The car that was following will be here in a moment. If you all take it easy no one will get hurt."

From the road they had left came the sharp crack of a police Webley, followed by the deadly stuttering of submachinegun. The pursuers were disposing of the police escort before they came on to deal with the occupants of the Rolls-Royce.

Snatching up his attaché-case from the floor of the car, the professor hit the chauffeur on the head with it. The little man was as brave as a lion, thought Julian sardonically, when it was Julian's life that was at stake. A pull on the trigger was all that was required for the reporter to embark on a painful and lingering death. But the chauffeur did not pull the trigger. Perhaps he was sufficiently new to the type of dangerous exploit on which he was engaged to have qualms about taking life. Snarling threats, he twisted his head to avoid another blow from the attaché-case. He kept the revolver hard against Julian's stomach.

If the professor was going to take risks with Julian's life, Julian decided to take one on his own account. He dropped his hand on the revolver and gripped the cartridge cylinder. If he gripped it tightly enough the gun could not be fired, because the cylinder would not revolve. If his hand was even slightly moist, it would be just too bad—

In a panic, the chauffeur tried to shoot, but he was too late. Julian held the cylinder grimly, his knuckles showing white through the skin.

With his free hand he hit the chauffeur on the chin. All his strength went into the blow—he wanted it to hurt—and it broke the man's jaw. Without a sound, the chauffeur fell back unconscious against the door of the car. Opening the door, Julian let him topple out on to the road.

The reporter was still holding the revolver by the cylinder. There was a chill emptiness in the pit of his stomach and his hands were shaking. With a sigh of relief, he put the gun in his pocket.

The pursuing car had turned the corner and was rapidly approaching. Sliding into the driving-seat, Julian switched on the ignition and started the car. He pressed hard on the accelerator. Looking in the driving mirror, he saw one of the men in the pursuing car leaning out of the window with the submachinegun in his hands. Ducking his head, Julian shouted to his companions to do the same.

The professor and Sydney Lanham threw themselves on the

floor. They were only just in time. A row of holes appeared in the back of the car where their shoulders had been; and the bullets sped on, to make a twin row of holes across the windscreen.

Tramping the accelerator pedal down to the floorboards, Julian swerved the big car from side to side in an attempt to dodge the stream of bullets from behind. It was hopeless, there were too many of them. They hummed about the Rolls like a swarm of bees, clattering on the coachwork like hail. One hit a rear tyre, which burst with a loud report. The back axle swung round, and Julian had to wrestle with the steering wheel to keep the car on the road. A one-sided struggle too violent to last.

At a bend in the road, Julian deliberately steered the bucking, rolling car straight at a hedge—at eighty delirious miles an hour. It went through like a shot out of a cannon, taking a chunk of the hedge with it. On the other side was a ploughed field. The Rolls ploughed it up as it had never been ploughed before. Momentum carried the big car for fifty yards, and then it skidded round to face the direction from which it had come and slithered to a stop, leaning on its side at an angle of forty-five degrees.

Julian jumped out with the chauffeur's revolver in his hand. Pulling open the rear door, he dragged out Professor Lochhead, who was bruised and shaken but otherwise unhurt. Sydney Lanham was lying unconscious on the floor of the rear compartment. Julian concluded that the secretary had received a blow on the head during the car's insane stampede across the field.

The pursuing car has stopped at the gap in the hedge and four men were clamouring through, three of them with revolvers in their hands, the fourth carrying the submachinegun. The man with the deadly 'typewriter' was Spider Marcovicz. Holding it to his shoulder, he directed a spray of lead at the derelict Rolls.

Julian knocked the professor's feet from under him and flung himself across the little man's body, remaining like that until the deadly fusillade had ceased. The car was between them and the machine gun but the bullets were coming through the metal coachwork as though it were made of cardboard. Raising his head, Julian peered round the radiator and saw that the four men had spread out and were advancing cautiously. Rolling clear of the professor, he aimed the revolver at one of them and pulled the trigger. His human target fell in a clumsy heap on the ground. There was nothing dramatic about the fall. Any movie extra could have done it better. Only a dead man could have done it so tamely.

The dead man's confederates, taking the warning, checked their advance. Another shower of machine gun bullets kicked up the earth on all sides of the Rolls.

"This is terrible," moaned the scientist. He raised his terrified face about an inch from the ground. It was coated thickly with mud. "Isn't there any way to stop them? If we held up a handkerchief as a white flag—"

"To the devil with white flags," hissed Julian. "You have bombs filled with your gas in that box on the back of the car, haven't you?"

"Y-yes, b-but—"

"Give me the key."

"N-no, c-certainly n-not. If you opened the box a bullet might s-strike inside and s-smash the b-bombs and t-that would mean c-certain d-death for b-both of us."

"That would be our hard luck," said Julian grimly. "This is war. Give me the key."

Wordlessly, the professor shook his head. Julian put the mouth of the revolver to the frightened little man's ear. It was cold and round and menacing.

"Give me the key—"

There was note of finality in his tone. Blinking with fear, the professor fumbled in a waistcoat pocket. After much groping he succeeded in producing a keyring, but his trembling fingers were unequal to the task of detaching the right key. Impatiently, Julian snapped the chain to which the ring was attached and crawled to the back of the car with the bunch of keys in his hand.

Before the attackers spotted him, he managed to insert the key in the lock. When they saw what he was doing the rat-at-at-at-at of the submachinegun started again. Flattening himself on the ground, Julian waited for it to cease. It could not go on for long. A new drum of ammunition would soon be required. The only question was whether the reporter would still be alive when the current drum was empty.

One bullet snatched the hat off his head, another scored a furrow along his elbow; his face was covered with gouts of earth thrown up by other bullets; that was all the damage he had suffered when the deadly stuttering ended at last. Looking up, he saw one of the men running back toward the gap in the hedge, presumably going for more ammunition.

Spider Marcovicz, hugging his machine gun, took cover behind the body of his dead confederate. The fourth man was crouching down, taking aim at Julian with his revolver. He took too long about it; he was still taking aim when a bullet from the reporter's weapon hit him in the shoulder, knocking him flat.

It was useless to shoot at Marcovicz, in the hope that a bullet would reach him through the corpse he was using as a shield. Julian did not know how many cartridges were left in the chauffeur's revolver; but there could not be more than four. He dared not waste one. Taking the chance that he was mistaken in thinking that the drum of the machine gun was empty, Julian stood up and turned the key in the lock of the iron box.

The machine gun remained silent, but Marcovicz began

sniping at Julian with a pistol. He was not a good shot. He obviously needed a weapon which could scatter hundreds of bullets a minute all-round the target at which he was aiming. With the pistol he failed to place a bullet within a foot of the reporter. Even so, Julian did not relish standing up to be fired at. Marcovicz might be lucky enough to fluke a bullseye.

Julian threw up the lid of the iron box. Inside lay a score of round objects like glass cricket balls, on beds of cotton wool. He dug one out.

The man who had run back to the gap in the hedge was now returning, carrying a drum of machine gun ammunition. Marcovicz jumped up and sprinted to meet him, with the machine gun under his arm. Julian sent the glass ball flying in a glittering arc through the air after the long, thin, racing figure. It shot past Marcovicz and broke under the feet of the man who was running with the drum of ammunition. He went on running for a split second, then fell flat on his face and lay still. He could not have had more than a whiff of the gas; but that had been sufficient.

"Deadly is the word for this stuff of yours, professor," said Julian in a tone of awe.

There was no answer. The professor had fainted.

Like a startled horse, Marcovicz shied away from the shattered glass. He ran in a circle round it, his feet travelling at incredible speed over the furrows. As far as he was concerned the battle was over.

Julian aimed his revolver at the fleeing man's back. By pulling the trigger he would be doing the world a service. Pull the trigger and that would be the end of Spider Marcovicz. A good riddance from every point of view except that of Spider himself.

And then Julian swore aloud. He could not do it. Something within him was repelled by the thought of planting a bullet in the back of a helpless adversary, no matter how thoroughly the adversary deserved to die. The man whom Julian had shot in the shoulder was now stumbling up and unsteadily followed his leader. Julian let them go. He called himself a yellow-livered fool, but he let them go. For the fun of seeing them run even faster he sent after them a bullet which he deliberately aimed high. They reached their car and went off in it without looking back.

Kneeling beside the professor, Julian propped up the white-faced little man in a sitting position. The professor looked lifeless, but his heart was still beating. In the heat of battle, he had swooned like any twittering spinster.

Pulling the car door open, Julian looked in at Sydney. Although the car was riddled with bullets the secretary had escaped injury beyond the initial blow on the head. His eyes were open but glassy, and his hands were groping feebly for something on which to take hold. He was muttering in a dazed voice. The reporter's eyes narrowed as he listened to that incoherent muttering.

Another car drew up at the gap in the hedge. It was the police

Bentley. There were only two men in it, Inspector Howells and another—and Howells had a trickle of blood running down his forehead. The inspector started climbing through the gap and Julian walked to meet him. The reporter recounted briefly what had happened to the Rolls and its occupants.

"Two of my men were killed by machine gun bullets," growled Howells savagely, "and another has a wound in the leg. I'll see Marcovicz hanged if it's the last thing I do."

"Perhaps now," said Julian bitterly, "the bigwigs will realise there's a war on."

They crossed the field to the battered Rolls-Royce and found Professor Lochhead fully conscious. He was sitting on the running board weeping hysterically. Julian bent down and slapped his face.

"Snap out of it," he said flatly. "This is no time for that. We've got to get on to the War Office test."

"The War Office test," whimpered the professor. "After what has happened? Are you mad?"

"I know you've been through the mill," said Julian, "but use your head—the thing to do is carry on. For today, Marcovicz is out of the picture. By tomorrow he may have gathered reinforcements. Let's take advantage of this breathing-space."

"Mendoza is right," agreed Inspector Howells. "We'd better carry on."

Without further parley, Julian helped up the frightened little man, wiped the mud off his face and half-carried him across the field. Inspector Howells followed, guiding the wavering footsteps of Sydney Lanham.

"Of what nationality is your secretary?" asked the reporter in a low tone.

"English," mumbled Professor Lochhead.

"You're sure of that?"

"Absolutely. Why?"

"I only wondered. When he was regaining consciousness, his first words were German."

"Nonsense," said the professor less weakly. "Rubbish! Sydney knows no German. You were mistaken."

"Perhaps. And again, perhaps not. How do you know he isn't German?"

"Sydney came to me with the best of recommendations. He is vouched for by the person whose opinion I value most highly."

"Who is that?"

"Young man," glared the professor, "there are limits to my forbearance. I deny your right to pry into my personal affairs."

"Have it your own way. But keep an eye on your secretary. Two eyes, for preference. By the way, where did you meet your wife?"

For a moment the professor was taken aback. "Young man," he said furiously, at last, "is nothing sacred to you?"

"Nothing," answered Julian complacently.

He seated the professor in the police car and returned to the Rolls. Inspector Howells joined him there. They relocked the iron box of gas bombs, carried it gingerly across the ploughed field, and securely strapped it to the carrier of the police car.

*

On a bleak stretch of moorland ten miles from everywhere, a wide space was fenced-in with barbed wire. At intervals of ten yards all around the enclosure, infantrymen with fixed bayonets stood on guard. Inside the enclosure, Professor Lochhead was greeted by the War Office technical experts and staff officers of high rank. They listened, in horrified bewilderment, to the professor's account of the adventure that had delayed him. In the background, Julian discreetly smothered a grin. To hear the professor tell it, the attack on them had been made by a force as large as any Great Britain had sent to France during the last Great War.

A flock of about a hundred sheep was browsing in the middle of the enclosure. These placid animals had been granted the honour of being the first to sample the professor's insecticide for humans. They had been chosen because they were diseased and would die soon, anyway. This seemed a quick and merciful way out for them. With four well-placed glass bombs, Professor Lochhead wiped out the entire flock. One moment they were cropping the grass contentedly; the next they were lying on their sides, very, very dead. It was as simple as that.

Staring at the still, woolly heaps, the technical experts and staff shook their heads in stunned amazement.

"This," said one of them, "is the greatest advance in chemical warfare in fifty years."

"A bomb filled with the gas and dropped from an aeroplane," said an officer delightedly, "could wipe out an entire regiment."

"If my figures are correct," Professor Lochhead beamed modestly, "less than a ton and a half would suffice to depopulate a small town."

"Amazing!"

"Terrific!"

"Incredible!"

"Darned awful!" added Julian—but he said it to himself.

Out of the corner of his eye he saw a man in the uniform of a staff officer detaching himself from the group and walking at unhurried pace towards the entrance to the enclosure. The others were too engrossed in their discussion of the gas to note this discreet withdrawal. Frowning, Julian followed at a distance.

At the entrance, the guard saluted stiffly and stood aside to let the man in uniform pass through. Julian started to follow, but the sentry blocked his way.

"No one is allowed out, sir, without authority from the general."

"I'm with him," said Julian easily, pointing to the back of the man in staff officer's uniform.

The sentry hesitated. With an air of smiling assurance, Julian walked past him. The man he was following was getting into a car parked in a long line of official vehicles. Julian reached it just as it was backing out.

"Half a minute," he said quietly.

The man stared up at him. "What do you want?" It was the curt tone of one accustomed to command.

"I happened to notice you pinching a glass bomb from the box," said the reporter calmly.

Swiftly the other man's hand dropped to the holster at his side.

Julian's hand had less far to travel. For some minutes, it had been wrapped round the revolver in his pocket. He knew it was either him or the other. He drew it and shot the man in the head.

Half a minute later Julian was backed up against the side of the car with an infantryman's bayonet almost prodding his stomach. Other guards came up at a run and formed a fence of naked steel about him. The staff officers and technical experts came pouring out of the enclosure. In level tones, Julian explained what he had seen and why it had been necessary for him to shoot the man who was slumped in the car.

"One of your staff, Brigadier," snapped a grey-haired man in the uniform of a field-marshal.

"But, Lord North, I thought he was with you. He came from Aldershot with your party."

"That is right," put in a major of the Guards. "He was in my car. I didn't know the fellow, but I'd seen him talking to Colonel Armstrong and presumed it was alright."

"He asked me some question or other," said the bewildered colonel. "I forget exactly what. I thought—"

"The fellow must be a foreign spy in disguise."

"There'll be the devil to pay over this," said another officer gloomily. "Dashed good job he didn't get away."

They searched the dead man. They searched the car. With extreme thoroughness, they searched the road to right and left and the cars parked on either side. They searched the enclosure and the open moor across the road. But the missing bomb was not found.

Julian aided the search. For some reason—perhaps because he was vouched for by Inspector Howells—they failed to search him.

It was as well. Otherwise, he would probably have faced a firing-squad one morning.

The Professor is Kidnapped

Several days later, in spite of the success of the test, the formula was still in the custody of the professor. It was a question of money. For this secret, worth millions, the War Office had offered five thousand pounds. Professor Lochhead was holding out for thirty thousand.

While War Office and the professor haggled like old clothes-dealers, matching stubbornness with obstinacy, Inspector Howells had his hands full guarding the paper on which depended the lives of half the youth of Europe.

The police dragnet had failed to entangle Marcovicz in its meshes. Nothing had been heard of that arch-scoundrel since the day of the test, which made Inspector Howells doubly uneasy. The Spider would strike again; of that he was certain.

Howells still yearned to surround Professor Lochhead's house with barbed-wire and machine gun emplacements, but that was out of the question, so he took the second-best course of keeping score of C.I.D. men constantly on duty in Elviston Square and its environs. In every conceivable disguise they patrolled the neighbourhood. Much to their disgust, the professor's neighbours were submitted to the more-or-less melodious noise-making of more itinerant musicians than ever before. Three detectives in caps and overalls went through the motions of working on the roof of an empty house; another drew crayon pictures of fish and Mr. Chamberlain on the pavement; another rounded the square at frequent intervals on a Stop-Me-and-Buy-One tricycle; and yet another pretended to hawk flowers from a barrow. Detectives in morning-clothes and top hats strolled slowly round the square, ducked into a building in the next street, and came back again in raincoats and bowlers. At all times of the night and day cars of assorted makes with several burly men in them came through at little more than walking speed.

Julian Mendoza had his own spy in Elviston Square; a reporter who had taken a room in a house facing that of Professor Lochhead and who spent most of his time with field-glasses at a window. Late one night this man put through a call to Julian at the *Morning World* office.

"You'd better get over here fast. There's something up at the professor's house."

Julian was there as soon as a taxi could take him. A policeman was stationed on the steps of the house, keeping unauthorised persons out; but he let the reporter in. Julian had been too close to the heart of things all along for it to be worthwhile to bar him now. In the library, he found Inspector Howells, Sydney Lanham, the professor's wife, and two plainclothes men. They all looked worried.

"What's happened?" Julian demanded.

"We think the professor's been kidnapped," said Inspector Howells curtly.

To one of the plain-clothes men, he added: "Go on with your story."

The man cleared his throat. "Well, as I said, about eight we saw this lady and gentleman go off in evening clothes in a taxi."

"We went to the theatre," said Sydney.

"About an hour later," continued the plainclothes man, "a little blue car drove up and a man and a woman got out. It was too dark to see their faces, besides, they both wore tweed coats with the collars turned up. The woman opened the door with a key—that looked as if it must be alright—and they went in. A few minutes later, they came out again with Professor Lochhead. I thought it was alright. Anyone could see with half an eye that he was going willingly."

"You fool," hissed the professor's wife. "The man and woman were Sybil Lochhead and her friend. He would never have gone with them willingly. They must have compelled him to do so."

"What makes you think it was Sybil?" asked Julian.

"'A little blue car'," repeated the professor's wife. "That sounds like Sybil's car. And the woman let them into the house with a key; Sybil has a key. She's been after the formula all along. Besides, I found this in my husband's study"—she held out her hand, palm up, and showed them a small silver brooch—"it belongs to Sybil."

"Looks conclusive to me," murmured Howells, rubbing his chin.

"When was the alarm given?" asked Julian.

"Mrs. Lochhead and I returned from the theatre about half-past eleven," said Sydney. "We found that the professor was not in the house. The servants knew nothing; they had been in their own quarters at the rear. When this policeman told me what had happened, I telephoned to Scotland Yard at once. I knew the professor would not have gone out willingly with his daughter."

"You're so sure it was his daughter," objected Julian.

"Of course, it was his daughter," snapped Howells. "That's obvious, Mendoza. Weren't you a witness to her first attempt to steal the formula?"

Julian drew the inspector aside. "Don't go off half-cocked," he said, in a low tone. "This looks like a frame-up to me."

"What do you mean?"

"These two could have set out for the theatre, changed their clothes somewhere, and come back in the little blue car."

"Why on earth should they?"

"Ever noticed the way Sydney speaks?"

"He speaks perfect English. Better than yours or mine."

"Exactly. His speech is meticulous. Never a word of slang."

"Well?"

"Englishmen don't speak their own language so perfectly," said Julian. "But a well-taught foreigner does."

"You're letting your imagination run away with you, Mendoza."

"The other day, when he was coming round from a knock on the head, his first words were German."

"Or so you thought," grunted Howells. "Do you suppose I haven't made inquiries about the man? The professor assured me that Sydney Lanham came to him with excellent recommendations."

"If I am not mistaken, it was the professor's wife who recommended him so highly."

"Well, what if it was?"

"How do you know she's on the level? I've made inquiries, too. The professor met her in Switzerland. Maybe she also was German travelling with a forged English passport."

"And maybe I'm a Martian," retorted Howells. "The trouble with you, Mendoza, is that you've fallen for this Lochhead girl and you're trying hard to cover up for her. Probably you'd like her to get her hands on the formula and destroy it. Maybe I don't blame you for that—but I have my duty to do. Sybil and her boyfriend are the ones who kidnapped the professor—and I'll have them in custody before the night's out or my name isn't Howells."

"As far as I'm concerned," replied Julian sourly, "your name is mud."

Inspector Howells strode to the telephone and dialled Whitehall 1212. Connected with Scotland Yard, he gave orders for a citywide hunt for Sybil Lochhead and Billy Menzies. Shrugging his shoulders, Julian went out of the house and across the street to his colleague's rented room. There he telephoned a number

Sybil Lochhead had once given him. In a few moments the call was answered by Sybil Lochhead herself.

"Your father's been kidnapped," said Julian without preliminary. "Know anything about it?"

A gasp came to him over the wire. "No, I don't."

"I didn't think you would. Where's your car?"

"At the garage where I always leave it, I suppose."

"Where's that?"

"Round the corner from Elviston Square."

"Does your stepmother know where you keep it?"

"Certainly. She used to use it sometimes."

"If I'm not mistaken," said Julian, "she still does."

"Do you think my father's in danger?" asked Sybil, with a tremor in her voice.

"Never mind that now. Leave your flat at once. The cops will be there to arrest you any minute. Know where Menzies is?"

"Yes, he's with me."

"Has he a car?"

"Yes, it's parked outside."

"Alright, get into it and beat it as fast as you can. Know Mott's Garage in Drury Lane? Well, drive in there and wait for me. Don't get out of the car. Sit in it and wait."

"But— About my father—"

"No questions. Do as I say."

Julian hung up. He went to the window, lit his pipe and sat down. In a little while he saw Inspector Howells come out of No. 29, followed by his subordinates. They climbed into a police car and drove off. Julian made no move.

Soon afterwards, Sydney Lanham came out of the house and walked along the pavement. He disappeared out of sight round a corner. Julian sat calmly smoking. In a few minutes, a coupé came into the square with Sydney Lanham at the steering wheel. It stopped in front of No. 29. The professor's wife came down the steps and entered the car, which drove away again.

Julian rose and went out. He hailed a taxi. "Mott's Garage in Drury Lane," he said.

He had an idea that, even if a car had been handy, following the coupé, it would have done no good. If his suspicions were correct Sydney and the woman with him would be on the alert for pursuit. There might be another way to find out where they were going; if there wasn't, it would be just too bad for the professor and his daughter.

As the coupé sped through the outer suburbs, the professor's wife kept looking back.

"At least," she said, in German, "no one is following."

"Why should we be followed?" said Sydney Lanham, in the same language.

"That reporter. I am sure he suspects."

"What does the reporter matter? It is the police who count. They, poor fools, suspect nothing."

They were silent for a while and then the man said: "What can the old devil have done with the formula?"

"He must have chewed it up as he claims. You saw him spit out the pulp."

"Yes, we both saw that. A pity you did not keep a closer watch on him, as I told you. But he'd never destroy it unless he had another copy."

"There was no other copy in the safe."

"True. But there must be one. He must have it on him."

"We made him strip. We examined his clothes."

"I know. Nevertheless, he must have a copy. We must give him another dose of that charming little torture you devised for him."

The woman uttered a laugh devoid of mirth. "This time," she said viciously, "we will work on him until we have the formula."

"I leave it you, Liebchen," said Sydney, smiling. His smile became a frown. "It is a pity his suspicions were aroused so soon. When he left the house with us so willingly, I thought it was going to be very easy."

"He thought we were taking him for a short run," said the woman. "He got the wind up when you wouldn't stop. That must have been when he started chewing the paper."

After a little over an hour of fast driving, the coupé passed through a slumbering hamlet, continued for about a mile up a narrow, rutted lane, and swung in through the open gates of a dark house that stood by itself in large and neglected grounds.

Sydney parked the car at the side of the house, and they walked to the front. Producing a key, Sydney unlocked the door and they went in. He turned on a light. Then he swore.

The professor was where they had left him; gagged and roped to a chair in the middle of the lounge-hall. But when they left him, he had been the solitary occupant of the dark house, and now he was not alone. Several grim-eyed men were standing round the room with their backs to the walls and revolvers in their hands. In a chair near the professor sat a man in a long black coat and a black hat drawn low on his forehead. Across his knee he nursed a submachinegun.

"Come in, Herr and Frau von Lanheim," said Spider Marcovicz. "Come in—and shut the door."

For a moment the man and woman who had walked into the trap were too paralysed with shock and horror to respond. A crooked and evil smile creased the Spider's lean dark features.

"My government has been able to give me a lot of information," he said. "For instance, Herr von Lanheim, it informs me that you allowed your wife to 'marry' the professor in the hope that she'd get her hands on the formula. She got you in as the professor's assistant for the same purpose. I told you to shut the door, Herr von Lanheim. Don't make me tell you again."

Sydney von Lanheim made haste to obey.

"If you have a gun," went on Spider Marcovicz, in a cold, dead tone, "take it out and drop it on the floor. Do not be rash enough to try any tricks."

Von Lanheim put a hand in his pocket, gingerly drew out an automatic and let it fall to the bare boards.

"That's right," said Spider Marcovicz. "Don't look so surprised. How I knew about this place is not really a mystery. My government again, Herr von Lanheim. Its agents watched you and found out about this house. I am obliged to you for bringing the professor here. I could not get at him myself while Elviston Square was so full of the police. He tells me you coaxed him to give you the combination of his safe. Did you get the formula?"

"It was not there," replied Sydney von Lanheim stiffly.

"You're sure of that?"

"If we had found the formula, would we have returned here?"

"No, I suppose not," said Spider Marcovicz. "So, now we will have to find a way to make him tell where the formula really is. That should not take long—"

*

Julian walked into Mott's Garage, looking to right and left for a car with two people in it. When he found it, he opened the rear door and climbed in. Sybil Lochhead turned from the steering wheel to look at him.

"Any news of my father?"

"None," he said. "But let's skip that pro tem. You told me the other night that you knew more about your stepmother than she imagined. You don't happen to have any idea where she'd have taken your father, if it were she who kidnapped him?"

"The Old Dark House," said Billy Menzies, who was sitting beside Sybil.

"Where's that?"

"Billy means a house about fifty miles out of London," replied Sybil. "We followed Sydney and my stepmother to it one day. You see, I had an idea they meant more to each other than they let on. I thought they were making a fool of father and I wanted to dig up evidence so that he could divorce her. So, we followed them when they went off alone to this house in the country. I didn't tell father about it, though. When I thought it over I realise that it might break his heart."

"Let's go," said Julian.

The car backed slowly out of the garage, and Billy Menzies flipped a coin through the open window to an attendant. Little was said as they raced through the crisp night air. After abut fifty minutes of furious driving, Sybil stopped the car at the side of the road and turned out the lights.

"The house is a hundred yards farther on. I don't know if you want me to drive up to it?"

"No," said Julian, getting out, "this will do. Wait here for me."

"Nothing doing," said Sybil. "We're coming with you. After all, it's my father we're looking for."

"Don't be a chump," snapped Julian. "We can't go marching up in a body. Wait here while I reconnoitre. I'll let you know what I find."

With that he was gone.

In awkward silence Billy Menzies took out his cigarette-case and offered it to Sybil. She shook her head. The young man lit one for himself.

"He thinks he's always right," said Sybil angrily. "The way his mind works, no one but him knows anything."

"Quite," said Billy uncomfortably.

He took three puffs at the cigarette and threw it away. In a few moments, Sybil opened the car door.

"I shouldn't if I were you," said Billy Menzies uneasily.

"Maybe you wouldn't," retorted Sybil, getting out.

With a sigh, Billy climbed out at the other side. In heavy silence they walked down the rutted lane to the open gates.

"Let's wait here," said Billy.

"If you're afraid—"

"I'm not afraid."

To do him justice the large youth did not know the meaning of fear. "I don't want to put my foot in it, that's all."

Just then they heard a shrill cry of pain from the house.

Without waiting for anything further, Sybil dashed up the path with the young man at her heels. She tried the handle of the door. It opened and they stumbled in.

Something hard—the butt of a revolver—hit Billy on the head and he dropped in his tracks. The nose of another revolver dug into Sybil's stomach, and a cold, unemotional voice told her not to move.

When Billy came to, he found himself lying propped-up against a wall. Sybil and the Von Lanheims were ranged beside him with their hands in the air. Several men with wary eyes and guns in their hands stood guard over them.

On a table in the middle of the room lay the professor. His gag and bonds had been removed.

"The big fellow has regained consciousness," said a voice.

"Make him stand up with the others," said a man—it was Spider Marcovitcz—who was bent over the professor.

A toe thudded into Billy's ribs and a voice said: "Get up!"

The young man rose slowly, clenching his fists and readying himself to spring.

"Don't, Billy!" cried Sybil. "It wouldn't do any good. They're all armed. They'd kill you."

Billy Menzies scowled—but relaxed.

"Maybe we'll kill him anyway," said Spider Marcovicz chillingly, "if the professor doesn't find his tongue."

The arch-crook raised a hand and struck the professor in the face.

"Talk," he rasped. "Tell me what you did with the formula."

Wordlessly, the professor shook his head.

"If you don't talk," snarled Marcovicz, "Igor will give you another taste of what you had a minute ago."

The professor quivered, but he still shook his head.

"You can kill me," he quavered between puffed and bleeding lips; "I'll tell you nothing."

"I'll kill you, alright," said Spider Marcovicz, his eyes glistening. "Make no mistake. I'll kill you. Perhaps you think I wouldn't. Perhaps you think I don't like killing in cold blood. Look at this."

He lifted the sub-machine gun and aimed it at the wall where his prisoners stood. He pulled the trigger and the gun jumped in his hands like a live thing. When the devilish clatter was over, Sydney von Lanheim lay twisted on the floor with enough bullets in his body to wipe out a platoon. With an inarticulate cry, the woman who, bigamously, had married the professor knelt beside him.

"That's one of them," said the Spider. "Unless you talk, I'll knock off the others." He meant it.

Professor Lochhead looked like a trapped rabbit.

Spider Marcovicz turned the deadly weapon on Sybil. "Your daughter next," he said.

A voice behind him said quietly: "Drop that gun, Marcovicz—or I'll wipe you out like the rat you are."

The arch-crook wheeled in his tracks.

On the stairs leading from the upper part of the house to the lounge-hall stood Julian Mendoza. Something round and shining was held aloft in his hand.

"One of the professor's gas bombs," he said grimly. "I pinched it on the day of the War Office demonstration. Drop that gun or I'll throw the bomb down. I don't need to tell you what will happen then."

There was a look of indecision on the dark, sneering face of Spider Marcovicz. He stood staring at Julian, the submachine-gun poised in his hands. He need only pull the trigger and the reporter would be riddled like a sieve.

On the other hand, there was the glass bomb. Marcovicz had seen what one of those could do.

In that moment of uncertainty, Julian threw what was in his hand at the feet of the killer. There was a loud pop. The Spider looked down in horror at the shattered glass and his face went green.

At the same moment, Julian launched himself from the stairs. He landed on the bent neck of Spider Marcovicz. There was a crack, and they went down together in a tangled heap. The sub-machine gun skittered across the floor.

His arms flailing, Julian struggled up and made another dive, this time for the sub-machine gun. A bullet from one of the other crooks chipped the floor beside him as he grasped it. Shouldering the gun, Julian pulled the trigger. The man who had fired dropped soundlessly before he could fire again. The rest of the arch-crook's accomplices threw down their weapons and raised their hands.

Julian glanced at the man at his feet. There was no need for him to look twice. The neck of Spider Marcovicz had snapped like a twig when the reporter's weight had landed on it.

Professor Lochhead was staring at the rounded fragments of glass on the floor. "I—I don't understand. You dropped the bomb—and nothing happened. We ought all to have been killed. I don't understand."

"I took the bomb that was missing the other day, alright," said Julian. "I'm darned if I know why I took it, and afterwards I didn't know what to do with it. It made me nervous, so I dropped it in the river. The 'bomb' with which I threatened Spider Marcovicz was an electric light bulb."

*

Later, the professor lay wanly in bed in a room in his house in which a fire was burning brightly. Two doctors had examined him and given the opinion that, although he was suffering from shock and bruises, he would recover in a few days, given rest and quiet. Inspector Howells and Julian were in the room, waiting to hear what had happened to the formula.

"In the car with Sydney and—and the woman I thought was my wife, I became suspicious," said the professor weakly. "I had the formula with me, so I slipped it into my mouth when they were not looking and chewed it to pulp."

"So that's the end of that," said Inspector Howells. He was not sorry.

"On the contrary," said the professor, with an air of pride in spite of his shaky condition, "before I destroyed the paper, I made some marks in pencil on the inside of the starched cuff of my shirt. Only a few scribbled symbols—but with their aid I shall be able to rework the formula. But for that, it would be lost forever."

With a studiously casual air, Julian sauntered across the room. He glanced round swiftly to make sure that no one was looking, and then, whipping out a knife, performed an operation on the professor's shirt which was lying on the back of a chair.

A few moments later Inspector Howells examined the shirt and found the cuff was missing. In the fire there was something square and black that looked suspiciously like charred linen.

The inspector looked hard at Julian, who returned his stare

calmly. Leaning forward, Julian kicked at the fire with the toe of his shoe and the charred fragment broke into tiny pieces.

"There'll be devil to pay over this," said Howells, with a backward glance at the professor, who was lying peacefully on the pillows, oblivious to what had happened.

"The devil to pay over what?" asked Julian innocently. "Have I done something? Can you prove it?"

"No," said Howells. "I can't prove it."

And no one else ever did.

But that was one 'passport' that was no longer a menace to the youth of the world.

THE END

PARTNERS IN CRIME

Mr. Benjamin Graves, senior partner of a long established and painfully respectable firm of solicitors, coughed dryly and glanced over the rims of his pince-nez at his distinguished clients. "I thought perhaps South Africa—"

"Australia's farther," muttered Bertie.

"The farther the better," declared Celia feelingly.

That seemed to be the general opinion.

"Then perhaps it had better be Australia," purred the lawyer.

"And of course," said Bertie viciously, "he must promise never to return."

"Of course," agreed Celia fervently.

"Of course," echoed Lord Eustace.

"Most decidedly," assented the Duke of Beaminster.

Mr. Benjamin Graves nodded solemnly.

The family had met at the Duke of Beaminster's magnificent country house to discuss the scandalous behaviour of the Duke's younger brother, Lord Charles Deignton.

Celia was not really one of the family. She was one of the Radley twins—the pretty one—but she was going to marry Bertie in a month or so and was, therefore, an honorary member of the family.

Bertie was the Marquis of Leasing, the Duke of Beaminster's only son. The behaviour of Lord Charles was so disgraceful that even Lord Eustace Deignton, the Duke's venerable uncle, was present, having dragged himself away from the cosy chair in the reading-room of his London club in which he habitually slept between meals. "Australia," he mumbled drowsily, "the very ticket!"

The door opened and Anne Radley came into the room. At a distance the resemblance between Anne and her twin was striking. They had the similar copper-coloured hair and almost identical figures; but when she came nearer the likeness was less pronounced. Anne's nose was inclined to be snub, while Celia's was pure patrician; Anne's mouth was—shall we say? —less like a rosebud than Celia's; Anne's eyes were thoughtful of expression, while Celia's had a babyish stare which Celia's many admirers found devastating. Perhaps there was rather more character in Anne's face than in that of her twin, but young men found the flower-like beauty of Celia infinitely more attractive.

Ignoring her sister's frown, Anne came forward to the large table about which the family council was grouped.

"I wondered where you'd all got to," she said pleasantly. "You look very solemn—as though you were judges about to sentence someone to death."

The others coughed and looked at one another, but no one spoke. Anne looked at the array of pink slips that were spread upon the table.

"What a pile of cheques!" she picked up one—again deliberately ignoring her sister's frown. "'Pay to the order of Curtis and Lewin, the sum of one hundred and eighty-five pounds,' signed 'Charles Deignton.'"

She glanced at another. "'The Ritz, seventy-five pounds.' Again signed 'Charles Deignton.' And another for three hundred!"

She smiled sweetly at her sister. "Celia, why are you kicking my ankle?"

With a slim finger she touched each of the cheques in turn.

"Fifteen of 'em! Charles has been busy! Why is he paying all his debts? Don't tell me he's going to be married!"

The solicitor placed his fingertips together and gazed discreetly out of the window. Bertie scowled and glanced anxiously at his fiancée.

"It's none of your business, Anne," said Celia icily, "but since you've pushed your way in here, I suppose you'd better be told. Charles has been giving cheques to heaps of people and he hasn't a penny in the bank. The Duke has had to settle them to keep the affair out of court."

"I see." Anne eyes the others thoughtfully, making them feel distinctly uncomfortable. "So, Charles is the condemned man. That's why he's coming here this morning, I suppose.

"You're planning to ship him away to some distant spot where he can't disgrace his sorrowing family. You will charitably allow him a tiny income. Just enough to live on—but not enough to allow him ever to save up the money for his passage home!"

His Grace said something not quite under his breath. Lord Eustace became raptly absorbed in the lighting of a fresh cigar. Bertie and his fiancée glared wrathfully at Anne.

The lawyer coughed dryly. "It is best for all concerned," he murmured, "that Lord Charles should be afforded—er—the opportunity to start life afresh in another country."

"And supposing he won't go?"

"He will if I ask him to," replied Celia loftily.

"Because he's always been in love with you?" said Anne coldly. "Don't you think it's hitting below the belt to take advantage of his affections for you, when you've decided to throw him over for Bertie?"

"Anne!" exclaimed Celia indignantly.

"Oh, I am not blaming you," said Anne coldly. "After all, Charles is a younger son, with no prospects and less than no money. Bertie is a much more suitable match for you, darling. Heir to the title and the estates and passably well off in his own right."

She looked appraisingly at Bertie. "But give me Charles. At least Charles has a chin—and a spine!"

Leaving them all gasping, she walked to the French windows that led to the garden. Celia had an unpleasant suspicion—she knew her sister of old.

"Anne!" she snapped. "Don't interfere!"

"Darling, do I ever interfere?"

"Do you ever do anything else?"

With a gay laugh and a mocking wave of her hand, Anne disappeared into the garden. Celia looked apologetically at the others.

"I'm awfully sorry. She's always been like that."

"Darling," said Bertie, soothingly, "we understand."

The solicitor coughed again. "A very—er—modern young woman," he pronounced.

*

Lord Charles Deignton drove his modest two-seater through the gates and up the drive of his elder brother's country house. Lord Charles was handsome young man, with a large Grecian nose, a cleft chin, smooth plump cheeks and blue eyes that were cheerful and friendly. He was bareheaded and his brown hair had a crisp wave; he was smiling to himself, revealing two rows of even white teeth.

Halfway between the gates and the house he saw the gleam of a white dress through the trees that flanked the drive. He stopped the car, climbed out, and ran noiselessly across the velvet turf to the slim girl with hair like burnished copper who was sitting on the grass with her back towards him. He was only a few paces away when she turned her head and he saw that it was Anne, not Celia.

"Oh!" he said awkwardly.

"Yes, it's the plain Radley twin," said Anne, with a smile. "Sorry, Charles. I suppose you thought it was Celia and your heart leaped with tender affection. You're rather fond of Celia, aren't you?"

"Frightfully. I—I want to marry her. Only, at the moment, I'm in rather a mess."

"I know. Those cheques. But even if you hadn't been a bad boy, Charles, I'm afraid you'd still have been doomed to disappointment. Celia's going to marry Bertie."

"Is she?" said Lord Charles gloomily.

"Yes, that's why I'm here. They didn't want me, and Celia had to have a chaperon—Lord knows why—and there was no one else. She's just sent off the announcement to the papers."

"Has she?"

"She has. Charles, she's gone over to the enemy. She's one of the judges who're going to try you for not having any money in the bank. It's going to be a life sentence. They're going to shoo you off to Australia or somewhere. Celia will kiss you goodbye—if you go quietly like a good little boy!"

Lord Charles' good-natured chin became suddenly very formidable.

"And supposing I won't be shooed?"

Anne jumped up with sparkling eyes and clapped her hands together.

"Charles, promise you won't let them chase you away!"

"Then you don't want me to go? Everybody else does. Why don't you?"

"Because I rather like you, Charles."

"That's rather nice of you, Anne."

She looked at him soberly. "Isn't there anything you can do for a living in this country?"

"Well," said Lord Charles doubtfully, "I'm not bad with cars. If I could lay my hand on five thousand pounds George Carmichael would take me in as a partner in his motor business. But what's the use of talking?—I can't raise five thousand farthings!"

"George Carmichael's a decent sort," said Anne thoughtfully. "He wouldn't sell you a pup."

"Not he! If I got in with him, I'd be in clover!"

"Perhaps the family will give you the money. I believe they would—if they were approached properly."

"Anne, you don't know the family."

Lord Charles looked at the plain Radley girl as though he were seeing her for the first time.

"I say, Anne—"

"Yes?" said Anne quietly.

Lord Charles smiled ruefully. "Oh, nothing. I'd better be trotting up to the slaughter like a good little lamb. See you later."

As he strode across the lawn towards the house, Anne Radley looked after his straight, square-shouldered figure with a certain mistiness in her eyes.

A truly penitent young man would have entered the house by the front door and come into the library with bowed head and tear-dimmed eyes. Lord Charles did neither. He came into the august presence of his assembled family through the French windows, with a wide cheerful grin on his pleasant features.

"Lovely day!" he said brightly.

This conversational effort was received in stony silence. Accusing eyes met his gaze wherever it wandered—even when he looked hopefully at Celia. He turned and glanced out of the window at the sun shining on the cool, green lawn, at the splashes of colour made by the trim flower beds, at the dappled shadows cast by the trees.

"Yes, isn't it glorious?" he answered himself.

The lawyer coughed deprecatingly and adjusted his pince-nez.

"Nasty cough you've got," said Lord Charles sympathetically. "I should take something for it if I were you."

The Duke of Beaminster leaned forward in his high chair and gazed sternly at his brother.

"Charles, this flippancy is out of place. This is an occasion of extreme gravity. We have here a number of your cheques—your worthless cheques—to the amount of—er—"

"Three thousand, eight hundred and forty-three pounds, eight shillings and seven pence," supplied the solicitor in a low whisper.

"Yes, three thousand, eight hundred and forty-three pounds, eight shillings and seven pence," repeated his Grace grimly.

"The amount," said Lord Charles, blithely, "is correct."

"To a penny," he added.

His Grace frowned.

"Your attitude, Charles, is in the worst of possible taste. I had scarcely hoped that you would have the decency to repent of your shameful—and dishonest—conduct, but I certainly expected that you would be—er—impressed and—er—subdued by the seriousness of your position. You are bound to realise that, but for my action in making good these cheques, the consequences would have been grave indeed. You would have been taken to court and a ghastly public scandal would have resulted. What on earth possessed you to write cheques when you hadn't the money at the bank to meet them?"

Lord Charles drew a chair forward, hitched up his exquisitely cut trousers, and sat down.

"The beggars were pressing me. At all hours of the day and night they were ringing me up and writing me letters saying: 'Please let us have a cheque at once.' Dash it all, I couldn't walk a hundred yards anywhere in the West End without some blighter popping up with an unpaid bill in his hand and demanding a cheque! I had no money and you refused to foot the bills, so it was all a rather disgusting mess. At least I could bear it no longer. An unpleasant little blighter collared me at the door of my flat and pushed a slip of paper under my nose. 'What about a cheque, my lord?' he snapped. I looked at him with a certain hauteur. 'You want a cheque?' I said coldly. 'That's it,' he replied. 'What about it?' 'You want a cheque,' I said with dignity. 'Very well, then, you shall have a cheque!' I wrote him one on the spot and he nearly fell over with surprise. After that, whenever a johnny wanted a cheque, I simply gave it to him. You've no idea the amount of unpleasantness it avoided!"

"But your cheques were no good!" roared Lord Eustace suddenly.

"I know it," agreed Lord Charles wearily. "But you should have seen how pleased they all were to receive them. Who could have had the heart to resist bestowing so much happiness with so little trouble? It was most touching."

"Idiot!" muttered Bertie savagely.

Lord Charles turned hard, glittering eyes upon him, and he shrank back.

"Not from you, my dear Bertie," hissed Lord Charles. "I must accept a certain amount of reproach from your father, but if my inky little nephew ventures to call me any names I will break every bone in his miserable body."

He turned with a suave smile to the Duke. "We were saying, my dear Beaminster?"

His brother made an impatient gesture. "This is absurd," he growled. "We summon you here to explain your outrageous conduct and you actually behave as though we were in the wrong!"

"I am almost inclined to think you are, my dear fellow," said Lord Charles reflectively. "The family reared me to exist with a certain decorative beauty but absolutely no utility. I was sent to Eton and Cambridge, supplied with a lavish allowance, and led to believe that there was plenty more where it came from. From early childhood I was taught that it would never be necessary for me to earn a living. Then Father died. He made no provision for me in his will, but on his deathbed, he asked you to continue my allowance as long as I lived. Six months after he died your solicitors notified me that you did not intend to continue the allowance. You were prepared to pay me a small quarterly sum—about enough to pay for my cigarettes—"

"Income tax…" muttered his Grace defensively, "the upkeep of the estate…"

"Income tax and the upkeep of the estate leave you about twenty thousand a year pocket money," retorted Lord Charles dryly.

"I secured you a comfortable berth in the City."

"Precisely. A job as a glorified office boy with a nasty little financier who practically expected me to lick stamps and address envelopes except when he wanted my presence in his private office to impress reluctant clients, so that they would leave their hard-earned savings in his slimy clutches. I had just sufficient conscience to punch his greasy nose and throw up the job."

The others looked at one another in despair.

"This is all beside the point," growled the Duke. "The point is that we are prepared to allow you a certain—er—adequate income on condition that you leave at once for Australia."

Lord Charles looked at Celia, who smiled wistfully—and a mite hopefully.

"Excuse me a minute," he said.

Before any of them could protest he strode across the room and vanished into the garden.

He found Anne where he had left her.

"I say," he asked, "would you care to live in Australia?"

"I'd loathe it," she replied with feeling.

Lord Charles came in at the window again, disturbing the family in the act of telling one another what an unprincipled blackguard he was.

"Wipe Australia off the slate," he said nonchalantly.

"If you don't go," said his brother sternly, "we wash our hands of you."

Lord Charles shrugged his shoulders and lit a cigarette with perfect sang-froid.

"No one will allow you credit," observed Lord Eustace sharply, "and then how will you live?"

"Oh, there are ways of making money." Lord Charles eyed his uncle shrewdly. "There are plenty of homely girls with large fortunes. I might make love to one of them and marry her. That's quite a genteel way, they tell me, of obtaining money under false pretences."

Lord Eustace turned a deep purple in complexion. His own wife—a painfully plain woman—had brought him a respectable fortune—and had lived to see him dissipate it on a succession of hungry chorus-girls.

"Or," said Lord Charles softly, "I might rent my name to financial sharks to attract suckers—there's money in that."

The Duke of Beaminster grunted angrily—although he knew nothing whatever about business or finance, he had for a period of seven years enjoyed an income of twelve thousand pounds as chairman of a number of companies which had all in the end been involved in a monumental bankruptcy which had ruined thousands of small investors whose savings had been attracted by his name on the list of directors.

"…I might even go in for pulling racehorses. That's a paying spec. Eh, Bertie?"

The Marquis of Lessing exhibited grave symptoms of being about to choke, but wisely refrained from uttering the angry rejoinder that rose to his lips.

"I don't suppose I could earn three pounds a week honestly," continued Lord Charles blandly. "But dishonestly—that's a different matter! And why not? The best people do it. I could mention the names of dozens."

"Good idea, Charles! Couldn't you use a partner in crime?"

Five pairs of eyes were turned to the French windows, where Anne stood against a background of brilliant sunshine which made he hair gleam like a new penny and touched with golden fingers her soft, rounded cheeks. She advanced into the room.

"I believe we'd do well together, Charles," she said. "We could go in for blackmail. I've always thought I had a flair in that direction!"

"With diamond robbery as a side-line," suggested Lord Charles enthusiastically.

"Of course. And—can you climb, Charles?"

"Like a monkey!"

"Splendid! We'll be cat burglars. I'll stand on the ground and catch the things as you throw them down to me."

Celia's cold voice cut the air like the lash of a whip. "What nonsense! Do you expect us to believe that you and Charles are going to marry and—"

"Oh, we shan't marry," said Anne quickly. "That would be a rotten advertisement. To live in sin will be much more intriguing. People will point us out to their friends and whisper: 'My dear, do you see that sinister couple over there by the palms? That's Anne Ridley, the Marchioness of Lessing's twin sister, and Lord Charles Deignton, the Duke of Beaminster's younger brother. They live together and they aren't married!' and the friends will be shocked and murmur: 'My dear, how awful!' and they'll all flock to meet us. Then we'll play cards with them and swindle them for hundreds!"

"Don't be absurd, Anne," snapped Celia. "You know you've no head for cards."

"I shan't need it. We'll play with marked cards and have a regular code of signals."

Anne looked calmly at the four incredulous faces that were grouped about the table.

"We'll probably be sent to prison once or twice just at first until we learn the ropes," she said thoughtfully, "but I hear a term at Dartmoor is essential if one is going to make a success of the profession. A sort of finishing school for promising young criminals."

"Very amusing, my dear young lady," murmured the lawyer dryly. "But I am afraid this is hardly the time for jesting."

"If you think we're joking, try us," snapped Anne belligerently. "We mean it—every word—don't we Charles?"

Lord Charles linked his arm in hers.

"Cross my heart and hope to die," he said fervently. "We'll have a shot at Aunt Agatha's pearls for a start. I've always thought the old girl was criminally careless with them."

It was impossible for those who heard them to doubt that they were in deadly earnest. Four pairs of eyes bulged at the two smiling but determined young faces.

"Bertie! What shall we do?" cried Celia suddenly. "She means it! I know she does! You don't know how far she'll go when she's trying to be awkward!"

"Oh, blazes!" squeaked Bertie.

Both Celia and her fiancé were foreseeing the devastating effect a sister and uncle engaged in criminal pursuits (and unhallowed by the marital blessing of the Established Church) would have on their social status.

"The deuce!" rumbled Lord Eustace.

The awful thought that he might be cut in Piccadilly by his oldest friends had just entered his rather dusty mind. He might even—shattering possibility!—be barred from his favourite chair in his club and be forced to seek some less hallowed spot for his sleep between meals!

"Good heavens!" was the Duke's unoriginal contribution to the combined consternation.

"When we've saved up five thousand pounds," continued Anne, calmly, speaking slowly and distinctly, "we'll retire and Charles will buy a partnership in George Carmichael's motor business—that is, if it isn't too late."

"We might even consider marriage then," added Lord Charles.

"I suppose we'd have to," agreed Anne gravely. "It creates a more solid impression in business."

The solicitor whispered something to the Duke, who listened with a frown. The Duke in turn passed on the whispered communication to Lord Eustace, who nodded his head vehemently.

"Anything to prevent a scandal," he croaked hoarsely.

The Duke of Beaminster sat up very straight in his chair and looked sternly at his brother.

"It goes against the grain," he growled. "Very much against the grain, but we have decided—to save a fine old name from disgrace—to give you the money to buy this partnership; on condition that you both agree to do nothing that will cause the slightest scandal—and that you marry each other without delay!"

"That's very nice of you," said Anne brightly. "Isn't it, Charles?"

"Very nice, indeed," agreed Lord Charles.

"Very stupid!" grunted Bertie.

"Bertram!" said his Grace sternly—and the Marquis of Lessing subsided.

"I believe we're making a mistake, Charles," remarked Anne, as she watched the Duke signing his name to a cheque for five thousand pounds. "We are obviously cut out for crime. It isn't everybody who can make enough money to retire from their first blackmailing venture!"

Lord Charles put the cheque in his breast pocket.

"If I push the old bus to her utmost limits we can just get to London before the banks close," he said.

"Splendid," responded Anne. "Celia, be a darling and send on my clothes to Charles' flat."

"Anne!" wailed the future Marchioness of Lessing.

"I hope," said the solicitor, sedately, "I hope you will both remember to fulfil your share of the bargain."

"Even we crooks have a stringent code of ethics," replied Anne breezily. "We'll send you a framed copy of our marriage certificate."

*

Anne sat in the car beside Lord Charles and watched the dusty white ribbon of road that unwound beneath their speeding wheels.

"I told you they would cough up if they were approached properly," she remarked demurely.

Lord Charles looked at her respectfully. "Anne!" he declared, drawing a deep breath, "you were wonderful!"

"Perhaps I was—a little," Anne admitted modestly. "At any rate, I've done Celia in the eye. I've always wanted to do that. You don't know how fed up I've been with just being the plain Radley twin.

"I wanted to show her that she couldn't have her own way

always. She thought that she'd only to tell you that she could never be more than a sister to you and you'd be glad to go to the end of the earth to hide your broken heart!"

"Then you didn't really want me?" asked Lord Charles. Quietly. "You—It was just to spite Celia?"

Anne blushed—yes, actually blushed!

"Don't be an ass, Charles!" she said. "I've always had designs on you. I could have choked Celia because you never had eyes for anyone but her!"

Lord Charles pulled up the car with two wheels perilously near the ditch on the wrong side of the road and proceeded to kiss her with an ardour that shocked a painfully respectable cow that was looking over the hedge.

THE END

JAMES RONALD STORIES OF CRIME & DETECTION

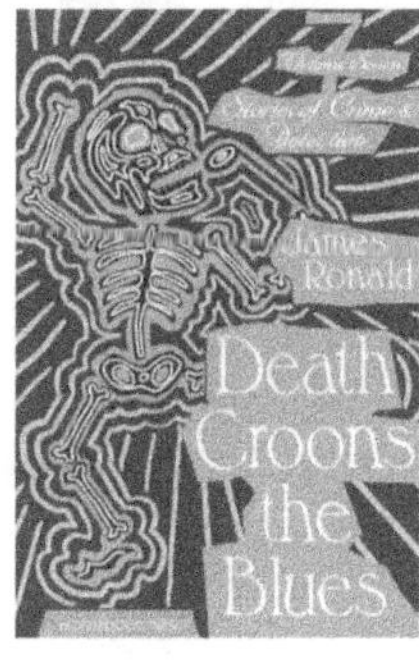